PRAISE FOR LAKE OF DESTINY

"Delightful, charming, and heartwarming!"

—NEW YORK TIMES BESTSELLING AUTHOR
WENDY HIGGINS

"I adored every page . . .Beautifully written, perfectly paced with traces of magical realism.

—AWARD-WINNING AUTHOR ERIN CASHMAN

"Well-written, well-crafted, well-paced and full of heart. . . . So much charm it's magical!"

—BOOKGEEK

"Martina Boone's gorgeous storytelling enthralled me from start to finish. The plot is captivating, whimsical, and full of surprises that kept me turning the pages."

—SINCERELY KARENJO

"I loved this!!! It reminds me of a Nora Roberts series, The Gallaghers of Ardmore . . . but a Scottish version with men in kilts!"

BOOKS

D0882401

PRAISE FOR COMPULSION

"Skillfully blends rich magic and folklore with adventure, sweeping romance, and hidden treasure . . . An impressive start to the Heirs of Watson Island series."

—PUBLISHER'S WEEKLY

"Eight Beaufort is so swoon-worthy that it's ridiculous. Move over Four, Eight is here to stay!"

—RT BOOK REVIEWS, RT EDITORS BEST BOOKS OF 2014

"Boone's Southern Gothic certainly delivers a compelling mystery about feuding families and buried secrets, not to mention a steamy romance."

—BOOKLIST

"Even the villains and not-likable characters were just so engrossing. I have to say I've already put the sequel on my TBR shelf."

—USA TODAY

"This Southern gothic mixes dark spirits, romance, feuding families and ancient curses into the perfect potion."

—JUSTINE MAGAZINE

ECHO OF GLORY

Also By Martina Boone

Adult Fiction:

Lake of Destiny: A Celtic Legends Novel

Bell of Eternity: A Celtic Legends Novel

Magic of Winter: A Celtic Legends Novel

Young Adult Fiction:

Compulsion

Persuasion

Illusion

Legend and Non-Fiction:

Welcome Home: Historic Romance
of the Celtic Legends

ECHO OF GLORY

—A CELTIC LEGENDS NOVEL—

MARTINA BOONE

MAYFAIR
PUBLISHING

Echo of Glory is a work of fiction, and the characters, events, and places depicted in it are products of the author's imagination. Where actual events, places, organizations, or persons, living or dead, are included, they are used fictitiously and not intended to be taken otherwise.

MAYFAIR
PUBLISHING

712 H Street NE, Suite 1014,
Washington, DC 20002
First Mayfair Publishing edition April 2018

Jacket design by Kalen O'Donnell
Interior Design by Rachel & Joel Greene

Published in the United States of America
ISBN 978-1-946773-09-8 (trade paperback)

For Ryan with all my love.

ECHO OF GLORY

ACCIDENT

THE SHOUT CAME FROM THE excavation site, and it was nearly drowned out by the roar of the ocean rushing through the slim channel that separated Dursey from Oileán Beag, the much smaller island that hugged the coast of its larger sibling. Niall Sullivan shifted the heavy box of chemicals and microscopes in his arms and hurried across the narrow temporary bridge. Gemma, their anthropologist, was famous for her temper, but she rarely raised her voice. If she was shouting before the volunteers had even arrived, it didn't bode well for the long, busy summer.

"Oi, Kieran! I'm talking to you, you slacker!" Gemma yelled. "Are you planning to do any actual work today?"

In the raw wind, the white nylon of the mobile lab tent on the other side flapped and billowed like the canvas of a sailing ship, as if the island on the southwestern tip of the

Beara Peninsula were a vessel with her prow turned determinedly into the Atlantic surf, an English frigate sailing away after the massacre, a pirate ship returning from sacking the monastery, or a Viking slaver carrying Irish captives off to be sold in the Middle East. Each of those had brought misery to Dursey through the centuries, but Niall's troubles since arriving on the island had been much more grounded in the present—and all of them centered on Kieran Stafford's general bolloxology.

Niall couldn't blame Gemma for her frustration. He'd have loved to have a go at Kieran himself, but he didn't have that luxury. These days, he needed to be responsible. Settle matters with leadership instead of a good lead hook.

His steps were slowed by the uneven, tufted grass alongside the lab, and the tent still blocked his view when Gemma raised her voice again. Not that her words required much in the way of visualization. "Kieran, Jaysus, come on! We need to get this done. Give James a hand picking up that sod instead of leaning on your spade. He's already put in six times as much effort as you have."

"Nothing new there, is it?" Liam's deep voice chimed in, the tone laced with resentment instead of his usual good-natured humor.

"Will you two leave off?" Kieran's words were drawled out, his accent more Oxford than Irish like the others, despite having been mostly raised in Dublin, too. "I'm entitled to catch my breath, and I've been hard at it all day."

Niall arrived at the front of the tent and scanned the area around the scarcely visible ruins of the Prince of Beare's last refuge. Where the dig team had marked it off with twine and orange tape, Gemma stood at the front edge of the excavation grid along the buried rubble of the walls. In front of her, strewn with roots and rock, the sour earth gaped bare, the sod newly cut away.

There wasn't much else to see. The foundations of the castle and fortress were mere bumps of history razed to the ground by the English at the time of the massacre and covered over by earth, grass, and clumps of furze and heather. Devoid of trees, the tiny island was an empty landscape, bare emerald green drifting toward the cliffs and white-capped sea. But to Niall, it was almost unbearably beautiful. Beneath the soil, anything and everything remained possible, answers and secrets still slumbering, waiting to be uncovered.

Gemma pushed the rim of her hat back from her face with a dirt-coated tattooed wrist. Her hair sprang forward in curls of deep red copper, and a galaxy of freckles shone beneath the gleam of sweat beading along her cheeks. A few feet away, Kieran—precisely as Gemma had said—leaned on his spade, talking to James, who, though forty pounds lighter and half a head shorter, merely shrugged his narrow shoulders, pushed his glasses up his nose, and continued lifting rectangles of sod from the stack by his feet and loading them into the wheelbarrow. Unlike the rest of the team, all of them caked with soil and sweat, Kieran still managed to look as though he'd recently stepped out of some glossy outdoor magazine advert aimed at the sort of readers who spared no expense.

Sunlight flashed on the blade of the six-inch knife Liam was using to hack away the last clinging roots from a square of sod, and then he swung himself out of his crouch. A gust of wind stirred the wheat-colored dreadlocks that hung midway down his back and made him look disconcertingly like a marauding Viking, but he lumbered over to where Gemma stood and made the tactical error of giving her his sweet, gentle smile and patting her on the shoulder.

Gemma swung to face him with her fists balled at her sides.

Niall stepped out from the shadow of the tent before the situation got any worse. "Right, that's about enough, all of you. Kieran, quit the foostering. Take over wheelbarrow duty and give James a rest."

"We're in the middle of a discussion." Kieran peered over James' head.

A muscle ticked along Niall's jaw. "Discuss it later. The rest of this grid needs clearing before the sun goes down."

Kieran straightened slowly enough for insolence. "The volunteers can finish in the morning. That's why we have them coming."

"Hardly." Niall shifted the heavy box in his arms. "You know better than that."

"I know I've more important things to do than manual labor." Kieran stabbed the spade into the grass and left it standing upright behind him as he stepped closer. "Is this how you're planning on running the dig? The staff catering to the hired help? To him?" He jerked a thumb back at James. "It's absurd, this whole site order that he's developed.

4

At this rate, we'll be checking half of Dursey before we get to the St. Michael's property."

"Which is what we all decided—four to one. I've no intention of overriding the vote. The odds of finding a burial site are slim, and it's not wild geese we're after, it's evidence to corroborate what happened."

"What happened according to Phillip O'Sullivan, which isn't the official record."

"The official *English* record barely addresses the massacre at all." Niall swallowed down a sigh. "Look, Kieran, you swore to me you were looking for the truth—whatever that turned out to be and whatever implications it would have for your father politically. I hired you on that basis. Now prove to me I wasn't wrong."

Kieran shifted his feet and the wind blew his blond hair back from a high, smooth forehead. He had the red-cheeked coloring of the Irish side of his family, coupled with dark brown eyes that sometimes made his thoughts and moods hard to read. "I didn't realize you would discount all my ideas."

"I'm not discounting them." Niall made an effort to soften the hard edge in his voice.

"As good as. You've given them such a low priority that we'll be lucky to start on the St. Michael's land before the end of summer. At least let me take the ground-penetrating radar out myself when James isn't using it."

"The equipment's not the point. We need to take the time to document systematically, and I need you here, helping with the volunteers, working toward the team priorities instead of haring off after your own agenda."

"It's a well-documented professional theory."

"Exactly. One theory. Not the only theory. This is my dig, Kieran. My team, and my responsibility, and I won't have you putting its success in jeopardy."

Kieran's chin came up, and he fixed Niall with a glare. "It seems to me you're the one doing that. And wouldn't it be a shame if you didn't get approval to continue digging here next year?"

It was a threat, possibly an empty one, but given that in a matter of weeks Kieran's father could well become the next *taoiseach,* the next prime minister of Ireland, it wasn't out of the realm of possibility. And Kieran's smirk said he knew Niall couldn't afford to take the risk.

Niall's temper was saved by a gull screeching into a dive too close overhead, which gave him a moment to curb the desire to wipe the smug look from Kieran's face. Seeing the shadow approaching, Kieran jumped back, and the gull flew past him with two feet to spare.

Niall was starting to have a genuine fondness for the island's seagulls. If he hadn't known better, he'd have sworn they'd launched a personal vendetta against Kieran in the past week since the team's arrival.

He tightened his grip on the box he held and managed to achieve a pleasant tone of voice. "Pull your weight, Kieran. That's all anyone's asking of you. You've put us behind schedule as it is."

He turned and walked away.

Beyond the tent and the temporary bridge where the

small island of Oileán Beag hugged the Dursey shoreline like a piece of a jigsaw puzzle, the sea curled white against the cliffs. The descending sun was edging down toward the island's spine, the old signal tower on the hump silhouetted like a postcard against the western ocean. Already, the evening light was changing, and the last of the day-walkers were hurrying to queue up at the cable car station for the return trip to the mainland.

Which was another problem to lay at Kieran's feet.

If they hadn't been so far behind—and if the tensions hadn't been running so high—Niall would have taken the day to drive to Dublin and bring his twin sister and her son down himself. Siobhan should have been here long since, but even with the spotty mobile coverage on the island, he'd received no message since a garbled call from Adam that morning—and no response to the calls he had made himself. After setting the box of assorted microscopes, testing sieves, and solutions down on the corner of a table, he gave in to the increasingly insistent worry, dug his mobile from his pocket, and tried again.

His sister didn't answer, and he could only leave another message. "Hiya, Siobhan. It's nearly eight o'clock. Where are you, love? The cable car's due for its last run in half an hour, and I hate to think of you and Adam stranded for the night. The weather won't be fit for a boat crossing from the mainland with the wind picking up. Phone me, would you? Let me know you're safe, at any rate, and if you won't be arriving straight off, I'll ring round to one of the nearby B&Bs. Just ring me back and tell me where you are."

7

Guilt swamped him along with a potent cocktail of fear and fury as he hung up and crossed to where the flap of the tent was tied back against a post. Kieran or no Kieran, he should have gone to get Siobhan. He should have made the time. Deep down, he'd known that even when she had sworn she'd be fine driving down on her own. She had already postponed her arrival twice by then and put off coming until the last minute. But she'd always had a gift for making him feel like he was worrying over nothing.

Until long after it was clear he wasn't.

Now all he could do was wait and regret—and try not to take it out on Kieran any more than the man deserved.

What he really needed was to replace Kieran altogether, although that would be a complicated prospect. It would be nearly impossible to find anyone else with a fraction of Kieran's familiarity with the historical material or archival research now that summer had begun. Anyone worth their salt was already committed elsewhere.

Then, too, he couldn't discount Kieran's threats.

The latest political shift had been only a cloud on the horizon when Niall had hired him, and the rumors of Kieran's father maneuvering toward becoming *taoiseach* had seemed like a distant—worst-case—possibility. But Callum Stafford'd had plenty of influence even then without being the actual head of government. And since the last of the approvals for the dig had been promised but not yet finalized, the advantage of having a bit of political influence on their side had crossed Niall's mind, he couldn't deny that. How much he had allowed the possibility to cloud his better judgment, he couldn't honestly say. Already at that first interview, there'd been a whiff of something in Kieran that suggested he was a bit of a chancer. Even more than the complicated tangle of his family motives and connections, that attitude had made Niall hesitate. He had convinced himself Kieran deserved a chance.

He should have listened to his doubts.

That was the problem, he thought as he emerged through the flapped opening of the tent and stood blinking against the light. When it came to the Dursey Island excavation, he kept letting emotion influence his own decisions. He'd spent his whole life thinking about this place, spent too many hours listening to his father's bitter stories, whenever his father had been in a mood to rail at injustice or wax poetic. Those moments were the memories of his da that remained the clearest for Niall, his father sitting in the old rocking chair beneath the window of the flat above the family's grocery in a part of Dublin far removed from the posh neighborhood where Kieran had been raised. With his powerful hands wrapped around a bottle of whiskey and his eyes alive with centuries-old injustice, the way Da could bring the brutality of what the English had done in Ireland— and to their own clan—to life had reduced Siobhan to tears, but Niall had walked away with questions about Dursey Island and the fate of the O'Sullivan Beares that demanded answers.

Those questions had been the saving of him. Years later, when he and Siobhan had been carted off to foster care and separated, Niall had been heading down an ugly road.

Malcolm and Valerie O'Rourke had taken him in, and they'd nurtured those questions of his and taught him the value of hard work and self-respect. He'd fought for it every step of the way, but he'd eventually gone on to earn his doctorate in archaeology.

Siobhan'd had no such luck. Niall owed her for that, and seeing her hurtling into darkness herself—yet again—he'd offered her an admin post on the dig in the hope of providing her the sort of second chance the O'Rourkes had given him. A chance to pull her life together, for Adam's sake, if nothing else.

With a sigh, Niall stopped halfway between where Liam was working and where Gemma had picked up her own spade to slice sod way from a new section of the grid. James bumped the empty wheelbarrow back along the uneven grass while Kieran jogged along beside him, still nagging, still trying to wear him down.

Niall shook his head. At himself as much as Kieran.

"Will you all gather around a minute?" he asked.

Liam came over, his movements loose and his large frame relaxed in a way that Niall had long since learned could be deceptive. "What's up, skip?"

"The cable car is about to stop running, so we have to make alternate arrangements," Niall began.

Gemma stopped at Liam's side. "Still no word from your sister?"

"Nothing," Niall said, "which is part of what I need to tell you. At this rate, I'll either be on the phone half the night bribing Pete to turn the cable car back on and bring them

10

over, or I'll be needing to get them settled at the house come morning. That means we'll have to take turns meeting the volunteers ourselves as they arrive and bringing them here to the dig site for the orientations."

Head cocked to the side, Liam studied him, and for all that he gave the appearance of looking like he had more brawn than brain, he'd always been perceptive. "I wouldn't worry yet, boss. You know how boys are at Adam's age. Probably took his time saying his goodbyes to twenty of his closest mates before leaving Dublin, then demanded feeding every half hour on the road. I was a proper nightmare to travel with at fourteen."

"You still are, so." Gemma grinned, raising her face to Liam's.

Niall ran a hand across the back of his neck and glanced up at the gulls circling overhead. "The point is," he said, eyeing James and Kieran as they wandered over, "whatever happens, Siobhan won't be here to help, which will make it doubly important for the rest of us to work as a team. One team, no squabbling, no letting our differences show. The volunteers are paying their own way to be here, and it's critical we remember that. We're the ones depending on them, so we owe them a good experience."

Gemma and Liam glared at Kieran, but if Kieran felt Niall's words were directed at him in any way, he gave no sign.

"What it comes to," Niall continued, "is that not one among us is indispensable. We can't afford to let our egos, tempers, or own opinions show in front of the volunteers, and I will—I promise you—replace anyone who treats a volunteer or another member of the staff with anything less than complete respect. Is that fair?"

"Yeah, boss," Gemma said.

"Understood," Liam and James said together.

Kieran buried his hands deep in his pockets and didn't answer.

For Niall, that was the final straw.

They should have been a solid staff. On paper, they still were. He'd worked with James and Liam before, and Gemma, their anthropologist, was among the best at reading bones. Liam had not only the training but the instinct to piece together fragments of battleground evidence, and James' skill at finding potential excavation areas was nearly supernatural. Niall had witnessed that himself once when James had veered two hundred yards off a plotted track to a patch of ground most archeologists would never have noticed without technology or research to point them there—and James had been right. The site had turned out to be a previously unsuspected Bronze Age burial.

With Kieran's knowledge of the sources, Niall had hoped to identify and finish preliminary instrumental explorations of all the potential excavation sites on Dursey Island before the excavation season ended. That would give him the winter to look for additional funding for the following year, and he couldn't let Kieran derail that.

Before he could weigh how to address Kieran's attitude and decide what more needed saying in front of the others and what could wait to be said in private later, his phone rang in his pocket. He turned aside and answered without looking at the screen.

"Finally," he said. "Where are you, Siobhan? Tell me you're phoning from the cable car."

The voice on the other end of the line wasn't his twin's, though. "Dr. Sullivan? Niall Sullivan? This is Sergeant Mahoney from the Dublin Garda."

The wind off the ocean raised chills along Niall's neck. "Yes?"

"I'm calling about your sister Siobhan. She is your sister, do I have that right?" The sergeant's voice was professionally gentle, the right blend of compassion and dispassion that allowed someone to deliver bad news on a daily basis.

Malcolm O'Rourke, when he'd taken Niall in as a teenager, had been an inspector in the garda, and the tone was one Niall had come to recognize. Dread slipped inside him like cold fog melting into his skin.

"Is Siobhan safe? What's happened?" he asked. "And Adam—"

"I'm afraid there's been an accident. The emergency crew did everything possible, but your sister died before she reached the hospital."

A gannet, soaring above the cliff, tucked its black-tipped wings and dove, a white blur disappearing beyond the rocks. Niall's heart plummeted with it, and he stood, locked in the moment as though his feet and his heart had turned to stone.

"Dr. Sullivan, are you there?" the sergeant asked.

Niall cleared his throat, but he couldn't form coherent thoughts, much less words. "I—yes. Sorry," he managed finally. "What about Adam? Was he in the car with her?"

"He's bruised a bit, and his arm's broken, but he's strong. He'll be fine. Physically, at least. Can you come and get him? We'll also need a formal identification. We phoned the boy's father, but he's . . ."

"Useless. Right." Niall closed his eyes and let the world spin around him. "Of course. I'll leave now—but I'm down on Dursey Island. County Cork. It'll be late before I get there."

"I'll stay here with the lad myself until you get here." The sergeant started to provide instructions to the hospital, but Niall, still staggeringly numb and disconnected, remembered he had to run to the station—literally run—if he hoped to catch the cable car off the island. He offered the sergeant a brief explanation and promised to phone back once he'd reached the mainland. Then he explained briefly to Gemma and the others.

"Don't give us a thought. You worry about Adam," Gemma said. "And yourself."

Niall didn't dare let himself think of Siobhan, not yet, though grief was already settling inside him like a hole, insatiable and dark. Kicking his feet into a sprint, he raced across the temporary bridge, and hopped into the rusting Toyota SUV they'd managed to negotiate the use of on the island. He drove full speed along the overgrown track, back toward the smallest of the three holiday cottages he'd rented for the staff in the abandoned village of Ballynacallagh.

Brian Sheehan, the farmer who'd recently fixed up the rental cottages—and purchased a good amount of the rest of

Dursey Island—was walking his cows in from the pasture as Niall raced past. "What's the rush?" Brian called, pushing a scratched pair of sunglasses up into his shaggy white hair. "You unbury someone's ghost already?"

Niall waved without answering, snatched up his wallet and the keys to his own car from the table in the kitchen, then drove the truck at an unhealthy speed to the cable car station. A rapid-fire explanation to the waiting tourists got him to the front of the queue, and while the lone six-seat metal crate made its slow traverse above the churning water of Dursey Sound, he stared at the bottle of holy water and the tattered copy of Psalm 91 that hung beside the phone box on the wall. He wasn't a religious man. He'd studied the aftermath of too many atrocities committed in the name of religion to allow for that, but for the first time since childhood he breathed a prayer.

Twice on the way to Dublin he was pulled for speeding, once on the outskirts of Cork and again on the M8 north of Cashel. Still, he felt as though he didn't draw a full breath again until he stepped into the waiting area at the hospital and Adam, spotting him as he ran through the door, rocketed uncharacteristically into his arms.

"Uncle Niall!"

Niall folded him in and held him close. "Hallo, mate. Steady on. We'll be all right."

Boys were fragile at fourteen, try as hard as they might not to let it show. Too well, Niall remembered what it had been like at that age to be ripped away from Siobhan and everything he'd ever known.

It struck him forcibly that Adam no longer had a mother. From one instant to the next, he'd been left with no one. Not a soul in the world, apart from Niall and a father so feckless Siobhan had long since named Niall as Adam's guardian. The weight of that responsibility settled on Niall's shoulders, and he didn't know if he was strong enough to bear it.

These past few weeks, he'd been afraid Siobhan was dancing herself toward a cliff. He'd tried to persuade her to go back to rehab, spoken to her sponsor, offered her the job on Dursey where he could be there for her. Clearly, none of that had been enough. If it had been, she would have been here with him now, her smile wide and bright, an invitation to trouble. As contagious as ever.

He should have known there was a problem when she hadn't been ready either the previous weekend or on Friday as she'd promised. He should have gone to get her himself, Kieran or no bloody Kieran—but that was a poor excuse. He should have found a way. He'd failed Siobhan, and now he couldn't fail her son. Whatever happened, he'd have to make sure he was always there for Adam.

BLANK STARES

*"The loneliest moment in someone's life
is when they are watching their whole world
fall apart, and all they can do is stare blankly."*

F. SCOTT FITZGERALD
THE GREAT GATSBY

NIGHTS WERE THE WORST. The job forced Meg Cameron into bed by ten each evening when the New York evenings were just beginning, and it forced her up again long before the term "morning" had any right to apply. Her apartment felt terribly lonely, then. The city felt terribly lonely. A place where people were obsessed with information and talked about compassion, but they walked past others without making eye contact in case the need for that compassion hit them face to face.

Outside, beyond her window, millions of people slumbered, lights off, streets deserted except for an occasional cab or small car taking a leftover someone home from the kind of job that kept them on the reverse of her own painful schedule.

The irony of it was, this had always been her dream job. And still was, she told herself sternly. Of course it was.

She slapped off the last of her three alarms—3:10, 3:20, 3:30—sickeningly upbeat notes of music spilling quietly between her pale white walls. The scrubbed oak floorboards were smooth and cool against the bare soles of her feet as she padded over to close the window she'd cracked open. After two weeks, the landlord still hadn't gotten around to fixing the air conditioning, but a crisp breeze billowed the sheer blue curtains and cooled her sweat-damp skin. She let herself stand a moment, reveling in the chill and knowing all too well that the temperature would shoot up to steaming before she'd signed off after her morning broadcast. Of course, Cincinnati had sweltered in the summer, too, but her schedule had been different there. She'd had time to run before work when it was still cool enough outdoors, and that was a routine she missed.

To get her blood flowing, she dropped down and did a few push-ups on the bare floor beneath the window, then padded into the bathroom, showered and put in her contact lenses. She squeezed in fifty pliés while she brushed her teeth, a few more while she hit her long dark hair with a flat iron, and a few squat-arabesques while she ate her yogurt in the kitchen after dressing and made herself a cup of coffee. This would be her only cup of the day, so she always made it count—the best beans, steamed half and half, a light dusting of cinnamon on top, all of it poured into a travel mug for her six-minute commute. She sent her usual text to the car company and drew back the living room curtains while she took the first blissful sip. Standing at the window, she listened to New York slowly coming awake and tried to will herself to love the view, the tiny green sliver of Central Park that was visible when she stood just here, the skyline, the feel of the city.

She wanted so much to love it.

That was partly what had drawn her to Ruben. Her brief marriage—long since ended—had been characterized by Patrick's distance from life. Ruben's enthusiasm for New York was so infectious that when she was with him she could nearly cloak herself within it. She loved discovering the out-of-the-way places he showed her: the neighborhoods set like gems within the vibrating, noisy, hub of the city, delicious hole-in-the-wall Greek, Italian, and Jewish restaurants, and the dim sum places she'd never before realized were byproducts of afternoon tea, the guilty-pleasure street vendor hot dogs that were about the last thing she should have been eating. Food had become such a big part of her outings with Ruben these past six months that she'd found herself spending twice as long on the treadmill in the gym every day, going around and around like a hamster on a never-changing wheel. But it was worth it. Getting away. Exploring. Indulging in curiosity. Maybe that all factored into her growing unease, the ever-ripening loneliness. There was increasingly a sense that the stolen moments with Ruben were waves churning along a beach, all froth and foam and undercurrent, retreating as much as they advanced.

That was the problem with secrets. They festered if you tried to keep them hidden too long.

But enough melancholy. This was a problem she would have to tackle later, because she couldn't afford to dawdle. She checked the time again on her phone, then hurried to the small desk she had renovated with elbow grease and chalk paint after she and Ruben had found it at a flea market. Gathering up her purse, keys, and the files she'd brought home the night before, she knocked over several of the travel books her mother had been sending her. They thudded to the floor, and the phone rang as she stooped to pick them up.

She hit the speaker button. "Are you at work already?"

"It's me, M," her youngest sister, Anna, said, calling from Scotland where it was a slightly more civilized hour. "Sorry if you're expecting someone else. Can you talk?"

"I'm on my way to the car. Everything all right?"

"I'm not sure. Mom sent me another email last night. I'm really starting to worry."

"We swore we were giving up letting her manipulate us." Meg set the books back on the table and frowned down at the cover of *Rick Steves' Ireland* with its green hillside sloping down to a turquoise ocean. "She can't expect you to go when you're six months pregnant."

"It's not me she wants," Anna said.

Meg felt the old wave of frustration crash over her, trying to pull her down into the rolling sense of helplessness that came from a lifetime of being the oldest child and cleaning up after her middle sister's feckless selfishness. And their mother's.

"What exactly does Mom expect us to do about

Katharine?" she asked. "If K thinks she's got a sliver of a chance at landing a part in that film, nothing anyone says is going to get her to leave Hollywood for some tiny rain-soaked Irish island with sheep and no internet and barely any cell phones."

"It's not Katharine Mom wants with her, either. Not really."

"Me? I can't take five weeks off." A half-hysterical snort of laughter pushed its way through Meg's throat. "Amazing how she kept telling me I shouldn't let anything stop me from taking this job at the network—and now that she wants me to do something for her, my work isn't even a consideration."

"I'm not suggesting it—but I don't know what else to do. I swear, I've never heard her so . . . quietly desperate. An archaeological dig, for Pete's sake? Dad's worried, too."

"Not enough to stop the divorce."

The phone was quiet for several beats before Anna spoke again. "Do you think he should?"

"No." Meg squeezed her eyes shut, then opened them again. "It's all too awful to contemplate." She picked up her travel mug and the files again, then scooped up the keys and her purse. "The idea that Mom could do something so horrible. I'm sure that's why she's afraid to face her friends— not that Dad would have told anyone the truth. It's just her own guilty conscience."

"That never bothered her before. Anyway, maybe her friends would be more inclined to be charitable if she'd spent less time gossiping about everyone else's divorces all these years," Anna said, sounding tired. Of the three of them, Anna was the sister who'd always had the closest relationship with their father, and their mother had made her pay the price for that.

It was both ironic and typical of their mother to try to make Anna an ally now.

"Don't let her guilt you," Meg said. "She can find something else to do. Somewhere else to hide."

"I suggested she could go on a cruise, or one of those organized tours. But she insists she's got it all arranged with her friend who's financing the excavation. Claims she can't back out now."

"She's a grown woman." Meg reached the door and started unlocking the first of four security locks. "How much trouble could she get into? No. Don't answer that."

Anna paused long enough that the silence grew ominous. "She says you aren't happy. That she pushed you into taking the job when you weren't sure."

"Of course I'm happy." Meg smacked the last of the locks, which had a tendency to stick, with the heel of her hand. She tried not to picture Anna, sitting in the tower office she shared with her gorgeous husband in their huge stone house at the end of a Highland lake in Scotland. Trying not to admit that the thought of Anna's life with Connal and his daughter, Moira, sent a small pang of something green and ugly twisting deep inside her. Her youngest sister pregnant. Anna living her life so richly while Meg couldn't help feeling as though, in spite of her own career success, somehow she was still waiting for her own life to start.

"I'm very happy," she repeated as she let herself out and locked the door behind her.

"You're a terrible liar, Margaret Mary Cameron." Anna sighed. "Maybe the job will get better as you get more seniority. Or couldn't they let you transition back into doing harder news?"

Meg crossed the hall and mashed the button for the elevator. "That isn't how it works, but I'm not complaining. I know how lucky I am. I love doing the interviews, and the people are great. There are a lot of compensations."

"I can hear the big, fat 'but' hanging off the end of that sentence. Is it more than just work? Is it that guy you've been seeing?"

Ruben wasn't a conversation Meg wanted to have with anyone. She'd always been so careful about who she dated— and dating your producer was about the worst sort of stupid cliché. Which was why it had made sense to keep things between them private.

"Nice try," she said, pacing in front of the elevator doors. "If he and I ever go toward something permanent, I promise you'll be the first to know. In the meantime, let's change the subject back to Mom. Couldn't Aunt Elspeth go over to meet her in Ireland? It's not that far from Scotland, and they have to get over being mad eventually."

"Elspeth is waiting for Mom to apologize, and Mom is waiting for hell to freeze over, so that's not happening anytime soon."

Meg checked the time as the elevator light stayed stubbornly stuck on the second floor. Giving up, she headed for the stairs. "Honey, look, I'm going to have to call you back later. I've got to go. Don't let Mom put all this on you. I'll talk to her. You have a baby to incubate—not to mention Connal and Moira and a growing business. Maybe we should both learn to be more like Katharine."

"Miserable excuses for human beings? No, thanks," Anna said, leaving Meg shaking her head as they disconnected.

Ten flights later, Meg was breathless by the time she exited the building. The black town car was still parked out front, though, and she knocked on the window and slid into the back seat with an apology.

"I didn't mean to keep you waiting, Azeez. Hope you at least snuck in a nap."

Azeez turned and flashed a smile. "Not a problem, Miss Meg. Bad morning?"

Not bad exactly. "Perplexing," Meg said. "But how's your daughter doing? Any better?"

"She will be better soon." Azeez put the car in gear and eased out from the curb. "Doctors say she can leave the hospital this week maybe."

"That's wonderful news," Meg said, beaming back at him. "Let me know how I can help. Even if it's sitting with her for a few hours so you and your wife can have a break."

"If I could talk Esther into leaving her, I would be a stronger husband than I am. Amina will not be allowed out of Esther's sight until she goes off to college."

They both laughed, though Meg couldn't help thinking she'd feel the same if her own child had been hit by a car on her way to school. Relieved that at least one story looked like it would soon have a happy ending, she switched on her tablet to check the morning headlines, trying to get a jump on the day's breaking news.

Fortunately—or unfortunately, for that was a matter of opinion—there didn't seem to be anything to preempt the segments they had scheduled already, nothing that required follow-up beyond the usual reading of the headlines and a bit of banter with her cohosts. Morning shows were cutthroat competitive, she had learned, far more so than the evening news. But then, the advertising revenue at stake was enormous and the networks watched every dip and rise in the ratings, however small. Worse still, every show was experimenting with format tweaks, doing their best to take advantage of the sexual harassment scandal that had left some of NBC's *Today* viewers up for grabs. Meg drained the last of her coffee during the drive and made a couple of notes to discuss with Ruben, then gathered her things to be ready as the car approached the back of the Times Square studio. Behind schedule by even the fifteen minutes she had lost, she felt as though she'd lost her grip on the day.

Compounding the feeling, Azeez had to wait to pull up behind a blue Mercedes that was double-parked in front while the passenger and the driver engaged in a kiss that had slipped from have-a-nice-day to hurry-home-for-lunch. "It's all right—I'll get out here," Meg said, opening the door. "Thanks, Azeez, and I promise I'll be on time tomorrow."

The couple in the car disentangled themselves at the same time that Meg slid out, and she found herself standing, cold and unable to move, on the sidewalk while the two cars pulled out from the curb. Tall and slim, the jacket of his gray suit folded over his arm while he juggled an overflowing laptop case and a Starbucks cup, Ruben looked equally shocked. His other hand froze in the farewell wave he'd intended for the driver as the Mercedes drove away.

"Meg," he said, going pale. "Um. That wasn't what it looked like. At all. Please, just hear me out."

Meg felt like both the cars had run over her, like all the blood was draining from her and leaving her freezing, her chest flattening so it was impossible to take in air.

Her voice sounded breathless, but otherwise she managed to keep control. "You mean it didn't look like you had your tongue down some woman's throat?" she asked. "Funny, because I'm not sure how I could be mistaken about that."

"It doesn't mean I don't care about you." Ruben walked toward her, frowning. "She doesn't—"

"Please don't say she doesn't mean anything, because you're a better writer than that."

"Let's not do this in the street. Please?" He straightened and glanced toward the studio, towering over her as he drew his free arm around her shoulders.

Meg shrugged him away. "Was that why you wanted to keep our 'relationship' under wraps?"

"Come on. Keep your voice down. There's no need to get angry—"

"Angry?" Meg whipped around to face him. "I'm not angry, Ruben. I'm furious. At both of us. Because I fell for the friend act when I knew better, or I should have, but you were charming and sweet and I was a lonely idiot who told herself I could keep business and personal separate."

"It wasn't an act, we are friends. More than friends. I'd never felt like this about anyone. All right—I should have handled it better recently." Ruben caught her arm again as she started to walk away from him. "The truth is, I didn't know what to do. You haven't been happy and professionally . . . well, it hasn't been exactly working."

Blood pounded through Meg's ears, drowning out the sound of traffic, and she couldn't move. "What do you mean, 'professionally'?"

"Not here."

"Yes, here. Right here. Tell me exactly what you meant."

He looked past her down the street. "The network's been on me about making changes, if you must know. But if you'll just be reasonable instead of storming in there and letting everyone see that you're upset, I'm sure we can work things out—"

"Is that a threat? You're threatening me because you *think* I would let this impact my work?" Feeling even colder, Meg looked down at where his hand gripped her wrist. "Threatening my job?"

"Of course not. I'm just saying the ratings haven't been as good as I'd hoped, but I've held off making decisions." Ruben's cheeks had gone an even deeper shade of red beneath his tousled sandy hair, and a series of expressions chased themselves across his features. His face had always been fluid, expressive. Endearingly so, Meg had thought, since it softened what was otherwise a somewhat studious but conventional form of handsomeness.

Feeling as if the day had somehow slid into a particularly horrible form of farce, Meg found herself shaking as she stood there processing what he'd said. The ratings? The ultimate card. The one that was seemingly empirical and unassailable on the surface—numbers didn't lie, after all. But they could say whatever Ruben and the network wanted them to say. Her own numbers had been steadily climbing, but "as good as I'd hoped" was hard to measure and even harder to prove.

"You're going to ease me out if I don't pretend you're not a snake," she said flatly. "Is that what you're implying?"

Ruben put his hands up in surrender. "Not at all. I— look, let's just have lunch later and talk it over. Be reasonable. We can work this out."

DETERMINATION

*"Life is either a daring adventure
or nothing at all."*

HELEN KELLER
THE OPEN DOOR

A T WHAT POINT HAD IT TURNED into sexual harassment? For two weeks, Meg hadn't been able to stop asking herself that question. Even now, driving along a narrow Irish road, her brain picked over every moment and conversation of her months with Ruben the way she'd picked at her scabs when she'd had chicken pox as a child. Two weeks after accepting that her position on the show was a no-win situation, she was no closer to answering the question, much less to deciding whether she ought to do something about it. Two weeks ago, she'd believed she knew what sexual harassment looked like. Now, the more she pulled the whole relationship apart, the more she questioned Ruben's actions in pursuing a relationship when he was in a position to influence the course of her career—and her own actions in being stupid enough to think that could ever be a good idea.

The clouds that had clung to the emerald green hilltops to the right of Bantry Bay descended to meet the road and settled into pockets, making visibility intermittent. Fantastic. Despite the hours they'd already spent on the route down from the airport in Cork, driving the rental car on the left remained disquieting. Not that there necessarily was a left or right by this point. The road was little more than one lane, constricted on either side by shallow stacked stone walls half-overgrown with brush or grass spilling over from the fields and pastures.

She still couldn't quite believe she was here, that she'd agreed—in a fit of weakness and despair—to come on her mother's mad adventure. But here she was, driving to what was just about land's end, the southwesternmost tip in County Cork, through some of the most beautiful country she'd ever seen.

So far, there were far more sheep and cows than people, and houses were usually sporadic. They were coming at decreasing intervals again, suggesting they might be approaching their destination. On the other hand, Meg had been fooled several times already. A single farm could contain many buildings on both sides of the road. Now, though, the buildings were all on the right, with only a narrow strip of sheep-dotted pasture and a spectacular view over miles and miles of misted sea on the left. Peering at the row of neatly painted houses, searching for a number, Meg had to veer sharply to miss a pair of children on bicycles zooming down a driveway.

Her mother chose that moment to wake up after having fallen asleep almost the moment they had left the airport. Predictably, Ailsa Cameron—she was refusing to take back her maiden name after using Cameron most of her life—sucked in a breath and sank French-manicured nails sharply into Meg's arm. "Slow down, for Heaven's sake," she said in a throaty voice that still held a lilt of the Scottish Highlands even after forty-odd years in Cincinnati. "It's raining."

Meg couldn't help a twinge of irritation. "I noticed."

"Don't go getting smart with me, Margaret Mary Cameron. I don't care what they try to call this, it's not a real road, is it? It's worse than driving in the Highlands."

"How would you know?" Meg muttered beneath her breath, anger sweeping in at the forced reminder of the strained trip back to Scotland for Anna's wedding, her father driving and her mother sitting in pale, fuming silence in the front seat beside him. That had been the beginning of the end.

"Don't think I didn't hear that," Ailsa said.

"Of course you did." Meg reached over and squeezed her mother's hand. Though she refused to give in to age and get the hearing aid she needed, Ailsa had always had an uncanny knack for tuning into anything anyone said about her. Glancing over, taking in the pale, slack skin of her mother's still beautiful face and the telltale bruised look of sleepless nights no amount of careful makeup had managed to hide, Meg felt a pang of remorse. "We must be almost there," she said. "Help me keep an eye out for the sign."

"I'll recognize the building from the pictures," Ailsa said, unwilling to be appeased.

Meg slumped deeper in the green Volkswagen's driver's seat. "I'm sure you will, but I'd love a little warning so I don't miss the driveway. The distances marked on the road seem to be either wild guesses or wishful thinking, and the GPS thinks I'm driving through Bantry Bay half the time. It's not inclining me to confidence."

They passed a small sanctuary along the side of the road with what looked, out of the corner of Meg's eye, to be a statue of the Virgin Mary, and beyond that a small building and parking lot that might have been the café she'd noticed on the map. From there, it hadn't seemed far to the small pocket of holiday homes and bed-and-breakfasts near the cable car terminal, but time and distance proved—as they often did—to be deceptive at the end of a journey. The road through stone-strewn fields from which a few placid horses followed their progress seemed longer than expected, dotted here and there by brightly painted farmhouses in startling shades of blue and brick and yellow, then yet another section where the road veered inland.

The view of Bantry Bay vanished behind rocky hills, and visibility went to zero. Shapes loomed eerily on the hillsides, appearing and vanishing again into the mist before Meg's mind could fully grasp what they had been.

It was a strange and frightening sensation, a landscape whose aching beauty was tempered by a savage history and its people's determination to survive. Meg felt the echoes of that desperation soak her skin, as if the mist and the landscape had been so saturated with it that it still leeched into the present.

The hills disappeared again. The sun spilled through the clouds in long-fingered shafts and glittered on the western bay as though a giant had opened a hand and scattered diamonds. The air filled to overflowing with the kind of light that made artists reach for brush and canvas, and though Meg didn't have an artistic bone in her body, she would have loved to paint the view. Best of all, a short while later, the neat row of holiday homes she'd seen in the photographs looked precisely as they'd been pictured, and then the Bay Point Bed and Breakfast materialized on a cliff-side ridge to the left of the road, a sprawling two-story white structure covered in climbing roses with a steep-pitched roof surrounded by a riotous tangle of garden.

Her mother released an uncharacteristically satisfied sigh. "I'll admit it looks all right from here. Not that we were exactly spoiled for choice."

"Oh, come on. It's gorgeous, and we won't be here much anyway. We're supposed to be at the dig all day—that's what you signed up for, remember." Despite agreeing to come, Meg hadn't lost her misgivings about her mother's enthusiasm for the project lasting the full five weeks that she had committed to stay. Given the work-study program she'd done on the archaeological dig in the Hebrides where she had met Meg's father, Ailsa was both confident in her skills and secure in the belief that, as a friend of the Irish-American couple who had funded the dig, she would get preferential treatment. Meg worried, though. Her mother was leagues away from the eighteen-year-old who'd spent long hours on her knees scraping soil with a spade and brush. Apart from the gardening that she had taken up the same year that her nemesis, Melissa Jenner, had won the Evergreen Country Club garden show, Meg couldn't remember the last time her mother had resorted to anything close to manual labor. Meg hadn't done much of that herself.

Perhaps these next weeks would be good for both of them.

She parked the rented Volkswagen in one of the available spaces, and by the time she and Ailsa had extricated themselves, the front door of the bed-and-breakfast had flown open and the oddly paired owners had emerged. Meg recognized them, too, from the website photographs, the man at least six feet six and thin as a pole, with an enormous head topped by curly red hair that rippled to his shoulders. In deference to the damp wind coming off the bay, he wore a turtleneck sweater that had stretched out around the neck and faded jeans tucked into rubber boots. The woman beside him was at least a foot and a half shorter, with dark cocoa skin that gleamed in the sunlight and a smile so bright it was impossible to resist smiling back.

"You must be the Camerons. That's right, isn't it?" she asked in a voice that was soft and not quite Irish.

"Meg and Ailsa," Meg clarified, taking the hand the woman offered.

"Wonderful. I'm Ari and this is Fergal, and you must both be exhausted."

"And gagging for a drink and a bite of supper, I'd

imagine," Fergal added. "Let's get you settled in, and then you can come to the bar whenever you're ready to meet the other guests. They're rather a mixed bag, a few cyclists, some stray tourists, a handful of other volunteers from the dig. You're the only ones coming in fresh—archaeological virgins, so to speak. The others have already been here for the first five-week session, so they can fill you in on the finds and gossip."

Meg's mother drew herself visibly inward, wrapping herself in the protective cloak of polite reserve Meg had seen her use so often. "I doubt we'd be very good company tonight after the long flight and the drive, and I'm not much for bars."

"Pish, love." Fergal dismissed both the excuse and the deflection with a grin and a graceful wave of his hand. "A glass or two of wine or a shot of whiskey'll soon set that to rights. I'll lay odds you've got a lovely voice. I can always tell, and we can use someone who can carry a tune, I don't mind telling you. Most of the current lot couldn't catch one if it slapped them." He gave her a conspiratorial wink. "We'll keep that between ourselves, though. Meanwhile, mind you two leave your suitcases in the boot, and I'll come back for them."

Meg felt slightly swept away as Ari snatched the keys out of her hand and ushered them down the path toward the door. "Carry a tune for what?"

"Singing," Ari said. "We like to have a pub session in the evenings, though technically we're not a pub. We just gather everyone together to sing and tell stories. What the guests lack in skill, they make up in volume and enthusiasm."

"Don't worry," Fergal said, laughing. "No one will mind if you only join in on the chorus so long as you're having fun."

Confused but already enjoying herself, Meg let Fergal's arm and the tide of his welcome sweep her inside. She couldn't help smiling inwardly at the mental image of her mother in a bar singing Irish songs with a gaggle of cyclists and sunburned volunteers with whom—by her own admission—she would have absolutely nothing in common. But if her mother had thought that she was going to coerce Meg into quiet evenings spent staring at each other in their rooms or traipsing off to restaurants in Bantry or Castletownbere after hours of backbreaking labor, she was very much mistaken. First, Fergal and Ari clearly had no plans to allow any guests to isolate themselves, and second— Meg decided there and then—she herself wouldn't allow it, either.

Her mother had wanted an adventure, but what she really needed was to learn to take herself less seriously. Have some fun. Wasn't it odd that that was a skill some people didn't possess while to others it came so naturally? Or maybe fun was a muscle that atrophied with disuse. Meg realized abruptly that it had been missing from her own life, too. She stole a glance at Fergal's profile, at the brackets etched around his eyes and lips by laughter and the sharp, intelligent brightness of him, and she suspected he'd be an excellent teacher in that department.

"I can't remember the last time I had a chance to sing

outside the shower," she said, though she remembered the moment very clearly. "I wouldn't miss it for the world, and neither would my mother."

REBELLION

*". . . believe in a love that is being stored up for you
like an inheritance, and have faith that
in this love there is a strength . . .'*

RAINER MARIA RILKE
LETTERS TO A YOUNG POET

F OR THE THIRD TIME IN ten minutes, Niall called up the stairs to Adam's bedroom. In the rental cottage, that was no great distance, but Adam still hadn't managed to come down. "Adam, get a move on. Your eggs'll turn to rubber."

Niall waited, listening, but since it was impossible to hear anything from Adam's room over the pounding music, he went back to the kitchen and turned the flame down on the cooker, leaving the pan still sizzling. With the full intention of marching upstairs and refusing to leave until Adam had finally strung more than a couple of words together for a change, he turned and was surprised to find Adam slouching through the door.

"Good morning," Niall said. "Sleep well?"

Adam grunted and dropped into a chair, instantly tipping the front legs off the ground and the back against the wall. With an insolent half-lidded glance at Niall, he popped a cigarette out of the pack with his left hand and fumbled with the lighter, then stared at Niall through a plume of smoke, daring him to object.

Siobhan had allowed him to smoke, and Niall had long since decided that was one of many battles he'd have to let Adam win—at least temporarily—so long as Adam confined it to the kitchen. He remembered himself how it felt to have no say in one's own life. And he'd learned the hard way where that kind of resentment and defiance too often led. If Adam needed a cigarette to feel he was seizing control in some small way of a life that had spun out of kilter, fine, let him smoke. They'd solve that problem together later.

Of course, letting Adam feel defiant meant Niall had to appear appropriately disapproving. He scowled and cracked open the window above the sink. "Do you need to light that up? We're about to eat."

"Coffee's all I want," Adam countered. "I'm going for a drive with Kieran. He said he'd be going to the university library for research."

"I don't think that's a good idea." Niall turned hastily toward the stove to hide his fury.

Adam slapped the lighter against the table. "That's what he said you'd say—said you'd told him to stay away from me. But I want to go."

Niall froze in the act of picking the spatula up off the counter. Glinting off the bay, the sun through the large window bored into his eyes, making him squint as he parsed how many things in Adam's casual statement were so, so wrong.

"Why don't you spend time with someone your own age?" He deflected all the deeper problems for the moment. "I can drive you and Soren to the youth center later if you like. Or swimming."

"Soren's a git. You don't mind when I'm talking to Gemma or Liam. Or even poncey James." The volume of Adam's voice rose dangerously. "You only hate Kieran because you're not allowed to fire him, and you can't stand it he's going to take the credit off you for whatever you're going to find."

Niall set the frying pan carefully back on the stove and turned around. "Is that what Kieran told you?"

Adam drew back, his face shuttering, and that was all the reminder Niall needed to rein his temper back in. He raked a hand through hair that was getting long enough to make him look as wild as he felt.

Adam's expression hardened, his jaw clenching and his lips tightening into a narrow line, compensating for even that brief flinch of uncertainty he'd dared to display. "Kieran said he'd let me drive his Porsche, only he was sure you wouldn't let me."

"Let you—" Niall shook his head and turned back to slide two eggs, over hard the way Adam preferred, onto the slices of fried bread he'd already dished out onto Adam's plate. "You're not legal. Come on, Adam. You can see through that. It's easy for Kieran to say he'd let you drive when he knows it's never going to happen."

"You're jealous of him, aren't you?" Adam snapped, flushing. "You hate him. Why don't you just admit it?"

Niall opened his mouth to deny it, but his desire to bloody Kieran's nose for him was growing day by day. At about the same rate that, despite's Niall's best efforts, Niall's relationship with Adam had been going steadily downhill ever since those few moments of vulnerability that Adam had displayed at the hospital when Niall had first arrived.

Freshly back on the island after Siobhan's funeral, Niall had been shocked at how much the wounded earth of the excavation had reminded him of his twin's raw grave, how raw he himself had felt, as if a part of his own familiar self had been cut away and Adam, unfamiliar and wounded, had been grafted in its place. Knowing Adam needed him but helpless to reach him, he'd tried to stay close, spending as much of his time cleaning and recording and studying the artifacts at the more permanent field lab they'd set up in Ballynacallagh where they were stored under lock and key. Maybe it had been easier to hide his own grief there as well, but he kept getting sucked back to the dig to mediate when Kieran picked arguments with James or Gemma. When even Liam had started losing his temper, Niall'd had no choice, and he'd told Kieran to pack his bags.

He should have known better. Stepping into a decent spot of mobile coverage this morning, his phone had dinged with several messages from the head of his university department demanding Niall phone him back.

"Are you insane, firing Kieran Stafford?" Graeme

O'Neill had come close to shouting. "The prime minister is setting a timetable for stepping aside and it would take a miracle for the party to choose someone other than Callum Stafford to take his place as *taoiseach*."

"I can't help that. Kieran's not pulling his weight, and he's bringing down morale." Niall had responded cautiously, wandering outside to stand in the overgrown yard of the cottage, looking out over the nubby patchwork quilt of fields and pastures that rolled down toward the sea.

"And you couldn't think to warn me?"

"I left you a voicemail."

"And if you weren't at the back of beyond, I might have been able to reach you before I headed off to a university fundraiser—one where Kieran's father happened to show up to hand over a generous check."

"Buying a career for his wee lad, is he?"

"Can't afford a whiff of public embarrassment, more likely," Graeme had said. "Not if he wants the nomination. But that aside, Callum Stafford can buy the lot of us with pocket change. Whatever you said to him yesterday, find a way to make your peace with Kieran. You don't need an enemy of that sort. Nor do I."

Niall had watched the silver-gray water of Dursey Sound swell and froth white where the wind slapped it into the tidal race. Before the advent of the cable car, the ever-present wind had often made the island unreachable, but Kieran Stafford had only to point his finger and his father's wealth and growing grip on Irish politics extended even here.

Niall couldn't let the rest of the team suffer for that,

though.

"He's a bully, Graeme," he said. "That's the short of it. The team can't work with him, and that makes him a liability."

"You're the one who chose him, so make it work. For God's sake, Niall. You're good with people. Bring him around. Frankly, you haven't any choice."

From Graeme, that statement had been a simple truth, but it smacked of repercussions. Without Graeme on his side, Niall didn't have much hope for job security. Not that Adam needed to hear all that.

Standing in the kitchen now, in the face of Adam's accusation, Niall struggled to balance diplomacy and truth. "It's not that I hate Kieran," he said. "But I don't like the way he takes pleasure in stirring things up, and we don't see eye to eye on how to treat people. I could forgive all that, but he's using you to get to me—"

"You're only siding with James like always."

"Can't you see how inappropriate it is, what's Kieran's doing? We have a plan that the team all approved. Kieran has a difference of opinion, but that's a professional issue. Not one he had any business discussing with you—"

"Because no one could ever want to talk to me."

"Because it's about his work. *Our* work."

"Because you think I'm a kid!"

Niall told himself to keep calm. Not to overreact.

Adam's behavior was only to be expected. Adam was grieving and angry and lashing out—trying to provoke reaction. His whole life had been upended. How often had

Niall reminded himself of that these past five weeks?

Every morning, Niall had looked himself in the mirror and sworn he'd take the good example Malcolm O'Rourke had set him and argue only over what really mattered. Hard as he tried, though, he was failing miserably at finding the line between giving Adam a taste of responsibility and keeping him out of trouble. Especially when that trouble came wearing Kieran Stafford's face.

With a quiet sigh, Niall carried Adam's plate to the table and sank into the chair beside him, all too aware that the dirty cast on Adam's right forearm was a reminder, frankly, of the least of the injuries Adam had suffered. The more serious ones ran deeper.

Swiveling in his seat until he was perpendicular to the table, he leaned toward Adam and tried to catch his eye. "Think, mate. You've got a good brain in your head. Ask yourself why Kieran'd be telling you what he's telling you. What's the point of it? If Kieran and James and I have a disagreement about our professional opinions, venting to you about it isn't going to get Kieran anywhere. And you're right, I did want to let Kieran go. Still do, given the way he bullies James and Gemma and can't be bothered to do his share of the physical work. I'd rather find someone who can be part of the team, but he went crying to his father, who pulled out the checkbook. That's a hard lesson. For me, and you."

Adam's jaw hardened, but his eyes were hollow looking back at Niall, hollow in a way that made Niall's heart ache for him.

Niall nudged the plate a half inch closer to Adam. "Come on, eat a bite or two." He settled back. "Look, Adam. The world is a different place for someone like Kieran than it is for the rest of us. That's the ugly truth, but that's why a dig like this—this particular dig—is important. Things like the massacre are important."

"Aye, right. It was four hundred years ago." Adam's voice was thin as he exhaled a lungful of smoke, supremely unimpressed.

Niall swallowed down a sigh. "It was, and that's a long time ago, but it still matters. Kieran's father and his political party could do with a reminder that if we're not careful, big business and the big farms can be built on the same ideas that caused what happened here. Policies that put money and power ahead of people. But truth matters more. When innocent people are slaughtered, women and children and those old enough to have earned some peace, we owe it to them and ourselves to learn what we can from it. The past matters because human nature doesn't change. I'm not perfect, mate. It's true I can't help resenting Kieran when he assumes that what he has is his by right, but if I feel that way, no one should ever see it—and it should never affect my decisions. If it has, I can only try to do better. That's one thing. When he tries to come between the two of us, it's something else entirely. You're far too important for me to let that happen."

"Then let me have some fun, why don't you? That's all I want. It's Saturday. *Saturday*, yeah? And I'm stuck on this bloody island without internet or telly!"

46

"You're right. Sure." Niall drew back. "Tell me what you want to do. As soon as I get the new volunteers settled in, I'll drive you and Soren wherever you like. Meanwhile, I could use your help—"

"Don't!" Adam let the front legs of the chair thud back down again, and the long ash of the cigarette fell off onto the kitchen floor. "Don't lie about how much you need me. Just let me go with Kieran. Least he talks to me like I'm not a kid."

Niall recognized the challenge in the blue eyes that were so much like his own. Didn't he remember himself at Adam's age? Brawling, smoking, challenging authority, doing whatever he could to push people away. To make them think he didn't care that life had double-crossed him. He'd very nearly ended up in prison for that attitude—would have done for certain if Malcolm hadn't seen through him to the fear that was all he had left to cling to.

"If you're thinking I'm not listening to you, I'm sorry," he said, "but I am your guardian, Adam. I'm responsible—"

"But I don't want you, do I? It's my da I want!" Adam jumped up out of his chair.

How was Niall to tell Adam his own father didn't want him? More so when that father had spent the last fifteen years blowing in and out of Siobhan's life whenever he needed money or a place to stay, playing the hero—for both Siobhan and Adam—and blowing out again whenever it suited him to go. Both of them had forgiven him every time and ached again when he inevitably left.

Niall tried to find the right words, but there were none.

"It's not ideal for you, all this. We're both trying to find our way, doing the best we can. All I can say is that I love you, and your happiness and safety matter to me above all else. I've never forgotten what it was like, being uprooted at your age. Feeling like I was on my own with only myself to count on. That's the last thing I ever want you to feel, but I do have a dig to run and a staff and the volunteers to manage. Still, if you need to get off the island, I'll find the time to take you."

"Like you found the time when I phoned you before Ma killed herself?" Adam threw the still-burning cigarette to the floor and ground it into the tile.

Niall stood up slowly, feeling old. "I made mistakes when it came to your mother, a lot of them. Not making sure I got hold of you that day is the one I regret the most, and believe me when I say you can't blame me for that any more than I already blame myself. That doesn't change the fact that you and I have to find a way together."

"You're still too thick to get it, aren't you? I. Don't. Want. You." Adam stared at Niall with his chest rising and falling heavily, then he suddenly snatched his phone off the table and crossed the kitchen in five long strides. Before Niall could guess what he was about, he'd thrown back the door and darted outside, and the door slammed behind him so hard it bounced open again.

A cold blast of wind blew a sheaf of Niall's excavation notes from the edge of the table to the floor. Too stunned to do more than try to wrap his brain around Adam's words, he didn't think too hard about where he'd gone at first. Where was there to go on the island, after all? Then again,

Adam wasn't thinking straight, and there were loose rocks and abandoned houses aplenty, and the cliffs—to say nothing of the orange bull that had gotten cross with a tourist just the day before yesterday when the bloody woman had tried to cross a field she'd had no business crossing.

Even on Dursey, there were a sight too many places where a lad who wasn't paying attention could get in trouble. Not to mention the toll of letting Adam keep thinking what he was thinking.

Jumping to his feet, Niall headed for the door himself.

The cottage was on the far side of the first of the abandoned villages. It was the smallest of the three properties Niall had rented for the staff, but it had a view of Oileán Beag and the dig site so he could keep an eye out. He'd imagined Siobhan loving the view, watching over the stone wall built in the distinctive local herringbone pattern while lambs chased each other in the adjacent field. The wall was meant for livestock, though—and it was all too easy for a boy of fourteen to jump, even with one arm in a cast.

By the time Niall had reached the patio, Adam was already halfway across the field en route to the road, heading away from the village, the dig, and the steepest of the Dursey cliffs. Headed toward the cable car. Which was just about ready, Niall confirmed with a horrified glance at his watch, to land the first visitors of the day.

Honestly, when he got his hands on Kieran Stafford, Niall intended to throttle the man. But he needed to catch Adam first.

Not bothering with the car, he took off at a dead run

across the field. After vaulting the wall on the other side, he jumped onto the road, and pounded after Adam, still shouting for him to stop. Adam glanced over his shoulder and put on an added burst of speed.

Niall cursed himself for being a fool. For letting Adam spend too much time following Kieran around like a puppy, taken in by his Porsche and his grown-up interest. For thinking too long—mistakenly, it was painfully obvious now—that Kieran would have the common decency to respect Adam's vulnerability instead of using the opportunity to turn himself into some misguided object of hero worship. For what? Because Kieran'd used his father's money to buy himself the sort of flash car no grown man needed unless he had something to prove to himself or someone else.

Pushing himself even faster, Niall topped the rise near the ruins of the old monastery near Oileán Beag and ran on. Up ahead, the pale blue and white box of a cable car was already descending toward the concrete platform that served as a station. If he'd had the car, he could have been there by now. But he'd thought he could outrun Adam—he hadn't been thinking clearly.

Gemma was already at the station, waiting to greet the arriving volunteers. If Niall'd had remembered his phone, he could have called and warned her. Not that she could have done much to head Adam off. Adam was too tall, too angry, and Gemma would have been no match for him. Pete in the control room, on the other hand, could have kept the cable car on the island long enough to keep Adam from slipping out of reach.

Day by day, Adam seemed to slip further away, and Niall never seemed able to catch him.

How had he made such a mess of the relationship between them in five short weeks?

EXPLOSION

"Why be the sheep when you can be the wolf?"

R.L. LaFevers
Grave Mercy

OUTFITTED HEAD TO TOE IN top-of-the-line outdoor clothing, Meg's mother settled herself on the wooden bench of the metal box that passed as the island's only regular form of transportation. Meg slid in beside her, and her eye caught on a tattered copy of Psalm 91 and a plastic bottle of holy water that hung beside the speaker to the left of the rickety doors. And the vague smell of sheep lingering inside the car explained the small sign she had spotted at the station proclaiming that livestock and islanders had preference over visitors. She hoped to goodness her mother noticed none of that.

The idea of her mother sharing the cable car with sheep or cows or pigs—Meg couldn't help smiling at the image—boggled the mind. She wasn't even sure how it would work. There was scarcely enough room for a livestock crate, just the floor and two narrow wooden benches.

With a rattle, the car shook into motion, conveyed along the cable overhead. Reaching the end of the mainland, it headed through a tower composed of steel bars formed roughly into the shape of a handheld mirror with a rectangular frame. Threading through the steel with mere inches to spare on either side gave Meg the momentary sense of traveling through Alice's looking glass. Then the car swung out over Dursey Sound and swayed wildly as it was struck by a gust of wind.

Beneath them, the channel was not much past low tide, water churning against sharp black rocks and white spray climbing the cliffs on either side. From this height, much of the four-mile-long island was visible through the windows in the cabin's double doors and the narrower ones above the seats. Brilliantly green, the landscape was a minimalist canvas of hill and stone and sea and sky punctuated by an occasional sheep or darker clusters of grazing cows. Myriad ancient rocks crouched exposed amid the sod, despite the enormous quantities that had clearly been collected through the centuries and stacked onto walls around the pastures or formed into the homes that stood in the three ghost villages that had long since been abandoned.

Beautiful desolation. Those were the words that came to Meg's mind, a land out of time caught in a tug-of-war between the elements and modern life. Unlike most places in the world, here on this wild island, the elements—nature—seemed poised to win. There was a quality to the stubborn green, green grass and even the very air that suggested it would all be here long after the last human inhabitants had done their worst. Meg shivered at the thought, and then the wind gusted again. She found herself flung sideways, tipped onto her mother's shoulder.

Her mother inhaled sharply and clutched her new lavender daypack against her stomach, staring out the window. "We're coming in too low," she said as the car slid toward the support structure at the island end that matched the one on the other side. "Doesn't it look like we're going to hit that tower?"

"It always looks like that, but it's safe." Gretchen Falsberg—one of the veteran volunteers Meg and her mother had met the night before—gave a jittery sort of laugh. Her narrow high-cheeked face was pale enough so the light dusting of freckles stood out on her nose.

"It's only an illusion," Gretchen's boyfriend, Marcus, said with an amused there-there-frightened-females look directed at them both. "See? We're exactly where we need to be."

Ailsa Cameron shut her eyes as they swept through the tower, her spine rigid and her grip on the daypack even tighter. A fresh gust of wind rocked the side of the car, pushing it into a support beam on the right. It gave a screech of metal on metal, and Meg's mother squeaked, like a cat in its sleep, then bit her lip as the car lurched away.

"It's all fine, Mom," Meg said. "We're through now."

Ailsa kept her eyes closed. "I was thinking maybe it wasn't a good idea to stay on the mainland. We should look for something in one of the villages. One of those self-catering rentals. There's not much point in paying for a bed-and-breakfast. We had to rush through the food this morning, and I barely had time for coffee. We'd save all that time waiting in line and the ride over here, then walking to the excavation site. That's close to an hour right there. Then we have to do it all again in reverse every evening—"

"What, and miss singing with Fergal?" Meg teased, smiling at the memory of her mother—after a third glass of wine—fudging her way through "Brown Eyed Girl" and "Molly Malone" with the other guests and laughing like Meg hadn't heard her laugh since . . . well, ever. Somehow Fergal had seemed to know just how much Ailsa needed a release, and from the moment they'd entered the dining room, he'd hovered over both her and Meg, keeping their drinks filled during the simple but delicious meal of Guinness stew and brown soda bread. Afterwards, once he'd introduced them to the rest of the lodgers and folded them firmly into the group, it would have seemed rude not to stay and sing for a little while. That little while, though, had quickly turned to hours.

Meg's throat still ached pleasantly from belting out songs she hadn't even known were Irish and many that weren't—the guests came from all over. She'd enjoyed it, loved the singing, loved not thinking. Not obsessing. Either over her own mess or her mother's divorce. She loved being with other people so she didn't have to pretend to be on her mother's side when she wasn't and couldn't be.

The idea of a place on the island, just the two of them in the quiet evening emptiness, with only the insistent voices of her mother and the churning ocean and her own insistent doubts for company, held no appeal.

"I'm sure we'll get used to the cable car, and we'll settle into a morning routine in a day or two. Anyway, you wanted an adventure." She took her mother's hand. "Think of the stories you'll be able to tell when we get home." She tried to drum up support from a pair of twentysomething students from Leeds who'd already been on the dig for the first five-week session. "It can't always be this windy, can it? Tell me the crossings get easier."

"Not really," one of them said. "But then I'm afraid of heights anyway."

"All things considered, the wind's not bad today. You could probably even cross over by boat. Can't do that most days," Marcus said.

The cable car descended steadily toward the tip of the island, where the land rolled steeply to meet the sea. Above the waterline, the civilizing cover of soil and grass had scrubbed away, leaving a snarl of bare, ruffled rock and, some feet to the right, a shallow bay nestled into the curve of steeper cliffs. It looked almost as if some other creature had taken a deep, wounding bite and swum away out to deeper water with the lash of a powerful tail. There was no station on this side, no attendant, only a narrow pad of concrete that sat on top of a stone tower surrounded by bare steel pipes fashioned into a rudimentary railing. A steel-pipe pen below the empty platform disgorged a group of seven or eight recently sheered sheep that were quickly moved up the ramp by a pair of black and white sheepdogs under the supervision of a stout, gray-haired woman wearing yellow shorts.

Fascinated by the dogs' efficiency, Meg watched them work as the cable car swayed to a halt. She stood back and held the door for the others to go through, then exited herself as the milling, bleating sheep reached the top of the platform, jostling each other. With a little "oh" of mingled alarm and irritation, her mother rushed to the other side and clutched the railing. Meg, stuck, retreated to the railing.

"Adam, stop!" Some distance away, on the road approaching the platform, a man shouted as he ran.

Simultaneously, a teenage boy with one arm in a cast rocketed past Meg's mother, darting like a track star through the sea of sheep, shoving them aside with both hands until he reached the cable car and dove through the open doors.

"Adam, get out of there!" the man shouted again from the road. "Mary Elizabeth, hold him, would you now? Don't let him go."

The voice was Irish but without the thick accent of the cable car operator or the local server they'd met at the bed-and-breakfast. Hearing the fear in that voice, Meg looked at the boy more closely. He was young, only thirteen or fourteen, with early pimples erupting on his cheeks and forehead and light eyes beneath dark, unruly hair. Even over the distance there was a strong family resemblance between him and the man running after him.

Seeing the man approaching, the boy's face filled with both fury and an ugly sort of glee that didn't bode well, especially when there was only the one cable car and it would be fifteen minutes before it made the round trip back again if the man didn't reach the platform before it left. An angry teenager determined to run away could be headed just about anywhere in fifteen minutes.

Meg acted on pure instinct. The farmer—the only possible candidate for a Mary Elizabeth in sight—was wading back up through the sheep, but the boy had them agitated. With Mary Elizabeth not guaranteed to make it, Meg ducked back inside the cable car herself and caught the boy's uninjured arm.

"Hi," she said cheerfully. "Is something wrong? Can I help?"

"Oi, get off!" The boy wrenched out of Meg's grasp and shoved her.

Off balance, Meg flew into the door and collided cheek first with the sharp metal latch.

Her cheek throbbed, but she had no time to dwell on it. The woman with the sheep had arrived at the platform, and she issued a sharp command Meg couldn't quite make out. The two border collies barked in an ecstasy of excitement and launched themselves toward her, sending the bleating sheep leaping and bumping each other to get out of the way. Meg had barely had time to duck aside with a hand pressed to her face before the dogs reached the top of the ramp, flung themselves into the cable car, and each caught a mouthful of the boy's jeans. Heads lowered, they put all their body weight into dragging him by the legs back toward the door. He kicked at one dog, and it gave a yelp and darted back.

"Lashing out at defenseless animals now, are you, Adam Sullivan? That's what you've come to? Haul yourself out of there. Come on. Leg it." The farmer, carrying a large, empty plastic bottle—on whose purpose Meg chose not to speculate—stormed over, shooing the sheep away. "Get a move on. I've got a full load of animals to get over to the farm, and it'll be you waiting your turn if you're going anywhere at all. There's poor Niall calling for you, too." Deftly reaching past the dogs, she grabbed the boy by the arm and dragged him out as though, used to hauling livestock, a teenage boy was no trouble at all.

He raised a fist to ward her off, then seemed to think better of it when she merely raised an eyebrow and the dogs growled low in their throats. Or perhaps he realized the cable car was already lurching into motion, leaving him nowhere to go. It departed the station, and they all stood on the platform surrounded by animals, the farmer's substantial chest heaving in righteous indignation and the boy fuming until his face looked as though it had been all but boiled in a pot. Meanwhile, the man—the boy's father?—arrived, shoving sheep out of the way and threading past Meg's mother and the bewildered volunteers who'd been pulled aside down below by a pretty young red-haired woman with both arms covered in tattoos.

Out of breath, he stopped in front of Adam, but it was the farmer he spoke to first. "Thanks for that, Mary Elizabeth. I owe you."

"You're all right, Niall," the woman said, patting him on the shoulder with a quelling frown in the boy's direction.

The boy had a suggestion of "city-dweller" to him, and Niall didn't look like a farmer, so Meg wondered if he could be the head archeologist whose name appeared in all the paperwork. He turned toward her. "Sorry about that," he began. Then he stopped and went pale. "Jesus," he said, "you're bleeding."

She had been transfixed watching the drama, and she lowered her hand and looked down at the blood that coated her fingers. There was quite a bit of it, actually, and the throbbing in her cheek had grown more insistent. She could only imagine her mother's mortification if she were to end up with a cut and a black eye that would have to be explained away to everyone they met in Ireland, and she had a sudden vision of herself, the self of two weeks ago that she wasn't even certain existed anymore, being shown a video of this moment with her standing here dressed in camping clothes in the midst of a crowd of sheep after getting into what amounted to a fight with an angry teenager.

The thought brought a sudden, hysterical urge to laugh.

She didn't, of course. Still, something of her thoughts must have shown in her expression because the man and the boy both gaped at her, their faces losing even more color beneath their tans. Digging into the pocket of her yellow shorts, the farmer produced a tissue and handed it to Meg. "Look at the state of you, now, poor girl. Here, take this. But you'll need to be having a doctor take a look at you. That'll need a stitch or two."

Meg looked down at the tissue briefly, wondering whether to wipe her hand or press it against her cheek. Her mother, hurrying up beside her, had no such qualms. "No, no." Ailsa unzipped one of the lavender daypack's many pockets. "Hold on. You'll need disinfectant. I've got some wet wipes here somewhere. And alcohol. Good heavens, what did you do to yourself?"

"I've no idea," Meg said, since she couldn't see herself. "It's probably just a scratch. Faces always bleed a lot."

"That's head wounds, not faces. But this looks rather deep." The man was staring at her, his eyes a dark, insistent blue, and then he blinked and raked a hand through dark hair that had a tendency to wave. "This is unforgivable. Adam should never have pushed you." He nudged the boy toward her. "Apologize, you terror. Right now."

"I'm sorry," the boy said, looking and sounding so shocked—and so much more like a child than an angry teenager all of a sudden—that Meg couldn't help pitying him, though she'd have pitied him more if he hadn't raised his fist to Mary Elizabeth, too.

But there was no sense in alienating him any further. "Honestly, I didn't help matters," she told him. "You worried me, trying to run off like that. I reacted without stopping to think."

Her mother gave a small crow of triumph and produced an alcohol wipe and a pack of gauze from a mini first aid kit. "See, I knew I had these in here somewhere." She pressed them into Meg's hand. "Now hurry up. Clean that before it gets infected."

"It's all right, Mom. I'm fine," Meg whispered.

"Fine? That's going to scar. You don't see yourself.

What you need is a plastic surgeon—a good one—or there won't be any way to hide that with makeup so the camera doesn't see it."

Her face heating with mortification, Meg carefully wiped her hand with the tissue that Mary Elizabeth had given her before reaching for the alcohol wipe, mostly so she wouldn't offend the farmer and wouldn't have to look at anyone. "I'm sure it will look much better as soon as I clean it off."

"You're lucky you didn't poke your eye out. And could you—for once—try not being stubborn?" Meg's mother dug out a mirror and waved it in front of Meg. "You see? Look at yourself."

Meg had to admit she looked like something out of a horror film. Blotches of drying blood were smeared across the right side of her face and the wound—more of a puncture than a cut—was raw, deep, and oozing blood. She dabbed it with the gauze, but that did little to help, and she tore the top off the alcohol wipe.

"I wouldn't do that, if I were you." Mary Elizabeth bent to nudge a fat lamb out of the way as it pressed between her and Meg. "Alcohol will only damage the skin and make the scarring worse. Salt water's what you're after, love. Clean it out good and proper, that will. But listen to your mother. No sense standing on pride, like. There'll be a plastic surgeon in Cork, or there's a hospital in Bantry. They'll have someone who can stitch you up."

"We'll be happy to take you into Cork. Adam and I will," the boy's father said, the words quiet and certain, an order rather than a question, as though he was used to giving orders. "It's the least we can do. I'm Niall Sullivan, by the way. You were coming to work with us at the dig for the next five weeks, weren't you?"

Meg nodded awkwardly and introduced both herself and her mother, who instantly agreed that Cork was necessary and Niall driving them made perfect sense.

"Good, that's settled." Niall squeezed Adam's shoulder. "Give me a minute, and I'll tell Gemma what's going on so she and the others will know to do without me."

Before Meg could even respond, he turned and pushed past the sheep again toward the cheerful, red-haired woman Meg had noticed rounding up Gretchen and the other volunteers. He moved confidently, his body lean-hipped but strong and broad in the shoulders, arms and the back of his neck tanned darker than his face from long hours spent bent over in the sun. Dressed in convertible outdoor pants and the sort of lightweight technical T-shirt that dried quickly and showed every muscle beneath it, he had nothing to be ashamed of in that department. His face wasn't bad, either. A solid face, full of character. The kind of face that was good on camera and held an audience's interest.

Meg's mother pressed a package of tissues into Meg's hand. "Don't try arguing your way out of this, Margaret. I know you, but you can't be stubborn and let this affect your career. Ruin your career."

She glared at Adam as though she would have liked to slap him. Adam shifted uncomfortably, watching with a pale, sweating sort of fascination as Meg changed tissues. He wouldn't meet her eyes.

Meg's career was quite possibly over anyway, so she told herself that her face was the least of her worries. Still, there wasn't much point arguing with her mother.

The thought brought a familiar flash of resentment. How was it that after all these years, Meg still felt betrayed and disappointed, like a child who had missed out on a coveted birthday present, by the realization that her mother still believed it was her looks that drove her career? Never mind Meg's other achievements, her degree, her awards, her experience, her hard work. Meg was an award-winning journalist with a good instinct for stories.

But really, how much did her mother's attitude differ from Ruben's? Not so very much. That was the simple truth. It wasn't only within the broken apparatus of news and entertainment where women were judged on their faces and figures more than men.

This—*this*—was exactly why Meg had decided not to stay and fight it out with Ruben. She'd seen too many women get the bad assignments, the lack of support, the subtle nudges that eased them out the door. Maybe it made her a coward, but she'd figured it was wiser to plead an emergency with her mother and take a break instead, give herself time to think it all through before she made her next move. Or a fresh mistake. Fighting for her job would have meant revealing the fact that she and Ruben had been having a relationship, and instantly, all of her accomplishments would have been discounted. By viewers even more than by the networks and producers. Women like her mother so often judged other women more harshly than they would judge the same mistake made by a man.

A not insignificant part of Meg almost welcomed the idea of a scar on her face. Not a large one, small, like this. One only large enough to become a crutch she could lean on for absolution. One she could use to cast blame on the industry's weaknesses instead of her own. Because the truth was, it had been her choice to date Ruben, her own loneliness and the mistaken belief that she was smart enough to know the kind of man he was—and sophisticated enough to navigate the complications.

When it came to salvaging her career, though, she needed to be smarter. Preserve her options. Otherwise, she'd eventually regret it. And Adam certainly didn't need the guilt of thinking he had left her scarred for life.

Turning back toward him, she searched for a way to soften her mother's words without absolving him of all the responsibility. He had, after all, kicked at the dog and barely caught himself from lashing out at Mary Elizabeth as well, and he certainly wasn't giving off a guilty vibe. In fact, he wasn't paying attention to Meg at all. His gangly limbs had stiffened, his eyes locking on a blond man just this side of thirty who was coming toward them along the road, his hands stuffed deep into his pockets.

Niall Sullivan had spotted the man as well. Breaking off his conversation with the small, tattooed girl, he veered toward the newcomer with tension written in the set of his shoulders and the forward thrust of his spine. As they met, he gestured back toward Adam, and though his back was still toward Meg, she could see the man stop a cautious few feet away.

For Adam's part, his entire body coiled, and he darted a look around, as though searching for a bolt hole or, failing that, a place to hide amongst the sheep. The same mask of resentful fury he'd been wearing earlier descended back across his features.

From whom had he been running earlier? Niall, or this other man? Possibilities shuffled through Meg's brain like playing cards, ugly possibilities based on ugly stories she'd reported throughout the years.

If nothing else, those possibilities absolutely ruled out subjecting Adam to hours with her mother in the tight confines of a car.

Having come to a decision, she turned back to Ailsa. "I'll make you a deal, Mom. I'll go to the hospital if you'll stay here and go through the orientation for both of us. I'd only feel guilty knowing you were missing out on meeting everyone, and there's nothing you can really do anyway if you come with me. Niall and Adam can help me figure things out at the hospital, and you can catch me up on what I missed here when I get back."

BEAN SIDHE

"The banshee (from ban [bean], a woman,
and shee [sidhe], a fairy)
is an attendant fairy that follows the old families,
and none but them,
and wails before a death."

W.B. YEATS
FAIRY AND FOLK TALES
OF THE IRISH PEASANTRY

THE SIGHT OF KIERAN STAFFORD ambling toward him, made Niall want to hit something. Especially given that the man managed to look as though he hadn't a care in the world, as if he wasn't cutting swaths through Niall's team and family like rot eating at roots, inch by insidious inch. Nodding vaguely at what Gemma was saying about the orientation lectures, Niall shifted over, ready to extricate himself.

"I'm sorry, Gem. I always seem to be ducking out on you when new volunteers are about to arrive, but I really do need to go. I'm sure whatever you arrange will be fine—you and Liam did a grand job the last time. If something comes up, just—well, no. That won't work. Even if the phones were halfway reliable, I didn't even think to bring mine."

"Take mine, boss." Gemma reached into her pocket and dug her mobile out for him.

"Thanks, but you keep it. You can try ringing Adam's number. I'll text you from it once we're on the mainland. Right now, I'm needing to have a wee word with Kieran before I go."

"Might have figured. Is he at the bottom of all this, then?"

Niall ignored that, because Gemma didn't need more ammunition where Kieran was concerned. "Will you thank Liam for pitching in, and James? I'll bring round a bottle for you later to make it up."

"Hold on, boss." Gemma laid a hand on his arm as he started off. "Go easy on Kieran, eh? Not because he deserves any kindness, but you'll be lucky enough not to have Adam up on charges without adding to your problems."

"Charges?" Niall did a double take. Gemma stood with the morning light spilling around her, catching in the fine mist that the churn of the sea sent up from the cliffs, and there was no hint in her expression that she was joking. "You think they'd have Adam on assault?"

"I didn't see it all, but it looked bad. It's probably good you're taking the poor girl to the hospital, that's all I'm saying, so have a care with Kieran. He's already looking for ammunition to use against you."

The warning poured memories like cold water down

Niall's spine. He knew from his own experience how easy it was, at Adam's age and with far less than Adam's troubles, to make a mistake that changed the course of an entire life.

Which was the very reason he couldn't ignore what either Adam or Kieran were doing. If he didn't stop Kieran winding Adam up, they'd end up with even worse than the poor girl standing on the ramp with bloody tissues pressed against her face. Shoving a woman? Raising his fist to Mary Elizabeth and kicking one of her dogs? None of that was excusable under any circumstances. Instead of getting better, Adam seemed to be struggling more and more, like a swimmer caught in low tide with crosscurrents pushing at him and sending him tumbling until he didn't know where to put his feet.

Meg Cameron. Niall turned back to look at her. From this distance, she was a slip of a thing with dark hair in a braid down her back, but it was her eyes he remembered. Solemn gray and wide eyes as clear as windows that seemed to swallow her entire face.

He knew who she was, of course. He'd had to approve her as a volunteer two weeks ago as a last-minute addition, and—given what Gemma had said just now—he realized abruptly how much trouble she could cause. Not only was her mother a friend of the dig's single largest financial contributor, which in itself carried an expectation of preferential treatment, but Meg Cameron was a presenter for one of the biggest morning shows in the States. Gemma and Liam had already been laying odds the past two weeks on what sort of daft American celebrity habits she'd be bringing with her—yoga at three in the morning or eating only a certain colored food on specific days. Still, she'd been a good sport about the injury so far. With any luck, for both her sake and Adam's, there wouldn't be any lasting damage.

Niall glanced back at the cable car to check its position. He still had time—it was barely to the station on the mainland. Until it came back to Dursey, there was nothing he could do to get Meg Cameron to the hospital any faster. He could, though, at least try to do something about bloody Kieran.

Adam was off-limits. He had to be.

"Problems?" Kieran smiled warily as Niall approached.

Niall gestured back to the platform where Adam and Meg Cameron waited. "Does it bring you some perverse sense of pleasure to use Adam to wind me up? Or are you simply too thick to grasp the effect you have on him?"

Kieran's face went red. "Hang on, you can't talk to me like that—"

"You far and away crossed the line from a professional relationship when you brought Adam into this." The last of Niall's hard-won patience swept away on a tide of red, and he closed the distance between them. "This is me speaking as Adam's guardian, not your supervisor. That's the line you've crossed. I asked you—begged you—to stay clear of him, Kieran. He's grieving, and he's hurt and angry. He needs family he can trust, but even that can't keep you from undermining me with him at every opportunity. Is it really so important to you that he see you as some sort of hero? Your ego's that fragile?"

"*My* ego?" Kieran stepped back and his expression hardened. "You'd be the last person to lecture me on that. You've ignored every suggestion I've made because it's James who sings your praises from morning to night."

There was a place inside Niall, a calm, deep place, where he'd learned to stand apart from the stream of life when things got to be too much. He dove into the sanctuary of it now, trying to control his temper. Still, he had to jam his fists into his pockets before they could connect with Kieran's jaw. "I'm not discussing this with you again. We'll get to St. Michael's when we get to it. Keep away from Adam. Understand?"

"You've never thought I might just feel sorry for the boy, have you?" Kieran called after him as Niall turned to go. "My mother died when I was fifteen. I know the kind of turmoil he's in, and I know what it's like when no one understands. He doesn't even have his mates here for company. Soren Johansen doesn't count. They hardly have two words to say to each other, and the closest thing to hardship Soren's ever faced is deciding which brand of cereal to eat. Adam has no interest in archaeology. He's here with nothing to do, and you've no time for him. I'd have thought you'd be grateful if I talked to him, kept an eye out—"

"Telling him you would have let him drive your Porsche but I wouldn't let you? That's your idea of keeping an eye out?"

"I didn't want him to think I was rejecting him, too, did I?" Kieran glared back at Niall with his breath coming sharply. "He already feels everyone hates him, like he's here with you on sufferance. You have any idea how that hurts? Knowing the one adult left in your life always has something else he needs to be doing. Something more important."

Niall's mouth opened to refute that, but he couldn't. Right or wrong, wasn't that exactly how Adam felt?

To a teenager, truth was about feelings instead of facts, about what they knew by instinct. It made no difference that what Kieran said wasn't true, and no amount of telling Adam otherwise would change how he felt.

Niall would never in a hundred years have imagined he could feel sorry for Kieran, but thinking of what he'd seen of Callum Stafford, he could imagine how hard it must have been for a motherless boy growing up in the shadow of a man like that. Kieran had the polished manners, the veneer of confidence, but underneath it, there was a vacuum of need that made it hard to like him.

Did Kieran even know how much hollowness he lived with every day? Possibly using Adam to lash back at Niall was entirely unconscious. It was possible, Niall conceded, that Kieran was also telling the truth as he saw it when it came to befriending Adam. It could be Kieran genuinely saw something of himself in Adam and was trying to reach out.

That was the basic problem with Kieran. Consciously or unconsciously, he managed to sniff out and exploit vulnerabilities with consummate skill. Niall'd seen him do that with both Adam and James, and he'd tried it with Gemma, too. Niall had to find a way to make him stop.

He studied Kieran, and—not for the first time—he wished it was easier to set aside his own resentment. No matter how many times he told himself it had been his own decision to let Siobhan drive down to Dursey on her own, though, he couldn't help wondering if she might still be alive if Kieran's attitude hadn't sent Gemma into a temper or James into a quiet sulk. Which wasn't fair, he knew that, but blaming someone else was always easier than accepting one's own guilt.

"I want to believe you, Kieran. I do," he said, running a shaky hand across the back of his neck. "And if you are genuinely trying to help, then give Adam time to heal. Give the two of us time to find our footing without inserting yourself into the mix. There's work enough for you to do without insisting you get your way all the time, and I promise that the rest of the staff will meet you halfway if you'll only make an effort. Your father can make it hard to fire you, but he can't make you part of the team. That's the one thing you have to do yourself."

Not waiting for Kieran to answer, he turned and headed back toward the platform where Adam stood sullenly by himself watching Meg Cameron talking to her mother. Mary Elizabeth and the dogs had herded the sheep back down toward the bottom of the ramp, where the dogs circled, keeping them from wandering off.

"I'll let you and that poor girl take the next car over," Mary Elizabeth said to him as he jogged past her. "With the drive to Cork, it'll be long enough before she's seen to, and it'd be a shame if she ended with a scar for her troubles. Now, you make sure to have her wash it out properly before you set off. Eamon at the caravan will have what you need." She peered at Niall with a motherly mixture of pity and amusement, then patted him on the arm. "She's a lovely thing, isn't she? Won't be a hardship for you to spend some time with your head out of the dirt for a change. And don't you worry about Adam. He may drive you to drink a while yet, like, but it's only natural it'll take time to see him right after all he's been through. I saw worse with my own boys, and now look at them. Both back here farming on the island and bringing their own sons up on Beara. Was a time I couldn't go a half hour without hearing how much they hated me—and this place. Now off you go. I'll stop around tomorrow for a cuppa, and you can tell me all about it."

Niall couldn't help smiling at Mary Elizabeth's phrasing, given that she'd gotten into the habit, these past couple of weeks, of bringing a thermos of tea and a sweet to share with him every other day. That and a tidbit of local history or folklore she'd dredged up from somewhere or remembered from growing up on the island before her parents had moved the family off. She had a sharp eye as well—too sharp, often enough.

"We all need help now and then." She patted his arm. "No shame in that, Niall. Don't you worry about feeling overwhelmed, and don't go doubting yourself. There's plenty of help to be had for the asking."

The cable car pulled up to the platform, and the door opened to disgorge the second batch of volunteers for the day. Niall squeezed Mary Elizabeth's hand and mumbled, "Thank you."

"I know, I know. Away with you," she said.

Niall jogged up the ramp and was waiting on the platform beside Meg and Adam by the time the last of the volunteers climbed out of the cable car. The three of them managed to duck inside and sit down before the box wobbled back into motion. Adam slid down to the corner, as far away from him as possible, with the sort of stubborn guilty desperation of a dog who's made a mess on the carpet and knows he deserves to get in trouble. Meg, meanwhile, still held a tissue to her cheek, and the bloom of blood on it continued to spread.

"Mary Elizabeth suggested we see Eamon at the fish and chips caravan before we set off. It's a good idea," Niall said to Meg. "We could get a snack for the road."

"Isn't it a little early for fish and chips?"

Niall swallowed back a laugh. "Eamon can offer something sweeter than fish, I promise, and he'll have salt and water so we can do a better job flushing out the wound. Unless you'd rather go back to your hotel and do it there." He cleared his throat as he said that, as she continued looking at him. "Clean the wound, I mean."

"Of course." She sat back further on the bench across from him. "The caravan is better. We're at the Bay Point, and Fergal's wonderful, but I think he's the kind to make a fuss."

"Oh, him and Ari both." Niall shifted in his seat so he wasn't staring at her. "But they're brilliant, aren't they? Nearly all the locals have stopped by the dig out of curiosity, but Fergal and Ari are regulars. They come by with cake or biscuits for the volunteers a couple of times a week, and Fergal's even been known to do a bit of digging."

"And singing," Adam said. "He makes the volunteers sing while they work. It's deadly."

Meg laughed—a good laugh, the kind that was natural and made a person happy to hear it. "He had us singing last night. My mother and I were ready to drop into our beds after the trip, but before we knew what hit us, we were in the bar instead. He even had my mother singing, and that's saying something. I haven't seen her enjoy herself like that in years."

Niall tried to imagine the aggressively elegant Ailsa Cameron letting loose at one of Fergal's *bothántaíocht,* but it wasn't an image that conjured easily. The type of woman who wore heavy silver jewelry with a top-of-the-range, neatly pressed all-weather camping shirt was more likely to be the sort who played at archaeology the way it had been conducted in the nineteenth century, when it had been the province of the adventurous rich traveling with sterling place settings, bone china, and native bearers. The sort who didn't play well outside her class.

"Fergal insists Adam and I should come out for his musical evenings, but we're hostage to the weather and the cable car schedule out here. I've heard great things, though. He ran a music school in Australia for years, which is where he and Ari met, then his mum died and left him the family sheep farm near Castletownbere, but he couldn't bear having to sell the animals off—and he felt sorry for the sheep when they were sheered—in case they got cold."

Meg laughed again, and Niall found himself searching for something else to say to make her continue laughing. "I picture him chasing after them with blankets," he said. "And staying up all night bottle-feeding lambs to make certain the ewes get a good night's rest."

"I can imagine that," Meg said.

Niall glanced at Adam, who was scowling insistently. Maybe a little too insistently.

"Anyway," Niall continued, "they sold the farm after a year and bought the bed-and-breakfast, and they've been fixing that up ever since. The evenings are Fergal's way of keeping people and music in their lives, somewhere between a pub night and the traditional gatherings at a neighbor's house that used to be a staple in the area. That and they're both smart enough to know tourists expect the 'Oirish' to be full of singing and drinking, eating corned beef and cabbage, and everyone saying 'Top of the Morning' to each other."

Meg laughed as he'd hoped. "You disappoint me. You mean that's not how it really is?"

"Sorry to be the bearer of truths, but there you have it. There's no such dish as corned beef and cabbage in Ireland, at least there didn't used to be, and if you say, 'Top of the Morning,' it's only one step up from asking if we've ever seen a wee leprechaun."

"Oh, don't tell me that. I was expecting one at the end of every rainbow—right beside the fairy forts and banshees."

"Fairy forts we have aplenty," Niall said. "No worries, there. About 45,000 of them, only in my profession we call them raths or hill forts. There's one on Dursey, come to that. Not much left, but I'll show you, if you like."

"And *bean sidhe* are real," Adam piped in, his eyes glittering with something between wistfulness and defiance. "I've heard one myself, singing on the island, haven't I? Seen her, too, in a gray dress walking in the field beside the cliff."

BLOODY GROUND

*"They give birth astride of a grave,
the light gleams an instant,
Then its night once more."*

SAMUEL BECKETT
WAITING FOR GODOT

A S MANY INTERVIEWS AS SHE had done in the course of
her career, it never ceased to delight Meg when she
got an answer she couldn't have anticipated. Nothing
in Adam's intriguing mixture of combativeness and
vulnerability had suggested anything like this.

"A banshee?" she asked.

Adam's expression tightened into superiority. *"Bean
sidhe,"* he corrected, splitting it into two words and adding a
slightly different—Gaelic—intonation. "I'm an O'Sullivan
on my mother's side. They dropped the O but the blood's
still there."

Confused, Meg turned from him to Niall. "Both you
and your wife are Sullivans? Or did you take her name?"

There was a brief silence, then Adam gave a disgusted

snort. "Niall's not my da, he's my uncle."

"Siobhan—Adam's mother—was my twin. She was killed five weeks ago in an accident," Niall said, his voice dropping in both tone and volume.

He didn't say any more, but the words were there in the way he looked at Adam, with a raw mixture of love and pity and bewildered exasperation that gave Meg's heart a painful twist.

"I'm so sorry," she said, not knowing which of them to look at. Seeing so much open anguish on a man like Niall, someone who didn't seem like the type to wear emotion on his sleeve, made her want to look away, to give him privacy. On the other hand, you had to be so careful with teenage boys. Vulnerability too often turned to anger.

She tried to imagine the enormity of losing a twin. Or a mother.

No wonder Adam was acting out and seeing ghosts.

"I don't think I've ever stopped to imagine what a banshee looked like," she said, summoning up a casual tone to keep him talking if she could. To help, if that was possible. "I'm Scottish on my mother's side. You might have guessed that—she hasn't completely lost her accent. But I'm not even sure if they have banshees in the Highlands, whether that's a Gaelic–Celtic thing or purely Irish."

"The Scots have their own version, but it's a little different," Niall said.

"And forgive me if I'm being dense, but what does seeing a banshee or not seeing one have to do with being an O'Sullivan?" Meg turned to Adam, watching him as he stared out the window, noting his body rocking back and forth. When Adam didn't answer the question, she glanced back at Niall.

He was watching Adam, too, almost visibly willing him to respond. After a long pause, Niall cleared his throat and answered himself. "The function of a *bean sidhe* is to call a spirit home. There's a certain school of thinking that claims they only appear to the original clans of Ireland, and that how they behave depends on their relationship to that family. If the family was one of their enemies, they scream in delight at the knowledge that another of their foes is about to be cut down. But if they're friendly, they can warn that death is coming or provide reassurance and welcome for a person who's meant to die."

"Ours watches over us," Adam said, turning to them with his eyes strangely empty. "Over the people she loves. Comforting them. Waiting for them."

That bleak look in his eyes as much as the words themselves left a shiver trailing along Meg's spine, and she had to force herself not to grip Niall's arm and make sure he'd noticed. She didn't know what to say. When she turned, Niall's eyes met hers and lingered long enough to let her see how deeply Adam worried him.

Hands clenched at his sides, Adam jumped to his feet as soon as the cable car pitched to a stop.

Meg had almost forgotten that they were moving, but she wished they had more time. More opportunity. Then Adam dove out the door and Niall bolted after him.

The two of them were both so clearly broken. Meg

wondered if Niall had gotten Adam a counselor or therapist, someone to help him cope with the grief and changes. Adam didn't really seem the type to take such a suggestion willingly, though. She thought of how hard it had been to hear that her parents were divorcing, and she was two decades older than Adam. And her own parents would both still be as close as her telephone if she needed them, not simply there one moment and gone the next. Except that in a way, they were gone, because they weren't the same people she'd always believed them to be.

Ducking through the door, she paused on the concrete platform with the wind whipping her hair and the crash of tide in Dursey Sound sending up a fine, chilling spray. Adam slunk off to a dusty white Peugeot station wagon parked at the edge of the lot not far from a red Porsche 911 and tried the passenger door. Unable to wrench it open, he hit the window with a fisted hand then turned and walked in front of the car and stood looking out across the fields, the picture of hurt and fury and loneliness.

Niall, still partway across the parking lot, stopped and watched him. Equally hurt and lonely, Meg suspected, though she didn't have any right to think so.

She tried to consider what to do, how to give them space. If she crossed the parking lot and walked up the path to the Bay Point, Fergal would sweep her inside—sweep them all inside—and the mood would change. Any chance of Adam continuing to talk would vanish, and he clearly needed to talk, if Niall could get him to open up.

Smiling at the volunteers and tourists who were queued

up waiting for the cable car to make the fifteen-minute round trip to the island, she edged past a tall woman in a wide-brimmed hat who was waving a steaming disposable cup of coffee in one hand and a sticky napkin in the other as her hands punctuated whatever she was saying to a friend. Several of the other volunteers were holding disposable cups as well, and the window at the blue-and-white fish truck parked near the station was open. Meg set off in that direction.

The truck's owner, a spry, balding man in what had to be his mid-seventies at least, had a line of what looked like bread machines lined up along the back of the far wall beside the fryers. Turning to Meg as she approached the window, her feet crunching on the gravel, he wiped flour from his hands with a rag and leaned over the counter on his elbows, beaming. The wide smile behind his long white whiskers faded as he took in the tissue she was still pressing to her face.

"You look like you could use some doctoring. Come around the back to the door and let's have a look at you," he said. "I have a first aid kit here."

Meg shook her head. "Thank you, but we're off to the hospital in a minute. I was hoping to get a cup of water and some salt, if that's all right?"

"Of course it is, bless you." The man dug under the counter for a container of salt and measured out a generous amount into a cup before adding steaming water from the enormous metal thermos. He filled the cup halfway, then stirred vigorously, his expression intent. Finally, he turned back to the sink and added more water before coming back to slide the cup toward Meg across the gleaming metal counter. "There. The tap water's safe. I've added cold to keep it from damaging the skin—don't want it too hot. Now what about gauze and tape? Or tea and a doughnut? All the above?"

A giggle bubbled up Meg's throat. "You had me at tea. That would be fantastic." She accepted the cup he'd slid over and poured some of the saline onto a folded napkin. Holding it pressed against her cheek, she winced as the salt soaked in and stung. Then, thankful her mother wasn't there to reproach her about empty calories, she decided to indulge herself. They hadn't eaten much for breakfast after all. "Did you really just say doughnut?"

"Deep fryers work equally well for that." The old man picked up a small blue trashcan from behind him and lifted it so Meg could throw the used tissue inside. "Makes sense when you think on it, like. Now, what'll you be having? I can do chocolate, strawberry, sugar glazed, or caramel toffee. They're all good, if I say myself. Or you could try the Nutella. That's my Eileen's favorite." He leaned in closer. "She swears it's the best thing I've ever given her. Mind you, we don't mention that to any of our seven children or eighteen grandchildren." He chuckled, and with his bald head, white whiskers, round rosy cheeks, and a family that size, Meg couldn't help wondering how many times he'd dressed up as Santa Claus. Of course finding a Nutella doughnut was pretty much like Christmas morning anyway.

"Eamon makes the best doughnuts in Ireland, as far as

I'm concerned," Niall said, walking up behind her. "Let me get you some. It's the least I can do."

Meg glanced sideways at him, then busied herself throwing the napkin in the larger bin beside the window and dampening another. "Adam might be hungry."

"Possibly, but fair warning—it'll take more than doughnuts to sweeten his disposition."

"Does he have a favorite flavor?"

"Toffee. And the strawberry. Though he's ordered chocolate a couple of times, too, come to think of it." Niall shook his head. "Honestly, I haven't any idea what's in his head. About doughnuts or anything else."

He smiled at her with a wry shake of his head, but it was a haunted smile that struck her as brave, though she'd never particularly thought of smiles in that way. She found herself studying, and he was the kind of man who drew one in the longer that one looked. It was one of those faces, Meg decided. The kind that was good looking without being pretty and changed with every thought and mood.

Less afraid of intruding than she was of stepping into something on the long drive out of ignorance, she worked up her courage to ask, "What was Adam—why was he—running away this morning? If you don't mind telling me. Was is something to do with his mother?"

"He won't talk about Siobhan. Not as much as he needs to. We argued, but one way or another, he's been running since he got here. He was glad to see me at the hospital after the accident, but he's been getting progressively angrier, and I don't know how to help him."

Something in the way he said that made Meg wonder whether it was only Adam who was having trouble coping. "It takes time for grief to sink in," she said. "All those stages."

"I know, and everyone takes it differently. I've read the literature."

"I can't even imagine losing a mother at his age. And his father?"

Niall leaned across the counter and ordered three teas and a mixed dozen doughnuts, evenly split, before turning back to face her. "His father's no use," he said. "I'm all he has, and I'm not much of an improvement. Every day that passes, I realize how much I don't know about teenage boys." He picked up another couple of napkins and folded them together into quarters, then gently took the cup of water from Meg and soaked the napkin with it. "May I?"

She nodded, and he set the cup down and stepped close to dab the wound. He was intent as he worked, and she had the odd impression he was the sort of man with the rare ability to focus all of his attention on a task. It made her uncertain where to look—it felt too intimate looking back at him, but impolite to look away.

His smile was sweet—kind—as he soaked the wound and then wiped gently at the blood that streaked her cheek. "Would you mind—" he began, then shook his head and started over. "What Adam said to you about the *bean sidhe* comforting the family, that's the closest he's come to talking about Siobhan in weeks. And what he said about waiting— that smacks of survivor's guilt. Or worse. I've no right to ask at all, but he seems to connect with you more than me. Would you see if you can keep him talking?"

"I'll try." Meg frowned at the bloody napkin in his hand, took it from him and threw it into the larger trash bin beside the window. She found Eamon taking out a sheet of parchment paper containing precut doughnut shapes and dropping them into the deep fryers, turning to watch her and Niall occasionally as he worked, his eyes bright and curious within their folds of wrinkles. "Now you realize you've created a dilemma by ordering all those different doughnuts," she said to Niall, changing the subject. "I've no idea what I want."

"I won't be much help with that," Niall said, grinning. "I happen to be a purist. With Eamon's doughnuts, anything more than a crisp dusting of sugar would only spoil the perfection of all that yeast and air and grease and goodness."

Meg found herself smiling at him again, at this big man who loved his nephew and talked about doughnuts in a way that made her stomach growl. Uncomfortable, she turned away as Eamon came back to snap lids onto the three steaming paper cups he'd set out on the counter earlier.

"In that case," she said, "I guess I'll have to make a point of working my way through every flavor in the next few days."

Eamon nodded, beaming widely. "Oh, a girl after my own heart, you are. And you'll be needing to try my fish and chips. After you get that pretty face of yours seen to, of course. How'd it happen, anyway?"

"I was clumsy, and I'm prone to sticking my nose where

it isn't wanted," Meg said easily. "This time, my cheek just got there first."

Niall's eyes focused on her and rested there, surprised. Then they shuttered, and he took the three cups that Eamon slid over and asked her, "How do you like it? Milk and sugar?"

"A hint of sugar and too much milk," she said, "at least according to my mother."

He added all that and gave her the hot cup, then doctored another for himself and one for Adam. Eamon went back to the fryer, and they both stood sipping and watched him work, the silence between them comfortable enough that Meg didn't feel the need to fill it. She wasn't even thinking anything in particular when Niall spoke again.

"You're being very good about all of this . . . Adam and—" He extended a forefinger, gesturing toward her cheek, making her go still at the thought that he meant to touch her. "Does it hurt much?"

"Not much." She raised one shoulder an inch or two.

In the fryers, the doughnuts grew and bloomed and turned a golden brown, like leaves changing from spring to summer to fall, and the scent of dough frying curled out through the open window in invitation, hinting at one of those food moments where everything in the universe conspired to make something ordinary unforgettable.

Meg imagined the segment she could have filmed about this marvelous Santa Claus of an Irishman and his doughnut and fish truck out here in one of the most beautiful places in the world. How quickly did the smell of frying doughnuts dissipate? If the wind blew westward, how far out into the Atlantic would the scent of Eamon's doughnuts travel? She was surprised that half the seagulls on the coast of Ireland weren't circling the parking lot like ocean-going pigeons.

But she didn't have a camera crew or even a place where the story could be told.

She watched, a little bereft, as Eamon removed the doughnuts with a spatula then set them on a paper towel while he eased the next batch into the fryer. When the last few were done and drying, he removed several large ziplock bags from the refrigerator, each with a small bit of a bottom corner cut away and, one flavor at a time, drizzled the toppings over the glistening doughnuts in even strokes. He stacked them in a box and slid it onto the counter as carefully as if the contents were the crown jewels of Ireland.

Meg reached for her wallet, but Niall beat her to it. Handing over a banknote, he added a smiling "Thanks, Eamon," and he picked up the box.

"Mind you don't forget to stop and tell me what you think," Eamon called after Meg as they turned to go.

"I won't," she said, and she followed Niall across the parking lot carrying her own tea along with the cup for Adam. He was still over in front of the dusty Peugeot, picking up rocks and throwing them hard into the nearby field.

Niall's expression went tight as he stopped beside the car and watched a moment. Adam didn't turn.

"Adam?" Niall prompted after a minute. "You ready?"

He opened the door for Meg, flipped the lid of the box

open, and handed her a napkin from the sheaf Eamon had tucked inside. She peered into the box, trying to decide, then the lid shuddered as Adam slammed into the back hard enough to make the vehicle shake. Plucking out one of the creamy, glistening Nutella-topped variety, Meg exchanged a glance with Niall, then dropped into the passenger seat.

Niall's voice held amusement. "I won't disrespect your unfortunate choice, but I will beg you to at least have a bite of mine. You'll thank me once you can actually taste the doughnut beneath the topping."

Meg had never imaged that doughnuts could be sexy, but somehow Niall made her think illicit thoughts. Which was ridiculous. Absurd. And *so* not what she needed to be thinking about Niall Sullivan.

He moved around to the driver's door with that easy stride of his and lowered himself behind the steering wheel before plucking out a doughnut for himself. He passed the box back to Adam. Glancing at Meg, he broke off a small piece of the pastry and handed it to her. As he'd promised, it was yeasty and light as a cloud as it collapsed in her mouth, like no doughnut she'd ever tasted, and the crumbs of sugar lingered like a kiss.

Behind them, Adam sat with the box on his lap, staring down at it without opening it to take one. He was brooding again, brooding more, and Meg thought about what Niall had said about survivor's guilt.

"So, Adam," she said cheerfully, hoping to pick up where they'd left off. "The banshee. I'm curious. Were there words or just a tune when you heard her singing?"

She didn't think Adam would answer, he let the silence drag so long. But he flipped the doughnut box open and ducked his face behind the lid.

"There are words, but I don't understand them," he said. "Can't even hear them, really. What she says is gentle, I know that much." He leaned forward, intent on making Meg understand as though that was important. "She's sad."

"Is the O'Sullivan banshee always sad?"

"*Bean sidhe*," Adam corrected. Then he shrugged, and just like that, the opportunity was over. He turned to look back out the window, leaving Meg wondering what else she could have said.

Niall switched what remained of his doughnut to his other hand as he shifted the car into gear and turned off onto the main road. Briefly, he watched Adam in the rearview mirror, then pressed his foot back down on the gas as a minivan rounded the bend behind them.

"The whole idea of *bean sidhe* is sad to me," Meg said. "It seems only fair that things like pain and hate and sadness should fall away once you die."

Niall flicked a look at her. "It'd be nice to think so, wouldn't it? But the old families—those were ugly histories. Cruel ones, with people fighting to survive any way they could. Some of the stories claim *bean sidhe* are messengers more than ghosts. Leftovers from a time when the first families arrived and they and the old gods divided Ireland between them, mankind above ground and the gods below."

"I'd have thought gods could negotiate a better deal," Meg said.

Niall's laugh was dry. "One would think. But good deal or bad, they kept their bargains. The fortunes of the families rose and fell—and kept falling once the English came. My father used to say the *bean sidhe* sang all the sweeter the crueler a family's fate had been, so the O'Sullivan *bean sidhe* sang the sweetest of them all." He slanted a wry smile across the car to Meg. "You know the story of the Dursey massacre and the O'Sullivan march?"

"Only what I looked up once my mother talked me into coming."

"Thanks to Mary Queen of Scots, people think more about Elizabeth I's problems with Scotland, but it was Ireland and the Nine Years' War that nearly bankrupted the English treasury. Many of the Gaelic chiefs came together to fight, and Donal Cam O'Sullivan Beare led a guerrilla war here in the south after the Irish defeat at Kinsale. But the Spanish who had fought with them there betrayed them and handed the local castles over to the English to save themselves. Donal Cam tunneled back into Dunboy and reclaimed it, and Elizabeth's commander, Sir George Carew, sent in an army of five thousand men with orders to show no mercy. Every one of Donal's men who wasn't killed in the siege was executed after they'd surrendered. Their families—the elderly, women, and children—had all been sent here to Dursey for safety, but the English came here, too ."

"They ran the babies through with spears and paraded them around," Adam said with the relish for the gruesome that was the particular province of teenage boys. "Tied the women and children back to back and threw them over the cliff. Then shot them while they fell."

He observed Meg while he told the story, and she couldn't help shivering as though he'd drawn the edge of a knife across her skin. The cruelty mankind could inflict on itself never changed, but every generation thought cruelty had been reinvented especially for them.

"The glory of war," she said, her voice laced with bitterness. She wrapped the doughnut she'd barely touched back into her napkin and held it on her lap.

"At the time, it was how wars were won and empires were made," Niall said, shifting gears.

"It still is. Shock and cruelty and displays of power." Meg examined his profile, which had grown sharp and cold against the green pillow backdrop of the surrounding Beara hills. "But I thought the Dursey fortress was destroyed at the time of the massacre, so what are you hoping to find?"

Niall pulled off to the shoulder to allow a black Ford that had been tailgating to pass, then he eased back onto the road. "There's no precise record of when the massacre took place. The English commander, Carew, and a nephew who served as his secretary, weren't shy about recording their own atrocities—to the contrary, they were matter-of-fact about them—but the particulars here are lacking. Mostly it was Phillip O'Sullivan, the son of the Diarmuid O'Sullivan who'd built the Dursey fortress, who recorded stories from the handful of survivors. There are some historians who claim the massacre didn't occur until a few months after the fortress was razed, in a second wave under Sir Charles

Wilmot with a mixture of English and Irish troops."

"Can you narrow an event timeline to months based on artifacts?" Meg asked.

"We might at least be able to tell whether it was mostly English soldiers or Irish who did the killing. That would help tell us which historical accounts are more correct."

WRAITHS

C HECKING IN AT THE EMERGENCY department in Cork, Meg said nothing about a plastic surgeon. In Niall's estimation, that not only defeated the purpose of having driven all that distance, but it also left her liable to get sewed up by the first doctor who came along. An overworked resident, most likely, that would have been, one who hadn't slept in thirty-six hours or longer. Niall waited until Meg had returned to her seat to complete the forms, and then he leaned across the counter and smiled at the woman who manned the desk.

"Is there any chance you could have my friend see a plastic surgeon or someone who could minimize the scarring?" he asked. "She doesn't want to be a bother, but she's a television presenter in America, and the injury is my Adam's fault. An accident, but I don't want him feeling guilty. He's only just lost his mother five weeks ago."

The receptionist was built like a rugby player and she had the long face of a dyspeptic horse, but her expression softened as she looked across the waiting room to where Adam slouched in a blue chair. Using his cast to hold the phone in place against his knee, his fingers flew one-handed, texting with his mates in Dublin or whatever he was doing while his head bobbed in time to the music coming through his earbuds. Meg's earbuds, more precisely, since she'd loaned them to him after he'd tired of conversation in the car and started to act the maggot.

"Poor lamb," the receptionist said. "Cancer, was it?"

Niall shifted on his feet, wondering if he'd ever get used to the explanation. If he'd ever feel less as though talking about Siobhan's death was disloyal or just plain wrong. The fact of it still felt soft-focused and fuzzy around the edges, like an old film technique for a nightmare. But saying it, discussing it, made it, word by word, more real.

"She rear-ended a bus not paying attention," he made himself admit with brutal candor. "Adam was in the car with her."

The woman's eyes flew to his, wide open in shock or maybe disapproval.

Shock most likely, since an instant later she thawed and said, "Let me see what I can do."

After tapping the keyboard of her computer, she half turned away and picked up the phone. A brief English greeting was followed by a rapid Irish conversation Niall had to concentrate to follow. Growing up in Dublin and not in the Irish-speaking western enclaves known as the Gaeltacht, he'd been bribed into learning the language by his father, a fact he'd hated at the time but had appreciated every day since choosing to study Irish archaeology. Honestly, though, he was better with the written language than the verbal, especially the urban verbal outside the Gaeltacht where phonetic and grammatical structure was morphing into something simpler.

The receptionist explained Meg's situation to someone on the other end of the line and asked if a Dr. Baqri couldn't work her in. "It'll be a handful of stitches, not much trouble."

An hour and a half later, Meg had a fresh pad of gauze taped over her cheek after having had the wound cleaned by a hospital doctor, and they sat in the waiting room at the plastic surgeon's office on the other side of town. Decorated in chrome and glass, the room smelled of incense, and there was a low, soothing gurgle of water cascading down a wide sheet of glass on the wall into a basin of river rocks. Three well-dressed women had spread themselves at equidistant points from each other in the far corners of the room, careful not to make eye contact or speak to each other. Each looked at Adam without bothering to hide their distaste.

In his outdoor clothes, the whole environment made Niall feel out of his depth and itchy. He no more fit in here than Meg's elegant mother had seemed to belong among the excavation volunteers. Oddly, though, Meg seemed at home in both environments. Or rather, she didn't seem to consider her place within the environment at all. The fashion magazine on her lap was a prop, forgotten as she studied the room and its occupants and tried—periodically—to keep Adam engaged in conversation. Adam would say a few words in response then lapse back into silence, which was at least an improvement over any reaction Niall managed to achieve. Every time Niall spoke, Adam only turned up the volume on his music until, even from two seats away, the tinny beat and throb of bass seeped out through the earbuds.

Hearing it now, Niall leaned forward. "Adam, could you turn that down a bit? It's loud enough to carry clear across the room."

Adam ignored him. Or maybe the music was too loud for Niall's voice to penetrate. Impossible to tell.

Turning back to Meg, Niall swallowed down a sigh. "Thanks for loaning him those earbuds," he said. "Obnoxious as this is, he'd be even worse without the music."

"Don't keep apologizing for him. There's no need." She set the neglected fashion magazine aside on the small table beside her and swiveled in her seat so she could look at him more directly.

And maybe, because he'd spent the past five weeks with Adam, who seemed sublimely uninterested in the world around him, it struck Niall how rare it was for someone to give so much of their attention to others. How kind. It struck him, too, that her curiosity could so easily have seemed intrusive, but it didn't come across that way. Maybe that was all a professional trick she'd learned as a television presenter, but he didn't think so. It seemed to be who she was—the sort of person who genuinely cared.

"What made you come out for the excavation?" he asked. "If you don't mind the question. Five weeks seems like a long time to take off in your line of work."

"It was a case of the perfect storm. I left my job, and I'm still deciding whether to go back, and my father asked my mother for a divorce a while ago. She's taking it hard—though not for the obvious reasons. She can do fine without him but being his wife has defined her whole identity for forty years. Maybe coming here is a way to reinvent herself, a way not to have to stick around the country club putting on a brave face for her friends. She hasn't done anything like this—anything on her own, really—since she was eighteen, though, so I came with her."

"I saw on her application she had done a dig in the Hebrides," Niall said.

"Yes, that was where she met my father."

"So this is what? Nostalgia? A pilgrimage of sorts?" He didn't mean to give anything away, nor was he trying to keep secrets, either.

Meg turned in her seat and searched his face, studying him as though something in his voice or his words had made her suspicious. "Did Kitty O'Sullivan call you?"

"She emailed." Niall found his eyes on Meg's lips, and he reminded himself to look away. "She wanted to make sure we had room to take your mother on."

"And let you know you'd be doing her a favor by making room," Meg said.

"A little of that. She and her husband did invest quite a bit of money in funding the excavation. Nice people—or he is. I met him once after a lecture I gave, and that's how we connected."

Meg nodded, picking at a spot of something—dirt or dried blood—around the edge of her fingernail. "What I said about leaving my job—my mother doesn't know yet, so I'd appreciate it if you'd keep it to yourself."

"Of course. A career change?" he asked. "Or changing networks?"

"I haven't decided." She bent her head, letting her fine, dark hair screen her face again.

Niall let the silence spin out in case she wanted to fill it. She hadn't said much about herself so far, and if he hadn't already noticed her genuine curiosity, he might have wondered if she didn't talk about others as a means of deflecting questions.

In the quiet, he could hear every beat of Adam's music, and he shifted around and tried again. "Adam, turn that down, would you?"

Without acknowledging him, Adam shifted over another seat, which put him only a handful of chairs from a too-thin woman in her fifties with improbably unlined skin. She sent Adam one of those stares that could chill a person at fifty paces, then shifted her eyes to Niall to make sure he understood it was him she blamed.

Niall rose and dug a banknote out of his wallet. Forearms splayed over his thighs, shoulders hunched, Adam raised his eyes and his forehead accordioned with horizontal lines, then he looked back down at his phone.

Niall nudged him and waited until Adam sighed and pulled one earbud out. "Yeah?" Adam said. "What d'you want now?"

"I'd like you to go down to the shop and pick up tea for the three of us. Maybe a bit of something to eat as well."

"What?"

"Sandwiches. Protein. Something to cut the sugar from all those doughnuts. Whatever sounds good to you."

Adam waited long enough for Niall to wonder if he would refuse. Eventually, though, he lumbered to his feet, his every sinew taut with resentment.

Niall tried not to mind. In a way, the day had helped already. Watching Adam, hearing what he had to say about the *bean sidhe,* seeing the way he interacted with Meg, it had occurred to Niall that Adam felt guilty the moment he even briefly forgot his grief or allowed himself even a small amount of pleasure. Guilt always made anger burn brighter, and survivor's guilt was hard to shake. Niall'd had enough incarnations of it in his own life. The very fact that he was sitting here now, alive when Siobhan was dead, was down to Malcolm and Valerie O'Rourke.

What if they'd taken Siobhan instead of him? Would she still have been alive?

What if he hadn't made the mistake, when he was no older than Adam, that had led to the loss of the family business . . . if he'd made different choices?

If he'd gotten Adam's phone call. Or hadn't accepted Siobhan's excuses delaying coming down to Dursey. If he'd handled Kieran better, or hadn't let her drive herself down.

So many choices and regrets.

He stood watching as Adam slammed his way out of the waiting room, wanting to go after him, but just about certain it would make no difference. What could he say he hadn't already said a hundred times?

"Family is hard, isn't it?" Meg asked him, watching him in turn.

He wondered how much she saw—rather too much, he imagined, but he didn't mind. He settled back into the chair beside her. "It must be hard for you, too, coming with your mother like this. A lot of emotional baggage?"

Her eyes widened. "Some, but I have nothing to complain about. Seeing Adam makes me even more aware of how lucky I was, getting to grow up the way I did. Two parents and every opportunity. I'll always have that. It's more a question of what you already pointed out, I think. I don't know why she came, what sort of a pilgrimage she's on."

"It's not unusual for people to come back to an interest in archaeology after they retire."

"Yes, but she was never interested to begin with. It was her sister who was supposed to go on the dig, but she broke her arm so Mom went instead. It's strange for her to want to do this. But she's never been one to be upfront about what she wants or why she does something. Layers of truth, my sister calls it."

"A bit like history," Niall said.

Meg smiled—a half smile that brought out the faint dimple in her cheek, and he liked that smile almost as much as he liked her laughter. "It's all perspective, isn't it?" she said. "The choices we hide—the choices we embrace. The things we can't control."

He'd been thinking about choices himself so hearing her words felt like an echo. She was right, too. One choice inevitably led to another. His mother's choice to leave their father, his father's choice to drink, Niall's own choice not to mop up the broken bottle of juice that had led to a customer falling and suing, and the insurance premiums going up until there was even less money. Even less dignity for their father, who had, in turn, chosen to drink himself into forgetting. Someone choosing two different foster homes. Siobhan picking a useless man with whom to have a child.

One choice at a time.

"My sister did her best with Adam," he said. "But one's best often isn't good enough. It's hard for people to change even when they want to."

"Was it drugs?" Meg reached over and touched his hand, gently—empathetically. "I'm sorry, I hope you don't think I'm intruding, but I got the impression there was something about her death . . ."

She pulled back, leaving the touch of her compassion lingering on his skin and making it clear she would listen, but only if he wanted to talk. It made him feel as though he could. As though he wanted to.

Did he? Niall choked down a breath of the humid, perfumed waiting area air.

"I thought it was alcohol—she'd been through treatment before, and she'd been doing well, but maybe she'd been under too much pressure. She'd had a job at a restaurant in Temple Bar, getting good tips, and she was saving money for a better flat. Then the couple who owned the restaurant split up and the new owners made her position redundant, at least that's what she told me. She got into trouble with money, and started drinking, so I offered her an admin job on the dig so I could keep her and Adam close. They were on their way down here when she died. But she wasn't fit to drive."

"So it wasn't alcohol, then?" Meg asked.

"Heroin." Niall closed his eyes a moment and shook his head. "I hadn't had a clue. Clearly, I should have been paying more attention, but I was trying to get the dig up and running—and our relationship wasn't always easy anyway. Adam was eight before we even found each other again when she moved back to Dublin. And the more my life came together, the less Siobhan wanted me to see she was struggling. Proud, that was Siobhan. And she had every reason for it—she always could light up a room."

"Taking the job with you must have been hard, then."

"I suppose, and the drugs gave her courage. Or oblivion." Niall's breath caught, and his chest ached at the thought. "She and Adam had a fight about it, and he refused to sit up front with her. That probably saved his life."

Meg tipped her head and studied him. "Did he know she was on drugs—driving on drugs?"

"He knew she wasn't right. He tried to phone his father, and then he called me." The guilt that had been gnawing at Niall for weeks had left vast, empty holes inside him. It made his voice hollow now. "But the mobile reception on Dursey is spotty. I got a garbled message I couldn't understand, and I couldn't reach him when I tried to ring him back. And his father's a useless git. He always was."

Meg didn't say she was sorry, the way ninety people out of a hundred would have done. Her face crumpled, and those wide eyes glistened with tears she neither shed nor tried to hide. She touched his hand again and squeezed it briefly, quietly.

Niall discovered he appreciated that more than he could have imagined. Apologies were always such easy, throwaway things. How many times had his own father been sorry, how many times had Niall been sorry? The adults had all been sorry after every bad situation in foster care, yet nothing ever changed.

Meg's fingers were pale and as fragile as bird's wings against his own scarred, sun-darkened ones that were permanently stained in Dursey soil these days. Earth and air, a good reminder of how far removed their worlds were from each other. She blushed and pulled her hands away.

"I think it's harder on boys when they lose their mothers than society likes to admit. You get the usual messages about being strong, being the man. We all gave those to Adam even while Siobhan was alive. 'Take care of your ma, now, there's a good lad.' I told him that myself, not knowing how bad things were for them. And I should have known—Siobhan and I both went through it. Our own mother left when we were young. Said she hadn't counted on twins and a man who was no better than a child himself. Siobhan never had much of a role model, and Adam's father's a drifter. Plays in a rock band and comes and goes when it suits him."

"So that's why you took him in?" Meg asked.

"I wish giving him a roof over his head was enough. He's so far away I can't reach him. Blames me for Siobhan's death. Maybe he blames all three of us, his father, me, and himself. Himself most of all."

"Everyone but his mother." Meg tilted her head and glanced at the door through which Adam had gone. "So he's looking for absolution," she said. "Or confirmation of his guilt. Which explains the *bean sidhe*, I guess."

"An external monster to go with the one that's eating him from the inside out? Something like that," Niall agreed, and even as he said it, he hated that he was still failing Siobhan, failing her all over again. Failing Adam.

Almost daily these past weeks, he'd woken up in the night, his body slicked in sweat and his heart beating wildly, having dreamed that it was Adam driving, Adam hitting the bus. Adam who was dead. Lying awake afterwards, with only the sound of the ocean battering the island for company, he'd become all too aware that the distance from self-doubt to self-hatred was dangerously short.

"I get the impression Adam's not the only one who has that problem," Meg said, her voice so soft he had to lean closer to hear it. "You can't blame yourself for other people's choices, Niall. We can always look back and see things we should have noticed, should have done. *Should haves* are in the past, though, and the present is all we can really change. Adam can't have any idea how angry he is with his mother.

Not yet. Whether he wants to admit it or not, though, it's a huge betrayal to find that someone he loved and trusted put making herself feel better ahead of him. That kind of betrayal makes it hard to trust anyone again."

She sounded like the counselors and the self-help books—Niall had done the rounds of all of those these past weeks. But understanding the problem didn't remove the helplessness of not knowing how to make Adam whole again.

On the opposite wall of the waiting room, a black-and-white photograph captured streams of morning light on the Kealkill standing stones on a hill overlooking the pearlescent glitter of Bantry Bay. Niall remembered standing in that precise spot with its eerie, ancient loneliness and the stark beauty that had nothing to do with color. It was the sort of place where fantasy slipped into reality like wisps of mist drifting along the hills.

Six in ten people saw or heard their lost loved ones when they were grieving. That was one of the useless facts Niall had picked up along the route to his archaeology degree. He'd often wondered whether it was true everywhere in the world, or whether the percentage was higher in Ireland where the connection to the past was something innate to the landscape and coded in the DNA.

If Adam saw a *bean sidhe* in the wraiths of fog that danced along the cliff, heard what his mind and heart were desperate to hear in the whisper of the ocean and the distant cry of birds, that was understandable. It was past time Niall stopped letting him off the hook about going back to see the counselor. Even if Adam still refused to do anything more than stare at the floor for the duration of the session, at least he'd know he had someone to talk to if he wanted to talk. Someone other than Niall—or Kieran.

The nurse finally came to the door and called Meg's name, and Niall glanced at his watch and rose along with Meg.

"I think I'll give Adam a hand with the food while you're in with the doctor. I'll meet you back here when you're done."

SLIVER OF HOPE

"There is a crack in everything.
That's how the light gets in."

LEONARD COHEN
"ANTHEM"

I T WAS STUPID, ALL OF it, Adam stood in the sandwich bar downstairs, paralyzed by the choices on the menu board. He wanted something—he always wanted something—but it was a smoke-and-mirrors wanting, gone the second he zeroed in on it. The morning's doughnuts sat at the bottom of his gut like lead, and sugar raced marathons through his bloodstream. He wanted to run, too. Run and keep on running.

"All right, love?" An old woman, a cotton-puff of white hair glistening damp from the mizzle of rain that had started outside, tapped him on the arm, smiling in concern. "Only you've been staring a long time."

"Go on, then." Adam stepped aside and waved her past him, and she hovered a second then hobbled to the counter, three shopping bags draped across her scrawny old-woman arm. But even as she leaned in to place her order, she glanced back at him with her eyes sharp, like they could see right inside him.

Adam's face went hot. He was sick of concern and pity. Sick to death of having to explain himself or make empty, pointless conversation. Why couldn't people just leave him alone?

He swung himself around to the door and met Niall just coming in.

Niall's eyes widened, and another of those concerned smiles spread across his face. Patient concern—that was the worst. Like Ma's dying had been a disease Niall had to nurse Adam through.

God, Adam needed out. He reached around Niall and snatched the edge of the door before it was fully shut.

"Hang on, mate." Niall caught his elbow. "Where d'you think you're off to?"

Adam jerked his arm away. "Away. All right with you?"

"Are you still waiting for the food?"

Adam hated the softness in Niall's voice. The understanding. "Haven't ordered yet. Food makes me sick. *You* make me sick."

Shoving past Niall, he let himself outside. A fine mist of rain cooled his skin and drained the afternoon of color, making red haloes around the brake lights on the road in front of him and muffling the city loudness. He stood breathing hard. Breathing.

But even then, Niall couldn't let him be.

"The food wasn't just for you." Niall came to stand beside Adam. "Look, I know it all hurts now, but not everything can be about you. It helps to remember that now and then, believe it or not."

Adam turned to the right and started weaving through the people on the sidewalk.

Niall's shoes squelched on the wet concrete as he hurried to catch up. "You going somewhere in particular?"

"I need a bleeding cigarette. Didn't plan on spending all day in stupid waiting rooms, did I?"

"You think Meg did?" Grabbing Adam's wrist, Niall spun Adam around. He let go straight off, but his nostrils flared in and out as he breathed, and Adam could almost feel his heart beating, though maybe that was his own heart thundering.

"You going to hit me?" Adam stared up at Niall, hating the fact he had to look up, hating the knowledge that Niall saw what he felt, hating Niall. He stepped forward until he couldn't anymore, until their chests were touching. "Go ahead. Go on, then. Hit me."

He *wanted* Niall to hit him, he realized, without knowing why. He didn't know why he did a lot of things lately, but he couldn't seem to stop himself.

Niall's eyes were steady on his, and his voice was quieter than most adults Adam had ever known. Deceptively mild and tightly leashed. "Hitting anyone isn't the solution. It doesn't make you feel better—either to hit someone or to be the one on the receiving end. Think, lad. Do you want to be the sort of person who reacts like this? You've been dealt a hard blow, sure. Life's not always fair. That's the hardest truth to accept, the idea that bad things happen to people who don't deserve them and there's nothing to be done about it. The fear that maybe we deserved it more than they did, or that our own choices, our own decisions, brought harm to the people we love. But punishing ourselves won't change what's past. All we can do is move forward, making better choices."

Adam stared at the concrete, where a pile of dog shite was slowly dissolving in the rain. "You about done? Because if you are, then get out of the way. Or stop me. Your choice."

"Adam, listen to me. I used to be like you. Just like you. Angry and afraid, and fear was the last thing I'd have admitted to. I thought I wanted to punish everyone around me, but I was punishing myself more than anyone else, and that's what you're doing. Just ask yourself if that's what your ma would have wanted. You're the one person in the world she loved more than life itself. She wouldn't have wanted to see you hurting—whatever mistakes she made herself. You want to do something for her? You behave in a way that would make her proud of you. Be better than she was."

Adam stole a look at Niall, and his eyes were sad and tired—tired like Ma's had been. Adam had never thought about how much Niall looked like her. They weren't identical twins. But that sense of sadness, the tiredness, that was what Adam'd hated most. Her moments of being desperately tired that alternated with days of being desperately hopeful.

He hated Niall for giving her hope without really helping.

Turning away, he dug his cigarettes out of his pocket. Shook one out and tapped it against his cast. "Go back to your new friend," he said. "I'll wait by the car until you're through."

Niall measured him, weighed him. Adam hated that, too.

"All right, go have your cigarette," Niall said. "Do whatever you're needing to do. Push me as hard as you like. It won't matter because I'm not going anywhere. I love you, and I'm not going to give up on you."

Adam's eyes felt hot and his throat closed in on itself. He couldn't think what to say, so he said nothing at all.

MUSIC

*"He was angry with himself
for being young and the prey
of restless foolish impulses . . ."*

JAMES JOYCE
A PORTRAIT OF THE ARTIST AS A YOUNG MAN

H AND RAISED IN FAREWELL, MEG stood in the driveway
of the Bay Point and watched Niall pull the white
Peugeot back onto the road. Barely an instant later,
the front door of the bed-and-breakfast opened, and Fergal
and Ari bustled out to join her. Meg's mother trailed them as
far as the top of the stairs, where she stopped with her arms
wrapped around her waist, the ends of the brilliant red and
pink pashmina wound around her shoulders streaming like a
battle flag in the wind. Seeing her there, Meg tamped down
a muddle of love and irritation, given that it was not quite
five o'clock and the cable car back and forth to Dursey ran
till eight. Talking to Niall had renewed her awareness that
she needed to do more for her mother, but honestly, she was
exhausted, too. She'd been craving time to herself, a chapter

or two of a good book, a chance to breathe.

"How are you?" Fergal and Ari both said at once.

"Good as new," Meg responded. "The doctor was great."

Fergal stopped beside her. "We couldn't believe when we heard what had happened. Adam's a good lad, mostly." Stooping from his great height, he caught her chin in his long-boned hand, turning her face this way and that to examine the tiny stitches visible on the surface. "But they did a grand job—I've seen designer clothing that wasn't as carefully stitched as this, and you're still gorgeous as ever."

"Well, so I'd hope." Ari wound her elbow through Meg's arm, her warm smile revealing one front tooth that overlapped the other. "Come inside. Have a drink and relax and let us spoil you a little. The rain will start coming down any minute, and you must be parched after spending the day in the car and in the hospital. It's a shame Niall's rushed off already. They never get to have fun, those two. And poor Adam stuck out there—at his age—without the internet. Is it any wonder he loses his temper now and then?"

Meg thought of how Adam had disappeared into his music most of the day. Avoiding silence, but also avoiding conversation. But of the two, she suspected it was Niall who was even more broken by the guilt and the loss of his twin after Siobhan's death. Losing a twin—Meg couldn't even imagine that.

She thought of her own sisters, the hard push and pull that came with being family. As the eldest, she had somehow abdicated the responsibility to rebel most of her life, always trying too hard, trying to keep her mother happy—*make* her mother happy—which she was only lately realizing shouldn't have been her responsibility. Katharine had been the polar opposite, never caring what anyone thought, and Anna? She had traded-in trying to please their mother in her early teens and had instead become a lawyer to please their father. Funny that both Meg and Anna had thought it was their own dreams they were pursuing all that time. Then Anna had met her husband, Connal, and his daughter and realized what she thought she wanted hadn't been all she'd hoped. It had taken Meg a little longer to figure that out.

The thought stole her breath away. Where had it come from?

She still wanted her career. She'd been happy.

She *was* happy.

As if to prove that to herself, she smiled and looped her arm through her mother's as they went up the stairs. "So, how was the dig? Fun? Anything like what you remembered?"

"Never mind that, what did the doctors tell you?" Ailsa asked.

"Nothing much. I'll be fine."

Her mother studied her cheek with a critical eye. "It doesn't look too bad, I'll admit. That's a relief. If it leaves a scar, at least you should be able to cover it with makeup. Honestly, that boy. What were you thinking, trying to stop him like that? It could all have been much worse."

"It could have, but it wasn't. It was my own fault, and Adam's just lost his mother. She died five weeks ago in a car accident, so he deserves our sympathy."

Her mother pursed her lips. "That's just like you, isn't it? He pushes you, but it isn't his fault. Nothing's ever anyone's fault these days. That's the problem. No accountability. No sense of responsibility. Everyone does exactly as they like."

Meg stumbled on the threshold. Coming from her mother, that was rich. "That's not fair—I don't think it's any different from how it used to be. People make mistakes. You weren't much older than Adam when you got pregnant."

"That's not remotely the same thing." Ailsa whipped around to look at her.

Meg sighed and shook her head, craving a glass of wine. "If you say so." She smiled at Ari and Fergal, who had paused in the entrance to the bar area to wait for them. "We need to make allowances, that's all I'm saying. Glass houses and all of that."

Her mother glanced away. "Do you want a shower before dinner? Or we could eat now. It's early yet, so it's up to you."

Meg doubted that she'd have the energy to emerge from her room again if she took the time for a shower, and on top of that, she suspected her mother wanted to talk. As it was, she'd had to go to the dig by herself and meet the other volunteers knowing no one, face the very thing she had been trying to avoid, the reason she had brought Meg to Ireland with her. She was probably dying to talk about it, and it was the least Meg could do. "Let's go ahead and eat. I'm getting a little hungry."

A few minutes later, seated in the quiet dining room with its enormous windows that overlooked the steel gray sea and the clouds that had burst into a steady rain, she tried to keep her attention from drifting off as her mother swirled wine in her glass and provided a person-by-person narrative about the staff and volunteers, most of whom were college students or recent college graduates. Ailsa's sharp observations were no more than her usual catalog of people's flaws and weaknesses, but maybe because she was fighting to do a better job of listening, or maybe because she hadn't heard her mother sum up a collection of strangers in quite some time, Meg couldn't help feeling more uncomfortable than usual. Did her mother really see everyone as potential opponents whose vulnerabilities she needed to probe? It was a defensive view of the world, the perspective of a victim, someone under siege.

She'd never considered her mother in that light—never seen her from anything other than a position of strength. But the way people saw themselves and the way the world saw them were often very different.

"You've gone very quiet," Ailsa noted, interrupting herself. "Did the doctor give you anything for the pain?"

"It's just a little sore. No, this is exactly what I needed." Meg raised her own glass, the deep bowl of it gleaming in the light and the pinot noir in it rich and dark and smooth. "The wine and the ocean and an opportunity to enjoy being here."

"Hmm." Ailsa studied her. "And what about Niall Sullivan? I hope you're not thinking about him. I'll admit he's more attractive than I expected. I assumed the photograph on the website had been doctored up a bit."

"I don't see him as the type to doctor photographs."

"Everyone's that type these days. In academia and everywhere else. The cult of celebrity. I doubt he even has much choice if he wants to have a decent career."

"He didn't strike me as particularly ambitious, either. Just dedicated."

"Well, Liam and Gemma sing his praises enough to make me wonder what's wrong with him."

"They could simply be telling the truth."

"Oh, please. No one is ever that nice about anyone else unless they have an agenda. Probably hoping to talk us out of suing. They do seem to like him, though. Not that I'm sure you can necessarily trust their judgment. Why do otherwise intelligent people feel the need to deck themselves out in dreadlocks and tattoos? I'll never understand that. Gemma could be very pretty, but those tattoos go from her wrists all the way up her arms. It must be a self-mutilation thing. Think what her poor mother must feel seeing her like that."

"She might just be happy that her daughter's happy. It's Gemma's body, after all, not her mother's. Maybe she's claiming it for herself. Asserting control. Expressing her creativity or her cultural or artistic identity. Honoring someone or something she loves. Proving she can take the pain involved. Did you ask her?"

Ailsa recoiled as if the idea set her back. "Why would I?"

"I don't know. Conversation." Meg took a slow sip of

wine. "To find out the answer before judging someone."

"I'm not judging. I never judge."

Their server, a young woman with a high-bridged nose and a mass of dark, glossy hair pulled back in a single braid, arrived with their meal and saved Meg from having to answer that. For a brief respite, there was a flurry of activity and polite conversation, and even after the woman had gone, Meg concentrated on cutting a bite from the flaking monkfish she had ordered, pan fried in a burnt butter glaze and served with a rice soufflé and crusty brown soda bread. Between the wine, the salt of the ocean on her tongue, her own bone-deep tiredness, and the warmth of the room in sharp contrast to the windswept white geysers breaking against the cliffs of Dursey Island across the sound, she wanted to savor the moment. The last thing she wanted was an argument.

Her mother set down her fork. "What has gotten into you, Margaret? I barely say anything to you, and you bite my head off. You've always been the good daughter. The one I could count on. I meant for us to come out here and have some fun together. Take my mind off of things and have an adventure. Just the two of us."

Meg refrained from pointing out that, in that case, it was a shame Ailsa had invited Anna first. But truth always had been relative to her mother, and the attempt at guilt, too, was a familiar tactic, often accompanied by an exquisitely formulated blend of defensiveness and accusation. Still, there was a note of wistfulness in her mother's voice that made her wonder. Ailsa so rarely revealed even a drop of uncertainty, much less vulnerability. It made her want to hold her mother close, much the way she'd wanted to hold Adam close, to swaddle her like a newborn child who needs to be wrapped tight when the world becomes too vast and overwhelming.

Without Meg's father, without the familiar life she had built for herself, her mother's world must have become infinite with possibilities, Meg realized. She couldn't help wondering if that wasn't the real reason Ailsa had begged her to come on this trip, because she'd needed to bring one familiar person with her, and Meg was the only one left in her family who Ailsa hadn't yet pushed away.

"Let's not worry so much about trying to have an adventure," Meg said, offering up a smile. "We could just enjoy whatever comes, couldn't we? Talk if we need to talk. Be together. I know all this has to be hard for you, but that's why I'm here. And look at this." She gestured around the room, where light spilled from whimsically painted chandeliers overhead and the clink of cutlery against china. A low murmur of polite voices muffled the sound of the rain that was sluicing off the roof outside and pouring down the gutters. "It's gorgeous. Now tell me more about the dig. Have they found anything interesting yet?"

Her mother studied her a long moment, her expression vacillating between being offended and the eagerness to talk. Fortunately, she opted for conversation. "There's not much left of the fortress," she said, "so that was a little disappointing, but they showed us the mobile laboratory where they clean the finds. The first week they were here, James—he's the one who handles most of the remote sensing equipment, the ground-penetrating radar and the metal detector—uncovered a small horde of coins and jewelry. They think it might have been buried by some of the women when they were inside the keep and realized the men had to surrender. Imagine being huddled in there with your children, cannons firing at the walls, knowing any minute the English were going to break through."

"If they tried burying their valuables, they must have hoped they'd survive." The red liquid in Meg's glass caught the light. "I don't know if that makes it seem better or worse. Or maybe you always hope you'll survive somehow. Especially if you have children with you."

Her mother looked down at her plate. "They've found some of the cannonballs already, along with bullets and some broken bits of weapons. There was a slave shackle, too—that was the most interesting artifact. James found it off the main dig somewhere two weeks ago, and they've marked the area to excavate in more detail later. Gemma says the shackle is Viking, though. Apparently, they used this as a collection point for the Irish women they captured before they shipped them off to be sold."

Meg looked up. "I thought they took them as wives. The Vikings were polygamous, weren't they?"

"Earlier." Ailsa's eyes half closed, pleased to know something that Meg didn't. "Then they traded men and women from Britain and the Slavic countries, mostly to the Middle East. They did that until the fourteenth century, then they traded in African slaves until the middle of the nineteenth. Naturally, they weren't called Vikings by then."

"Naturally," Meg agreed, smiling.

Her mother ignored her. "James—you'll like him— knows a lot about all that. He's a sweet boy, really, though more Bill Gates than Indiana Jones, if you know what I mean. I suppose one Indiana Jones is enough." She glanced at Meg with a faint lift of her brows. "There were a lot of disappointed volunteers when Niall wasn't there today. But then again, most of the college girls were giggling over Liam. Especially when James mentioned Vikings since Liam looks a bit like one."

"Maybe that's the dreadlocks. Vikings and Celts both wore them," Meg said, changing the subject. "I wonder why, come to think of it, whether it was some kind of symbol of manliness or a matter of convenience."

Ailsa picked at the salad on her plate. "I don't understand why people have to try to kill each other."

"Survival. Or lines on a map. Wealth. Power. It always comes down to that. One person trying to take what someone else has or keep what they have themselves. Killing's only one side of it all. You know that from your own family."

"Campbells and MacGregors and MacLarens." The Scottish burr Ailsa had tried to leave behind with everything else when she'd left to marry Meg's father came back with the familiar names. "It was interesting," she said. "Niall Sullivan is supposed to be related to the O'Sullivans who were killed and one of the other archaeologists—he wasn't here today for the orientation, though—is descended from the man who ordered the massacre. He wants to prove it wasn't his family who was responsible for the massacre, but the others all hate him. I could tell whenever they mentioned him. It made me wonder if it's the same here as it is back in the Highlands, my father distrusting every MacLaren because his father hated them, and people only now starting to forget all that."

Meg studied her mother, but there was only a clouded look in Ailsa's eyes, no specific emotion that Meg could read. "Was that why you were so desperate to leave? Why you married Daddy instead of John MacLaren?"

"Water under the bridge. All that was a long time ago." Ailsa took another long sip of wine.

"Dad doesn't think so."

"Things aren't always what they seem, Margaret. The people we think are guilty. Sometimes they're just caught up in events."

Meg took a deep, long breath. "Are you saying you didn't get pregnant on purpose after all?"

She didn't know why she'd asked the question that way, so baldly, except maybe because she so much wanted it not to be true. Or maybe because having spent the day with Adam and listening to his silence, she'd realized that silences could be filled with too many terrible things. Driving back from Cork, there'd seemed to be an uneasy truce between him and Niall, a pause like two boxers retreating to their corners and waiting for the bell to ring again.

She didn't want it to be like that with her mother. She wanted the air cleared, the truth told.

The truth mattered. What her mother had done—the

accusation her father had made before filing for divorce—
had changed the way Meg looked at her mother's entire life,
at her own childhood. Everything that she'd always thought
she understood. It changed the interpretation of every piece
of advice her mother had ever given her.

Afraid to see the truth while she waited to hear it, afraid
her mother would lie to her, she looked anywhere except at
Ailsa, at the single drop of butter glaze that had fallen on the
pristine white tablecloth, at the storm that was getting worse
beyond the windows, the ocean whipping into froth and
clouds shearing flat beneath a driving wind.

When she looked up, her mother's face had pinched
itself into tight, hard lines. "I'll put that question down to
you having had a hard day. Maybe you should go straight to
bed after dinner."

"You didn't answer me."

"I've no intention of answering you. It's none of your
business."

"I guess that's answer enough, then, isn't it?"

Ailsa opened her mouth then closed it again as Fergal
came to clear away the plates and drop off the dessert menus.
"Can I take these for you? How was the meal?" he asked. "I
can get you something else if you'd rather."

"No, no. It was wonderful. I'm just tired—I should
probably have an early night," Meg said.

He put the menu down on the table and picked up her
plate. "Don't say that. At least come sing for a while. You
have to end the evening smiling. It's a fast rule around this
place. Singing together makes you happier—that's proven

science. It fights depression and boosts your immune system, makes you handle pain better. So you see, you have to come. Doctor's orders."

The way Fergal smiled at her with his entire face, with every neuron in his body, Meg couldn't bring herself to say no. And having said yes, she found herself happier already.

She thought of Adam disappearing into his music at the hospital, and she pictured him over on the island now with no television or the internet, stalking his room like a caged dog, or sitting on his bed, his head bobbing to music while he threw a ball against the door. She imagined Niall listening on the other side of the wall, not knowing how to reach him.

"Do you suppose it would it be all right if I invited Adam and Niall to come for the music tomorrow?" she said to Fergal. "If getting them back to the island's a problem, they could take my room if you don't have any vacancies. I could stay with my mother."

"You might have thought to ask me first," Ailsa said, frowning, once Fergal had gone again.

Meg leaned forward. "I'm sorry. Do you mind?"

"I think it's dangerous getting involved with them." Her cheeks reddening, Ailsa bent her head to scan the menu. "That boy's unstable, and Niall's attractive. That's a dangerous combination. For you especially."

Her voice had gone ragged, and Meg wondered for an instant if that was all the answer she was ever likely to get to her previous question. But she couldn't help prying at it anyway. "Do you regret it?" she asked. "Meeting Daddy on the excavation. Marrying him?"

"Ruining his life, is that what you're implying?"

"I never said that. *He* never said that. Just that he needed honesty going forward."

"I gave him a good life—it was a good marriage! A partnership. It wasn't as if I meant for it all to turn out like this. I hoped for everything when I married him. I wanted the fairy tale, and I miss the idea of that kind of love. I lost out on that as much as he did. But I did love him. You should know that. I still do love him, in my own way."

Hearing the selfishness in those words, Meg felt another hot curl of anger wrap itself around her heart. Or maybe it had been there all along, and she had simply tried to ignore it. Maybe she'd had no idea how angry she had been these last months since the truth about her parents' marriage had all come out, and she wondered if that was the emotion she had mistaken for loneliness, the kind of loneliness she hadn't seemed able to fill, no matter what she did. Or maybe the loneliness came from realizing she'd never had a good example of how to love someone. How to fill the emptiness inside herself.

Deciding that retreating to her empty room alone was the very last thing she needed, she squeezed into the bar after dinner, and in the cozy room with the firelight casting clawed shadows on the wall and twenty strangers around her, she sang to the accompaniment of Fergal's guitar and a local farmer's *bodhrán* drum. Not sure what she was trying to drown out, she let her voice ring out free and heedless. She barely even noticed that other voices were dropping away to listen, until on the last verse she was singing all alone.

"You've had some training, then," Fergal said, when he'd played the last notes of Van Morrison's "Wild Night" and laid his palm across the strings to still them.

Meg felt a little wild, too, high on the music and the determination to let loose. She missed performing, she discovered. Music was something she'd left behind deliberately along with her sashes, tiaras, and sequined gowns after winning the Miss Teen Ohio pageant. After a lifetime of having her mother cart her and Katharine from one to another, even after Anna had refused to do them anymore, that had been Meg's last pageant. Her mother had always sworn winning a big one would help when it came to a career in broadcasting, and it had. Already in college, though, Meg had come to hate how the title made people see her. How so many people—men and women—had let it flatten her into one dimension.

Her music training had been part of the pageant world, and so she'd let it go. After years of developing her voice and writing songs, of expressing herself in notes and phrases that said things she hadn't been able to say in any other way, she'd given it up because it had been the "talent" her mother had chosen for her. Funny, she hadn't realized that, either. Not completely.

She turned and looked down the bar to where her mother had drifted away to talk to some of the volunteers. Seeing her there nursing another glass of wine, it struck Meg how much of their childhood and adult decisions—hers and Anna's and even Katharine's—had been driven by Ailsa's choices. Living with them, affirming them, rebelling against them—or failing to rebel.

"You're right," she said to Fergal. "I haven't sung in ages, but it feels wonderful. I'd forgotten how good it can make you feel."

Fergal reached into the guitar case beside his chair and plucked out a music book, coffee-stained but otherwise with little sign of wear. Then he pulled out another barstool and set it beside his own. Ari, with her sweet smile, produced a violin case from somewhere behind the bar then came around to nudge Meg to the empty seat.

"You sing, and I'll play," Ari said. "I've a feeling you've got a lot inside you that needs to be let out."

LONGING

*"Wasn't it hard that you did so much for children
and loved them so deeply
and they seemed so indifferent to you in return?"*

Maeve Binchy
Chestnut Street

AILSA CAMERON DRAINED ANOTHER GLASS of wine and laughed at something one of the women said. Janice something or another—Ailsa couldn't be sure, but it didn't matter. There was always so much to remember, and all she wanted to do was forget.

Why had Margaret insisted on dredging everything up again tonight? The divorce. The pregnancy. All the long, interminable years of Ailsa's marriage and its ignominious end.

That was the thing about children. When they were little, they were always on your side. You could count on them to look up to you, to believe in you. They thought you were wonderful, and their own wonders, all the good things they did, you could count those as accomplishments. It was only when they got older that you would look over and catch them judging you from behind a mask of their old love, and you realized you didn't know quite when they'd decided that everything you did—everything you had ever done for them—was wrong. Just wrong.

Margaret had been the only one of her children who hadn't made her feel that way. Until lately. Until this trip. Well, until Anna's trip to Scotland, to be exact, when Elspeth had spilled the beans to Anna and everything about what she'd done had trickled out. Nearly everything anyway. Because even Elspeth didn't seem to have realized that the accident that had resulted in her broken arm hadn't been entirely an accident. Ailsa had just needed *out*. That was what Margaret would never understand, how trapped you could feel by a place, by a past, by the weight of destiny and expectation.

The room around Ailsa seemed to shrink at the thought, the clink of glasses, the hum of conversation, laughter she wasn't sharing. She should have nudged herself into participating, but it felt like too much effort to drag herself out of the past into the present, to try to make meaningless small talk.

She would have ended up marrying John MacLaren if she hadn't gotten out. She'd have become one of those helpless women, trapped in a marriage. A farmer's wife. A MacLaren. That future looming over her day by day had made her claustrophobic until she couldn't sleep, couldn't eat. Couldn't think. Margaret and Anna—even Katharine—had all judged her for what she'd done, but if she hadn't married their father, where would they have been?

Sometimes, you had to do whatever it took to change your fate.

Around her, the bar descended back into a hush as the good-looking man who'd been playing the Irish drum picked up the beat again. She turned to see Meg seated on a barstool between Fergal with his guitar and Ari with a violin, and they both started to play. Meg frowned down at a music book on her lap, her concentration fierce the way only Meg out of all three of the girls could concentrate, as if whatever she was doing was always a matter of life or death. Then Meg raised her head and looked out across the room, made eye contact with the audience and connected in the way that came so easily for her. She'd always been able to draw people in, and she began to sing.

Ailsa slumped back against the silk smooth wood of the bar, feeling the edge press into her back. She'd almost forgotten how Meg's voice could roll out into a room, pure and clear and sweet as honey, but with a hint of mist around the edges of the emotions that could play tricks with the listener. You'd think the words she was singing meant one thing, then you'd discover, listening to her, that you felt something else entirely.

"Fields of Gold." That was the song Margaret sang. Hearing her, Ailsa's throat grew tight.

How had she let so much slip away from her? One small decision bleeding into another, a step here, a step there, and when she looked back, there was a lifetime gone, and where were all the things she had promised herself? All the things she had meant to do?

Many years have passed since those summer days among the fields of barley,
See the children run as the sun goes down among the fields of gold,
You'll remember me when the west wind moves upon the fields of barley,
You can tell the sun in his jealous sky when we walked in fields of gold.

More and more often lately, Ailsa's mind went backward, to before the Hebrides. Back to the braes of Balwhither and the glen where she and Elspeth had grown up. Back to a time when all her choices had been in front of her and the world still shone with possibility.

If she was honest, that was the reason she'd wanted to come when she'd found out that Kitty O'Sullivan and her husband were providing funding for an excavation. It had seemed fitting, somehow, to mark the end of her marriage with an excavation when that was where it had all begun. She hadn't meant to dig up her own past along with history, but maybe that was inevitable, too. Maybe what she'd really hoped for was a chance to make Margaret understand the choices she had made.

Making her understand, though, that would require telling her about it all—and how could Ailsa even begin to do that? Where did she find the words?

TERRIBLE BEAUTY

"All changed, changed utterly:
A terrible beauty is born."

W. B. YEATS
"EASTER 1916"

AFTER THE NIGHT'S RAIN, THE tufted grass had been scoured into an even more unearthly green set off by occasional cotton-puff dots of sheep. The air smelled of salt and wind and the honey scent of heather as Meg emerged from the cable car onto the platform clutching the box of doughnuts she had brought along for Adam. Beyond the rise that limited her view, the spine of the island continued some four odd miles past the excavation site to Dursey Head at the far end. Just off the coast there, the natural sea arch on Bull Rock had been called *Teach Duinn* by the Irish long ago, the House of Death. They had believed it was the gateway to the underworld, and Meg thought that name was fitting—at the moment, she felt ready to die. Death warmed over.

She should have gone to bed hours before she had, or at least gone to sleep once she'd crawled between the sheets. Her brain had been too busy, still singing, still reliving and thinking. Finally, she had snapped the light on and read up about the island on the internet. And about Niall and the other excavation staff, about Kieran Stafford and his father and their distant ancestors, Sir George Carew and Thomas Stafford, George's bastard son, who'd both been so proud of what they called the "pacification" they'd done in Ireland in the service of Queen Elizabeth I that they'd had no qualms writing about the atrocities. Not that the English had been alone in doing terrible things. Just as there had been in the long march to the loss of Scotland's independence, there'd been plenty of Irish who saw opportunities taking the English side, including Owen O'Sullivan Beare, who had fought his own nephew in the hope of taking Donal Cam O'Sullivan Beare's place as Lord of Beare and Bantry. In turn, Donal had held Owen's wife hostage on Dursey Island, and Owen had condemned every man, woman, and child there when he colluded with the English to get her back.

The history of Ireland was full of betrayal, but even among those, the O'Sullivan part at the end of the Nine Years' War had been a mess. One treachery, one tragedy, following another.

The cable car shuddered to a stop on the island side, and Meg rose from her seat in the corner and waited, her body inclined at the waist, until the other volunteers had all shuffled out onto the platform. After the close quarters in the metal box, it felt good to be out in the fresh air, and she paused at the railing, taking in the beauty of the landscape that, through years of war, oppression, famine, and abandonment, had been bathed in blood and steeped in tears until only a handful of permanent residents remained.

"Come on. Don't dawdle," her mother called back to her.

Juggling the container of doughnuts, Meg nodded and pushed her dark sunglasses further up her nose as she turned to follow. Cars and even a few small trucks were parked near the base of the platform for use by the farmers who came over from the mainland to work in the fields and villages, but the site of the fortress wasn't far from the station, and the volunteers were all supposed to make their way there on foot each day as they arrived.

The gravel road led past an old harbor, boathouses, and a dark, narrow fishing boat hauled up on the grassy bank. A steady wind gusted around them, churning up whitecaps along the surface of the Atlantic where the water shifted from turquoise to jade to pewter beneath the drifting clouds. A short while later, they came to the ruined monastery and graveyard whose broken walls overlooked Oileán Beag, the tiny island just offshore where the O'Sullivan fort had stood.

The English had set cannon behind the monastery walls and on the road above it to fire down on the fort, then brought in ships along the backside of Oileán Beag and bombarded the fortress from a second side. Meg could only imagine the terror of the four hundred people who'd taken shelter inside, children screaming, their mothers trying to provide comfort while the walls were shot apart around them.

Protected by cliffs on every side, Oileán Beag had been meant to provide a last, impregnable refuge for the most vulnerable among the O'Sullivan clan. The drawbridge that had once given access to the small island from Dursey had long since been destroyed, but its foundations were still visible at the base of the temporary bridge Niall and the dig crew had laid across the chasm.

Spray from the waves crashing against the cliffs below had dampened the narrow planks, making the bridge dangerous as they crossed, and Meg kept a wary eye on her mother. If the traverse made Ailsa nervous, though, she didn't allow Meg to see it. Even on the trip over in the cable car, she'd been cold and quiet, one of her favorite forms of punishment, although Meg wasn't quite sure what she was being punished for this time. For having asked about the pregnancy? For talking about the past at all? For letting loose afterward and having fun while Ailsa sulked?

Releasing a sigh, Meg followed her mother as she stepped from the bridge onto the springy grass. In front of them, the sides of a large white tent crackled in the wind, and farther ahead, clear sheeting on the ground glinted with water that had collected overnight. It wasn't until they had reached the front of the tent that the rest of the site was visible. Orange plastic tape flapped from stakes that marked off the outline of where the castle and its outer fortifications had once stood. The turf had been peeled off from various sections along the perimeters of the structures and in the spaces within, and staff and volunteers already knelt in the newly exposed dirt, scraping centuries away layer by careful layer. Sometimes thick walls cut through the trenches, jutting a few inches above ground level here and there but mostly below the surface. It was shocking how little remained.

"Is there a place where we're supposed to check in? What should we do?" Meg turned toward her mother. But Ailsa had already walked away to speak with the one older couple who was working nearby. Feeling a bit lost, Meg stood uncertainly, trying to get her bearings since she'd missed the orientation.

She was relieved to see Niall emerge from the white tent beside her. "Hullo," he said, giving her a wide smile. "I've been keeping an eye out for you."

Meg's pulse had given an odd jump at the sight of him, and she took a breath and held up the box. "Hello, yourself. Is Adam around? I brought some of Eamon's best over for him."

"What? None for me?" Niall clapped one hand across his heart and sent her a wounded look.

"There might be a sugar-crusted in there somewhere. I'll flip you for it." Spotting Adam standing sullenly near where the castle would have been within the heavier outer walls, she set off in that direction.

"Are you trying to say I converted you?" Grinning, Niall strode after her.

She threw him a smile across her shoulder. "Converted? No. They're doughnuts, not religion."

He caught up with her and took the box from her. "I wouldn't be so certain. Eamon takes his pastries seriously."

"He fussed at me for not stopping by last night to tell him how I was feeling."

"Well, he's Irish—he has an eye for a beautiful woman and an Irishman's charm."

"Charm, is it?" Meg asked in her best imitation of an Irish accent. "Is that what you're using now?"

Niall grinned even wider, his eyes laughing into hers. "That depends."

"On what?"

"Whether or not it's working."

Meg blushed warmly and told herself there was nothing wrong with flirting. People were meant to feel good, not hurt and empty all the time.

"It may be working," she admitted. "Just a little."

"In that case, you can have my sugar-crusted doughnut. And having tasted one, you'll know the caliber of sacrifice I'm making."

"Not as significant as you think, as it happens," she said.

He gave her a steady look, and then he opened the box, laughing as he saw the row of golden doughnuts crusted in glistening crushed sugar crystals. "You really have been converted."

When she had taken a pastry, he plucked out another for himself and held it up for a doughnut toast. She tapped hers to his. Their eyes met, and she watched him as they each took a bite, the sweetness and yeast and grease and pillowy, silken pastry all melting together inside her mouth. There was something illicit and a little reckless about watching Niall eat. He continued smiling down at her as he chewed, and there were crumbs of sugar left along his lips that she found herself wanting to brush away.

She broke eye contact awkwardly. "So how is Adam this morning?"

"As charming as he ever was. I wish I knew how to tell him . . ."

"Tell him what?" Meg prompted when he didn't finish.

"That no one is whole, I suppose. I remember being his age and bouncing between extremes, feeling like the worst person in the world one minute and feeling maligned the next, as if the universe itself was conspiring against me. We all have stains on our conscience that feel unbearable. We're all hurt and angry and confused, but we muddle through the best we can while making mistakes that we regret. That never goes away."

Meg wondered whether to say anything—it wasn't her place, but she hated thinking of Niall carrying so much weight, not for himself but for others. It was another thing she liked about him, the way he seemed to assume it was his responsibility to make people happy, but it was a hard burden even for his wide shoulders. "You can't hold yourself accountable for other people's choices," she said. "Not Adam's, and not your sister's, either. All you can do is be ready to listen whenever he's ready to talk—and I think he knows you are. If he doesn't, it's because he's too hurt to admit it yet, not because you haven't made it clear."

He sent her a swift unguarded appraisal that showed there was a great deal more emotion underneath the calm exterior. His eyes were a lighter blue in the sunlight, surrounded by a fan of wrinkles from long days working in the sun. But he only gave a brief nod and changed the subject. "I haven't even asked how you feel," he said, his voice pitched low over the rumble of the ocean and the whipping wind as they approached the dig site where several groups of volunteers were working. "There doesn't seem to be much bruising."

She started walking in Adam's direction again. "I know," she said, "and here I was looking forward to having a shiner and starting a new and disreputable chapter in my life."

His laugh was low and warm. "Feeling a little dangerous, are you?"

"I might be. Of course, that could just be the sugar rush talking along with the hangover from singing last night. Then again, my mother did insist this would all be an adventure. And that reminds me—I had an idea. I know it's hard to get back here after the cable car stops running, so I thought I could share my mother's room with her if you and Adam wanted to use mine tonight. You could have dinner with us and stay for the music afterward. Adam might enjoy it."

"I'm not sure it's wise to subject him to fine china and multiple courses just yet."

"Fish and chips, then. Or pub food. Whatever. Take him somewhere by yourself, but come back for the singing. It's clear he loves music, and you mentioned his father is a musician."

"He is, but it's Siobhan who has the gift. Had. Was," Niall corrected with a pained look, as if the reminder of his twin's death still snuck up on him now and then.

Meg refrained from apologizing. She hated when people did that to her, apologized to fill emptiness, for things that weren't their fault. "So would you mind if I invite him?" she asked. "I'd love for you both to come."

It struck her after she'd said it how the words would sound, as if she was asking both Niall and Adam on a date. Well, but wasn't that what she was doing? She'd had fun singing with Fergal and the guests at the Bay Point, and she wanted to share that with Adam and Niall, but maybe it was also a chance to spend more time with them. She couldn't deny she wanted that.

She decided not to overanalyze. Shining a light in the darkness, you could never be sure you'd like what you saw.

"You can ask, of course, and I hope he agrees. I'd personally love to come. Only don't expect much in the way of enthusiasm, so." Niall frowned in the direction where Adam stood inside what had been the castle's inner keep. He'd moved again, edging closer to the excavation trench.

Twine and more orange plastic tape tied around wooden stakes separated the trench into uniform squares, within which volunteers knelt to scrape dirt away with trowels and brushes. Adam, dressed in ripped jeans hanging low enough to reveal the top of blue plaid boxer shorts, had his arms folded across his narrow chest as he watched.

Meg walked over to him. "Have they found anything interesting yet?"

"No." Adam flicked her a glance then shifted his attention to the box Niall was holding.

Niall flipped the lid up and offered the doughnuts to him. "Have any plans tonight, Adam?"

"Me? I was thinking I'd watch the paint peel off the walls, seeing as how I'm spoiled for choice where it comes to nightlife." Adam snatched up a strawberry doughnut and turned away.

Having grown up with Katharine as a sister, Meg wasn't daunted by sarcasm. "Your uncle's asking because we thought you might want to come to the musical evening at Fergal and Ari's. You and Niall could spend the night so you wouldn't have to worry about getting back."

Adam's thin face tightened into hungry attention, like a child watching a birthday cake being brought in and knowing that would be followed by presents. Then he looked away as if he couldn't give himself permission to show even that hint of softening.

"I wouldn't mind," he said. "If Niall wants to."

He slouched away then, moving farther down the excavation toward a plywood board laid over a section of the trench where two men were engaged in a heated but quiet argument that looked one-sided. The larger of the two—the same tall, blond one who had been arguing with Niall back by the cable car station the day before—loomed over a slighter, sandy-haired man with glasses and a faintly nerdy appearance that made Meg remember her mother's comment about a staff member who was more Bill Gates than Indiana Jones.

"Sorry about the rudeness," Niall said. "But I don't think Adam's as unenthusiastic about the music as he made out, for what it's worth. It was a good suggestion. And thanks again for the doughnuts." He fitted the lid back onto the box.

"Who are those two men arguing over there?" Meg asked as Adam sidled still closer to the argument to eavesdrop, his back stiff and the doughnut forgotten in his hand. He seemed to be glaring—not at the larger man but the smaller one.

The furrow deepened between Niall's brows. Then, tucking the doughnuts beneath his arm, he gave Meg the kind of perfunctory smile that said there was nothing to smile about. "The taller is Kieran Stafford, our historical archaeologist, and the other's James Donovan, who does the geophysical archaeology. That's metal detection, ground-penetrating radar, and so on, all the techniques we use to determine where there could be something of interest so we don't have to dig up the whole ten square miles of island. Or, more importantly on Dursey, to help us separate what's interesting from what's both worthwhile and pertinent to what we're investigating."

"Do you know what they're arguing about?" Meg asked.

Niall clenched his jaw. "Everything and anything, I imagine. They're both set in their opinions, but the main issue is that Kieran has a pet theory about a site he wants us to investigate, and the rest of us have other priorities to cover first. James has charge of the instruments, so Kieran spends a not insignificant amount of his time and energy trying to bully him into agreeing."

James seemed to be holding his ground physically, but

he had a belligerent hunch to his shoulders that suggested he felt cornered. "Poor James," Meg said. "That can't be easy."

"It isn't." Niall's expression darkened into a frown. "I've been trying to find a solution, believe me, but my hands are tied."

His eyes had grown hard, remote, and Meg wasn't sure whether that was because of what she'd said or because of the situation. She hastened to apologize. "I'm sorry. That was more of a physical observation. I didn't mean to criticize."

"You weren't. It's complicated," Niall said, relaxing a fraction. "Then, too, James is patient about it all, which only makes it that much harder and more frustrating."

"And Adam? He seems to be siding with Kieran. Or am I missing something?"

"I wish I understood the attraction," Niall muttered almost beneath his breath. "Kieran is like a magnet for him, and on Kieran's end . . . I can't be sure. Either he genuinely likes Adam or he wants to get back at me for not taking his side. Perhaps a bit of both." With a brief sigh, he shook his head. "Never mind all that, though. Give me a moment to go have a word with them—my daily useless effort—and I'll take you around to introduce you properly to everyone so you can be getting to work. It's time we gave you some of that adventure you were craving."

He resumed walking, but James suddenly straightened and his head snapped up. "Because I don't have to listen to you, that's why!" James cried. "Leave me alone!"

The red-haired girl with the tattoos—Gemma, according to Meg's mother—pushed herself up from her knees where she was working nearby and launched herself at Kieran with a snarl. "Right, that's it. What's it going to take for you to get the message? Leave off him, Kieran. I mean it."

Niall ran after her, though whether that was to intercept or assist her, Meg wasn't sure.

"Me?" Kieran spun around toward Gemma. "You're the ones nagging at me, all of you. I can't even offer an opinion or ask a simple question. And spare me the lecture, please. He does this on purpose, look at him. Playing on your sympathy, begging you to leap to his defense."

He had a symmetrical face with a long, aquiline nose and narrow chin. Above this, his lips were out of balance, his upper lip stretched thin into a sneer, while the much fuller lower lip seemed more inclined to pout.

Gemma, seeing that expression, hissed like any angry mother cat. She snatched the soil-stained bucket of dirt that James was holding and shoved it into Kieran's solar plexus. "I'm impressed you could say that without laughing, Kieran. Really. Now get to work. Take that over to the sifting screens."

The whole site had gone quiet around them, and the cries of the gulls swooping overhead and the roar of the wind and the sea had grown too loud. Niall stopped beside Kieran and dropped a hand on his shoulder. "Might be best to do as Gem suggests, Kieran. Give everyone an opportunity to cool off."

"I don't work for her. Or him," Kieran snapped, nodding at James.

He'd grabbed the bucket out of reflex when Gemma shoved it at him, and he stood there with it pressed against the pale blue cotton of his oxford shirt. Breathing hard, he darted a furtive look around, as if he'd remembered they weren't alone and realized for the first time that the volunteers had all stopped to watch what was going on. Mottled patches of red crept up his cheeks, and he stormed between Gemma and James. But his foot caught on a severed root at the edge of the excavation trench, and he lurched into Gemma's shoulder, knocking her so that James had to reach out to keep her from falling. The bucket tumbled from Kieran's hands, scattering dirt across the trampled sod and Gemma's feet.

Kieran stared down at it, fuming. Then to add ignominy to humiliation, a gull let fly its bowels overhead, and a long, thick cream of excrement plopped on the front of Kieran's shoulder and oozed along the cloth. Kieran swore and kicked the bucket away. With Gemma and James in front of him partially blocking his path, he shoved them aside and headed back toward the tent. A ripple of shocked laughter followed in his wake.

Niall's free fist clenched as he strode the remaining paces to where Gemma stood.

She was shaking as she looked up at him, but she tried to smile. "Somebody find me that seagull. I want to give it a big fat medal." She shook her head. "You have to do something, Niall. He's about as useful as a chocolate teapot, and if you don't sort him out, one of these days, I'm going to have to murder him."

"I'll have another word with Graeme," Niall said, raking a hand through his hair. "And I'll speak to Kieran again once he's had a chance to think. Try to reason with him—"

Adam whipped around to face him. "Why can't you just let him use the ground radar like he wants? That's all he's asking, and you're all being unfair—"

"Unfair? This dig isn't Kieran's personal playground," Gemma snapped.

"But James—"

"James is only doing what we all agreed to do," Niall said with an edge to his voice. "I don't know what Kieran's been telling you, but his opinion doesn't get to count any more than anyone else's, no matter how often or loudly he offers it. And that, mate, is the end of the discussion. As much as I love you, this is a problem for the staff to settle between us—which we will. Later." He turned and smiled around at the volunteers. "I'm sorry, everyone. Clearly, we're all passionate about our work, but I think that about concludes the entertainment portion of the morning."

People evidently needed a release of tension, and there was an appreciative round of light laughter. Gemma crouched down to scoop up the dirt Kieran had spilled onto the grass, and Niall handed the box of doughnuts to Adam while he bent to help. Meg had already started to bend as well, and they collided on the way down, so that they both jumped back and rubbed their heads.

Gemma wiped her curls out of her eyes. "I'll get this. It's my own fault for letting my temper get the better of me, which happens a sight too often." The smile she sent Meg was both good-natured and wry. "You'll have gathered I'm Gemma—the other member of staff here—and that's James."

"Howya," James said. "You must be Meg. Sorry to hear about yesterday."

"It's nice to meet you both," Meg said, smiling at them.

James blushed, ducked his head, and gestured at the spilled soil on the ground. "Sorry about all this, too. I try to ignore Kieran, most days—"

"You shouldn't have to," Gemma snapped. "You're a bloody saint, if you ask me."

Adam, listening, snorted, and spun on his heel to hurry after Kieran, who, instead of heading to the sifting screens that stood on the far side of the tent, was marching in the direction of the bridge that led off Oileán Beag back to the larger island. Niall called after Adam. "Hold up, mate. I was going to ask you to help out at the cleaning station today. What do you think?"

"My stomach hurts," Adam said without stopping. "I'm going back to the house. Or can't I even do that without a lecture?"

As Adam spoke, Kieran reached the far corner of the white tent and crossed the remaining yards to the bridge just as a large, muscular man with sandy blond dreadlocks gathered into a ponytail was stepping off it. As narrow as the path and the bridge both were, there wasn't room for two. Kieran and the other man both stepped aside in the same direction as they sought to avoid each other—and then they both moved the other way. Finally, the larger man stopped, laughing as people did in that situation, but Kieran—either because he mistook the object of the laughter or out of sheer frustration—lashed out and shoved the man, trying to move past him. With legs the size of tree trunks, the man didn't budge and Kieran instead only succeeded in pushing himself off balance. Stumbling, he lurched off the path and onto the rocks above the cliff until the man yanked him back to safety. Kieran slapped his hands away, stomped over the bridge in a huff, and veered left along the road that led into the nearby abandoned village.

"Good riddance," James muttered.

Adam snapped around toward him, his expression mutinous. "Why do you always do that?"

Seeing everyone looking at him, he froze, then he took off at a run toward the bridge, the dirty cast clutched against his stomach, his agitation transmitting itself to the gulls that had perched along the top of the tent as he pounded toward it. They launched into flight in unison, screeching and wheeling in the air.

"So, that went well." Niall stared after Adam with every muscle clenched. Head bent, he ran a hand over the back of his neck, and he gave Gemma a slow, reluctant grin. "I hate to ask, but—"

"Sure, I'll look after things here."

He nodded. "Not that going after him will make things any better between us, but I don't have much choice. The mood Kieran's in, there's no telling what he'll say—and that's the last thing Adam needs."

"What if I went instead?" It wasn't any of Meg's

business, none of it, so she wasn't sure where the suggestion came from. She knew only that Niall was in a no-win situation and both he and Adam were miserable. And clearly there was something going on between Adam and Kieran, something that made Adam identify with Kieran, which could be both a problem and an opportunity.

Niall studied her. "Are you sure?"

"As long as you don't mind trusting me with him. I can say I feel guilty about his stomach because I brought the doughnuts. And you have things here that need your attention."

Niall clasped her arms, looking down at her with so much warmth and worry and gratitude that it was hard to meet his eyes. "Thank you. Honestly. I'm afraid I'll push him toward Kieran even more if I go after him—or signal that I don't trust him. If he is with Kieran, don't try to intervene. I don't want you in the middle of that. But if you do get a chance to talk to him alone, just make certain he's all right. I hate that I spoke to him the way I did just now, and he seems to open up with you more than he does with me."

Meg loved how much Adam mattered to Niall, not only as a responsibility, but as a person entitled to self-respect. She loved, too, that he wasn't afraid to let her see his pain and fear, at least not where Adam was concerned. Niall's own pain, she suspected, was buried a great deal deeper.

"Strangers are easier to talk to sometimes," she said, "because they matter less. It's the people we care about who are hard to face."

BLACK SKY

THE ABSENCE OF TWENTY-FIRST-CENTURY sound
seeped gradually into Meg's awareness as she followed
Adam down Dursey Island's single road. Grass
growing in the middle of the track cushioned her footfalls,
which would have, in any case, been muffled by the wind and
the white crests of the waves along the cliffs. Adam had
disappeared around a bend, so ahead of her there was only a
row of power lines, the green hillside broken by yellow furze
and lichen-flecked rocks, and the gray ocean changing colors
beneath a racing cloud, and by the time she had rounded the
edge of the slope, Adam had slowed from a run to a jog. A
trio of sheep wandering on the road trotted awkwardly out
of his way, but then they paused to watch him pass, their ears
flicking and their mouths still ruminating on the grass they

had been chewing before he'd come along. Meg wondered whether they had been deliberately let loose to graze on the commonage or if they'd escaped from one of the ancient fields, the outlines of which had probably been marked in stone a thousand or more years before and had since remained essentially unchanged.

Time on Dursey seemed altered once she'd stepped off the cable car, as if a decade was little different from a century, or even a millennium. Looking across the fields that hung off the spine of the island and sloped to the very sheer edge of the cliffs, she could imagine herself standing here the day before the O'Sullivan massacre, seeing these same sheep trotting along the track, hearing the same mournful calls of gray-winged gulls who called out as they circled overhead like echoes of long-dead voices crying out in joy and pain and grief. The ancientness of it all dwarfed her own life, her own concerns, and she wondered if Adam felt any of that here, whether it was a help or a hindrance. Most likely, he was too young and locked inside himself to notice.

The village of Ballynacallagh, when she reached it, was eerily quiet, too. A few scattered houses with blank, abandoned windows stood shoulder to shoulder with the roofless stone husks of earlier dwellings. Some of these had been converted into additional livestock sheds with roofs of painted tin, and the fields around a small cluster of buildings were speckled with cows and sheep. A few chickens scratched in yards where Mary Elizabeth and others like her commuted every day from their homes on the mainland to tend the farms that had been in their families for generations.

Apparently, more people lived full time on the island now than at any time since the 1970s. A handful of the old farms had been purchased in the past two years, Fergal had said, some by a local farmer who was converting them into holiday cottages and others to transplants who didn't have children and were looking for solitude: a writer and his wife, a graphic designer, a retired couple down from Dublin. And a few of the farmers still stayed overnight now and then. The habitable houses were spread between two of the island's three villages, Tilickafinna on the distant end and Ballynacallagh closest to the cable car, while Kilmichael not much beyond that was completely vacant. But walking on the empty road with only Adam in front of her, Meg had the eerie feeling of being entirely alone and remote from her usual life, as if, at any moment, time could peel away without her having noticed and leave her stranded in another century. She wondered if teenage boys had been any easier to reach in a different age, or whether they had always been the same.

Afraid to spook Adam, she didn't call out to him, and he didn't seem to know she was hurrying behind him until he turned onto a path in front of a two-story yellow house with chimneys on either end. Catching a glimpse of her as he paused to unlatch the gate, he seemed visibly surprised to see her coming up the road.

"Hey," she called out. "I wanted to make sure you were all right. It wasn't the doughnut, was it?"

"No." He stood with his hand on the latch, but he didn't go in. That was something.

Meg increased her pace and was breathing hard by the

time she reached him.

"You didn't need to come," he said, not quite looking at her.

She hadn't fully worked out what she was going to say, but it was easier, sometimes, to get someone to open up if she confided in them first. "It was a little awkward for me, to be honest, after missing the orientation yesterday. Everyone else knows each other already, which leaves me as the odd man out. Do you ever have that feeling? Can I come in a minute? I'm more out of shape than I expected, so I'd love a drink of water."

Adam gave one of his trademark shrugs, but he fumbled with the latch, then pushed the gate aside and held it for her. "They're mostly all right. The volunteers anyway."

"But not the rest?" Meg picked her way along a path of mossy stones set into pads of soft tufts of grass.

Adam edged around her to shove the door open, and she followed him inside, where the living room was painted the same shade of yellow as the exterior of the cottage but wide, wood-framed windows looked straight out toward Oileán Beag and the endless Atlantic. A staircase climbed to what must have been the bedrooms overhead, and Adam moved through into a narrow kitchen. Making a point of not making eye contact, he removed a glass from a cupboard and went to the refrigerator. "Water or lemonade?" he asked. "Both are cold."

"Lemonade sounds great."

He poured it out for her, then got another for himself. She leaned back against the counter while he slumped into a chair at the table.

The drink rested pleasantly on the verge of sweet and sour, and Meg allowed herself the luxury of savoring it in silence, but then she moved to sit beside Adam without looking at him. Like the angels from her favorite—terrifying—episode of *Doctor Who*, some people seemed only to come to life when you didn't look straight at them.

"It's nice out here," she said. "Quiet."

"That's not my idea of nice."

"*Too* quiet?" Meg laughed. "I guess I would have thought the same thing at your age. I remember my dad dragging us camping one summer—by which I mean something nowhere near as rustic as this. A rental house at a lake in Virginia. Four bedrooms, a motorboat, jet skis, and a big screen television. My sisters and I spent the whole time arguing, and my mother finally drove us three hours away to go shopping so my dad could have some peace. I think back now and wish I had it to do over again."

Adam flicked a look at her, then stared down into his glass.

Meg tried again. "Was your mom a peace-and-quiet kind of person? Or did she love the city?"

"She couldn't bear silence. Played her music all the time."

"What kind of music did she like?"

"All sorts. Whatever she could sing with."

Meg took another sip of lemonade and, rummaging into her toolbox of questions, it struck her that, for the first time in a long time, this wasn't a staged interview with someone posturing to look better on television while she fought to get anything genuine to offer her viewers, most of whom didn't really care anyway. Maybe that was part of the problem with the world: there were so many stories all bombarding everyone at once, so many tragedies, so many choreographed truths, that it was hard to allow oneself to feel them. But people needed—deserved—to have their pain shared. That compassion was part of being human.

"Would you like to tell me about your mother?" she asked. "What was she like, Adam? What do you miss most about her?"

"I don't know." Adam blinked as if he'd never considered that question before. "She was my ma. She liked doing things. Singing. Writing poems. Music. Dancing. She read books all the time—everything. Politics, romance, history. She'd get an idea, want to go somewhere, and we'd just go. That was brilliant. She wasn't much good at the rest of it, the cleaning and paying bills part. She was crap at cooking. Seriously crap. But she tried to be my friend. Wanted to be."

"Like Niall?" Meg asked.

"Naw. Niall yells, doesn't he? Tells me when I've been a maggot. I hate him sometimes," Adam said without sounding quite convinced. He looked away again, his chin collapsing into tiny strawberry-dimpled wrinkles as he tried not to cry. To steady himself, or maybe as a reminder that he wasn't a child, he pulled a crumpled pack of cigarettes from his pocket and shook one out so he could close his lips around it.

Meg waited until he'd lit it, the flame of the lighter wavering in a draft as the faint crackle of tobacco burning the only sound in the silence. He took a deep pull and tipped his chair back against the wall.

"Did you hate Niall before your mom died?" Meg asked.

Adam blew out a stream of smoke. "Naw, he was all right, then."

"But you didn't want to come here?"

"Why would I? Jaysus, look around." Adam gestured out the window at the patio and the fields and the sea, where one lonely sailboat was being pushed by the wind. "Even Ma didn't want to come. I think that's wh—"

He stopped himself and shut down, his hand shaking as he lowered it to the table.

The blood in Meg's veins turned to frozen sludge, and she wrapped her arms around herself, both for warmth and to keep from reaching out to hug him. "Are you afraid she did it on purpose?" she asked as gently as she could. "Is that what you meant?"

Adam took another drag of the cigarette and looked away. "Who says I'm afraid?"

"I would be in your shoes."

"But you're not me, are you? Your ma's not dead."

Meg let her eyes drop to the condensation rolling along the outside of her glass, watched it descend in a crooked little stream. "It's not the same thing, but my parents are in the middle of getting a divorce, and my father just moved out. That's why my mother and I are here. She's running away from facing her friends, from feeling like she failed, and I guess I'm running away from my job and a decision I need to make. From a mistake I'm just now seeing I may have made because I didn't want to deal with the idea of losing my father."

She kept her voice neutral, but she had almost felt the air sharpen around Adam as his attention focused, so she was encouraged to continue. "The funny thing is, I feel like I should be a grown-up. I should accept that they're responsible for their own mistakes and I'm responsible for my own. But no matter how much I remind myself of that, deep down, I wonder if I could have done something different, been a better daughter, been *not-me*, somehow, I could have changed things. And since I can't go back, it makes me angry. Do you know what I mean?"

It was, she realized, the truth. What every child felt, however old. But it was also a gamble because Adam was smart. Street smart as well as intelligent, and he'd probably see right through what she was doing.

Maybe, though, he needed to talk more than he needed to be cynical.

"I rang my da before the accident," he said, drawing in a deep breath of smoke. "He told me she'd be all right. Said not to worry, because she was just making drama like always. Only I knew she was afraid."

"Afraid of what?" Meg asked, not daring to move now that he was talking.

"Everything, lately. She was tired of being scared. Then after, you know, when they called my da from the hospital, he said he'd have come to get her if I'd only told him how bad she was. He said it like he believed it. But I did tell him. I *did.*"

"Oh, honey. I believe you." Fury pooled in Meg's stomach and threatened to erupt, making her stop and catch her breath. The thought that anyone could say that to a child—that Adam's father had tried to absolve himself at Adam's expense—made her physically ill. She caught Adam's hand beneath the grimy cast. "Let me tell you something, Adam. Whatever your dad said, it wasn't your responsibility to stop your mother getting in that car. That was all on her, and you can feel sad about her choices, or about the events that made her take the drugs, but you can't take the blame for her decisions. Parents are supposed to be the responsible ones, not the other way around."

"But I knew, didn't I? I shouldn't have let her drive. I should have called the garda. Done something. Then she was weaving all over the road. I told her to pull over, and she wouldn't. Only kept driving faster." Adam was still shaking, the trickle of smoke from his cigarette making tiny, incriminating contrails. "My da sat at the hospital staring at me when they made him come. Didn't say anything for a long time, just sat there. Then he told me he didn't have room for me and Ma had wanted me to live with Uncle Niall anyway. I knew he didn't want me, but he didn't want to say it. And Niall doesn't have a choice."

Meg searched for words, feeling out of her depth. This time, he was the one who needed answers, and there weren't any she could offer to take away so much pain.

"I don't know either you or Niall well," she said with

her stomach churning, "but I know there are always choices. Niall wants you more than anything. He's said as much to me, and I'll bet you if you think back, he's said the same to you in a dozen different ways. Believe him, Adam. All he wants is for you to be happy, and he knows you aren't. He's just frustrated because he doesn't know how to make things easier for you. How to fix it."

"He can't fix me."

"Not you—you're the only one who can do that. The situation between you. Your sense of having a place here, with him."

Adam drew his hand away and took another pull of his cigarette, then he dropped it to the floor and crushed it with his toe. He studied her, his cheeks still holding on to the last of their baby fat and peach fuzz hair still soft on his jaw in the light through the window. A teenager teetering on the cusp of childhood and having to grow up too fast.

"You like Niall, don't you?" he asked.

"Yes." Meg's response was automatic, but it hit her then how much she did like Niall. He was probably one of the most fundamentally decent men she'd ever met. Not that her instincts had been solid in that department lately. Still, thinking about her mother and father, about her own short marriage, maybe there was no such thing as solid. How could you ever know what anyone was, deep inside them? What they would do when they were pushed? Maybe like or dislike—instinct—was all you had to go on. "Yes," she repeated. "I like him quite a bit. I like you both."

Adam continued staring at her as if he was trying to

decide whether she was lying or telling the truth. Then he bent his head and picked at the plaster around the edge of his cast. "Sometimes, I get so mad at him I think it's going to swallow me up inside the way the sky out here eats up the whole world at night. There's no lights. Just black."

Meg thought of the sky beyond her window as she'd lain awake the night before, a bowl with pinpricks of stars so bright they were like light filtering in from another universe, so many stars she'd scarcely seen the darkness. Yet Adam didn't see the light at all.

"Is that why you like to hang out with Kieran?" she ventured. "Because he's angry, too?"

Adam was quiet a long moment. "He talks to me like I'm the same as he is. His life's been crap, too, so he understands how it is when you're trying to get through. The others would laugh if he said that to them. All they see is he has money and a posh name and who his father is. But his father never had time for Kieran, either, and his ma died like mine. He tells me things because no one here wants to listen to him. They all hate him and they think he picks on James, but it's only because James makes them choose sides."

"What do you mean?"

Adam shrugged and looked away. "He just does."

"So you like Kieran better," Meg said, in part because she was curious, and partly because she felt if she circled back to Niall or Siobhan she risked pushing too hard. It was a fine line when you wanted someone to keep talking.

Adam stared out the window, and a faraway expression slipped over his profile. In the sunlight, he sat between everything, Meg thought, the ancient concept of *between* that meant a gateway betwixt two things: two times, two seasons, two worlds, two planes of existence. Adam was caught between childhood and manhood as well as between grief and anger, struggling to balance with one foot on either side and no way to steady himself as the ground shook beneath his feet.

"Kieran's no worse than anyone else," Adam said. "Everyone lies. Everyone."

Meg decided that he was working very hard to defend Kieran to himself. And that was always tricky to deal with. Too often, the more you pushed someone into justification, the more they were able to justify.

"That depends," she said.

His hungry eyes, meeting hers, gave him away. "On what?"

"On what he's lying about."

HOSTAGE

NIALL HATED EMBROILING MEG IN yet another family crisis, but he had to admit that if he'd chased after Adam himself it would have made the situation worse. Honestly, having Meg volunteer to speak to Adam was a relief on many fronts—he'd already had to duck away from the excavation too many times and left Gemma and the others to clean up Kieran's messes. It was part of his responsibility to keep everyone getting along.

He waited until Meg had crossed the bridge, then walked to where James was scraping the last of the spilled soil back into the bucket and clapped him on the shoulder. "All right, James?"

"No, I'm bloody not. Kieran's out of control."

"I'll speak to Graeme again and get it sorted, only it

might be easier to take the instruments over to the Kilmichael cemetery this afternoon for the sake of keeping peace."

"That's giving in to blackmail." James flushed red and glared at Niall. "Anyway, what's the bloody point? We'd have seen if there was a mass burial—that many graves from the same period or one large one. And someone would have remembered. There'd be a place name, a mention somewhere. But all Kieran has is an idea because he doesn't want the bodies to have been thrown over the cliff. Or he's trying to delay us finding anything until after his father's nominated in case we find something that proves it was Carew's men who did it."

"That may be," Niall said, stifling an exasperated sigh. "But if you go out with the metal detector and find nothing unusual, it will be easier for me to stand my ground."

"He still won't be satisfied. There are still thirty-odd acres of land that belonged to St. Michael's. He'll insist we have to scan those, too, and he'll say we should use the GPR in case there wasn't any metal in the graves, and he won't stop until we've done what he wants. Then we won't have time for proper documentation or spot excavations where we really need them before the season's finished."

"Assuming there's anything to find elsewhere."

"There is," James said, his eyes gleaming. "I feel it."

He turned away as though that were the end of the conversation—and in his own way, he was no less stubborn than Kieran. He'd been treated as a prodigy so long, he expected his opinions to be taken as gospel, but unlike

Kieran, he had the track record to back it up. As usual, Niall was left scrambling to know how to appease them both when neither was willing to give an inch.

"Go to the cemetery this afternoon—for me, James. Have a poke around. Do another quick walk through the fields. Then when you don't find anything, you can at least say there's nowhere to start and we'll be able to move it back down to the bottom of the list. The old tunnel's meant to be out that direction anyway, if it was ever there. You could take a walk toward Corr Áit and see what you think."

"Fine," James huffed, and he picked up the bucket and walked toward the far side of the tent where the big sifting screens had been set up. Every square inch of soil that was removed from the ground had to be sifted. Teeth, bone, and bits of wood wouldn't have pinged with the metal detector and could be too small for the volunteer to notice.

Niall rubbed the back of his head and watched him go, then he took time to do a walk through the dig site and try to lighten the mood. At last, he hiked over to one of the more reliable spots of mobile signal and left a message for Graeme O'Neill to ring him.

Heading toward the laboratory tent, he heard Gemma and Liam arguing by the sieves and veered off in their direction. He'd barely rounded the corner when they fell silent.

"Something I should know?" he asked.

Gemma's face went crimson. "Nothing. Sorry, boss. Sorry about this morning, too. But I can't take much more. He's a bloody menace. He's lucky Liam pulled him up and kept him from falling in the sea. Should have let him fall, that's what I say."

Niall wandered over to the screen where Gemma had been sifting dirt and ran a hand over the contents that had been caught inside, bits of roots and rock, nothing special. "I'll need you both to put in some public relations effort getting the volunteers back on our side after this. But first, I'd like you to tell me what happened—from your own point of view. How you came to stumble."

Gemma's hair was blowing in her face, curled strands the color of the red copper that had once come out of the Beara copper mines. Despite her best efforts with hat and sunscreen, the freckles on her cheeks and nose had darkened in the past five weeks so that she had twice as many. "What d'you mean?"

"You're within your rights if you want to write up a report. All three of you are."

"Because he pushed us?" Gemma asked.

"Is that what he did?" Niall kept his face expressionless.

Gemma had gone still, and then she looked from Niall to Liam and back again. "He pushed me twice, actually." Her voice was thoughtful. "The first time might have been an accident. The second was deliberate. He shoved both me and James, and he meant it. That should have a report, shouldn't it?"

Niall felt guilty even raising the issue. The moment the problem was even mentioned, it would set a chain of events in motion. True, Kieran had pushed all three of them in front of witnesses, but what if it had been James who had lost his temper? Would any of them consider documentation at this stage? On the other hand, if Niall didn't get the situation sorted, he'd be responsible if anything worse went wrong.

"If you feel you want to write it up, it would be a good idea," he said.

Liam lowered his chin and folded his arms, the thick black bands of his tattoos standing out across his biceps. "You want a report for when you talk to Graeme O'Neill, is that what you're saying? Something to give you leverage?"

"It's difficult, and it seems excessive, but there are rules."

Gemma plucked a small, pale rock out of the sifting screen and rolled it between her fingers. "And Kieran hasn't listened, however many times you've talked to him."

"But if we report it, I'd hate having him in the house with Gem after he finds out." Liam put his arm around Gemma's shoulders, his usually gentle expression replaced by something fiercely protective.

"It might not be for long, but we could clear out part of the other cottage, if you'd rather," Niall said. "We'd need to shift the storage and lab equipment, but that could be done."

"Don't be daft, the pair of you." Gemma's eyes flashed, and she glared at Niall and Liam. "Kieran's not going to hurt me, and I think I can just about manage to keep from stabbing him in the eye with my knife. Worry about James if you want to worry about anyone. He's reached the end of his tether."

Niall sighed again and gave a reluctant nod. "We'll figure it all out. Now go get a start on that PR campaign. Smiles and cheerful conversation, you both know the drill. And hope like the devil there's something good that comes out of the ground today."

He'd no right to hope for that at all. Together with the small horde of coins and jewelry, the slave shackle James had found buried near the place that the locals called the Place of the Massacre, Áit an Fheoir, was already a better find than anything he'd expected. The kind of important find that museums would salivate over, though there was still a lot of work left to do in the lab before they proved exactly how important it would be. Nevertheless, maybe the gods were finally smiling down at them, because it wasn't an hour later that Ailsa Cameron, of all people, called Gemma over to check an oddly shaped stone near the inner keep.

Gemma knelt to work the object out of the soil, and then she sat back on her knees with a queer expression. Niall was already on his way over before she called out, "Niall! You'll want to come and see this!"

Resting on a plastic bag in her palm, the object was about two inches by a half inch deep, oval in shape, with rounded planes on the front and back. Four small protrusions were evenly spaced along what might have been the right, left, top, and bottom.

"It's man-made, isn't it?" Ailsa asked, standing with her hands on her knees outside the shallow trench to watch Gemma work.

Niall crouched alongside Gemma. "Good eye, yes. The shape's too regular to be natural. Could be a piece of jewelry—a pendant or a brooch maybe."

"Want a go, then?" Gemma handed the bag over to him with the artifact cradled on top while she took a couple of additional photographs. Then she extracted soil from the area around where the item had been found and placed that into a second bag.

Niall turned the object over, his blood quickening as it always did when he held a fragment of history, a missing piece of an intricate puzzle that finds like this and modern science were only now beginning to fill in. He handed it back to Gemma. "It's all yours. I'll record while you do the assessment. And Ailsa, good job spotting this. You might as well come along and see the lab work in process."

The timing was an enormous bit of luck, and Niall seized the chance to gather the volunteers around. "This may turn out to be one of those rare moments when the ground offers up a glimpse of something that hasn't been seen in a few hundred years," he said. "You witnessed tensions running high this morning, and I'll admit that happens more often than we'd like. We spend too many days working with little to show for the effort, so people get anxious. That's why, when we do make a find, it's important to take a minute out to celebrate. And I want to use the opportunity to thank you all for your hard work. In this case, we have Ailsa Cameron to thank for her keen attention, but a find belongs to everyone—to all of you."

Gemma took the artifact back to the lab and after a bit more consultation, they agreed it was too risky cleaning the object with anything but a dry, soft brush. They couldn't afford to damage it or lose any clues to what it was, how it had gotten left in the ground, or who had left it there. Even the dirt embedded around the item might hold traces of blood, and metal in it could have picked up useful contaminants.

It was the first potentially significant find of the current five-week session, so Niall split the volunteers into smaller groups and let them take turns watching the cleaning progress. Gemma worked patiently, using one-directional strokes with a paintbrush and letting the deposits fall onto a white cloth she'd laid out on the table. The earth packed around it was relatively soft, easing away to reveal a silver and gilt pendant with glass affixed to the metal surface on both sides.

"What do you think?" Gemma bristled with energy that she tried to hold back as she finally set down the brush.

Niall felt his own pulse quicken as he turned the object over. It was double-sided, two small paintings—or possibly two objects—covered in protective glass, and he'd seen something similar to the first image in the collection at the Royal Irish Academy, a face blurred by an obscuring cloth.

"I'd say it might be a personal reliquary, if I had to make a guess. It could even be a double reliquary, and there's a symbolism to those. This covered face could signify that it's meant to contain a piece of the Turin shroud on one side—"

"The actual shroud that Jesus was wrapped in?" Gretchen Falsberg's face held a reverent hush.

History and religion didn't always play well together, so Niall was careful in how he phrased his answer. "I would doubt it," he said, "but whoever wore it almost certainly would have thought so. Relics were big business back then—holy objects, splinters of the true cross, bits of bone from various saints. The validity of the claims would have been impossible to prove but faith made them worth a lot of money to the people who believed."

"And the other side? That could be the Virgin Mary, couldn't it?" Gemma asked, turning the pendant over, but the image there had faded and darkened more, making it harder to see. It looked—possibly—like the figure of a woman in a veil, with her head bent. A trace of blue in the veil remained, but blue colors often faded more slowly than others.

"If it's another reliquary, I wouldn't even want to guess who the figure is meant to be. We'll need more tests to find out if there is anything inside—or ever was. With an object like this, we may never know anything for certain, not unless we find a written record."

Ailsa Cameron shifted closer, peering down at the object with one fragile blue-veined hand clutching the chain of the necklace at her throat. "It's important, though, isn't it? Whatever it was?"

"No doubt." Niall was surprised at how much she seemed to need affirmation—she was one of those women who came across as if they had all the confidence in the world. "Something like this would have belonged to someone with money. We know Owen O'Sullivan's wife was held hostage here for Owen's part in helping the English and betraying Donal Cam O'Sullivan Beare. She was freed by

Carew's men when the fort surrendered."

"Then it was a hostage rescue before the massacre?" Ailsa asked.

"Carew wouldn't have wasted a single soldier on that. He meant to destroy Donal Cam's last refuge, but Owen provided the intelligence that let them take it. Whatever happened to the other people on the island later, we know she was released and the soldiers who surrendered after the fortress fell were taken to Dunboy for execution."

"He means Sir George Carew—Kieran Stafford's ancestor," Gemma added. "He was Lord President of Munster and acting for Queen Elizabeth."

"The massacre was either done by his men or troops under Sir Charles Wilmot, the Governor of Cork, who came through in December of that same year. The records aren't clear."

"But Wilmot's mother was a Stafford, too," Gemma said, her eyes glinting with malice. "They'd still be related."

Niall sent her a quelling look, and she gave him a defiant shrug, then bent to sweep the debris that had come from the pendant into a plastic bag. The nape of her neck was flush with sunburn where her hair fell on either side.

In the excitement of the find, Niall'd had moments when he'd been able to let what had happened that morning slip to the back of his mind. Meg and Adam had returned, and they stood together near the entrance of the tent, neither one of them appearing the worse for wear. If anything, Adam looked marginally less in danger of exploding. James had taken the metal detector out to Kilmichael, but there'd been no sign at all of Kieran. Graeme hadn't returned Niall's message, either, but on checking his phone, Niall realized he had no signal. And it was going on three o'clock.

He studied Adam across the room, then pulled Gemma aside, out of earshot of the volunteers. "I know I shouldn't have brought Kieran up," she said. "But I won't apologize. No one would even care if he and his father are related to George Carew—if he wasn't making a point of insisting it was Irish men who'd done the killing."

"I'm not here to be your conscience, Gem. I wanted to ask a favor. Adam needs a bit of fun, and I need to get somewhere with better mobile coverage to speak with Graeme."

"You want me to hold the fort again?" Gemma gave him a wide, elfin grin.

He couldn't help smiling back. "As long as that's the one and only time you use that joke."

She glanced across the tent at Adam. "Yeah, go on, then. We'll be fine here, and I'd like to have a look around where we found this and see if there was a chain that went with it."

Her voice was level, but their eyes met and he recognized the sense of mingled excitement and awe in her, the enormity of holding history in their hands. "I know it's not the bones you were hoping we would find," he said, "but it's a start, isn't it?"

"Maybe James' certainty is contagious, but I've a hunch this is only the beginning," Gemma answered. "I think things are looking up."

JUSTIFICATION

"I lie to myself all the time.
But I never believe me."

S.E. HINTON
THE OUTSIDERS

F LUSH WITH THE SUCCESS OF her find, Meg's mother
objected as soon as Meg said she was going to eat with
Adam and Niall and drive down to the site of Dunboy
Castle with them. Ailsa had been crouched at the edge of the
trench, watching Gemma brush away the soil from around
the area where the pendant had been. Now she straightened
and her lips narrowed into petulant lines.

"But I thought you and I could celebrate. I thought you
would want to celebrate with me," she said.

Meg's conscience stirred uncomfortably. "I do—but I'll
be back later. Or better yet, you could come with us."

"They're strangers."

"Not really. Not anymore. But if you don't want to
come, you have plenty of people here and at the Bay Point

to help you celebrate until I get back. I wasn't even here for most of the action."

"All the more reason to stay now instead of running." Ailsa stood up and dusted off her hands, then pulled Meg away from the rest of the volunteers who were watching Gemma work. "Is it Niall?" she asked. "Because I don't want you making a mistake that you'll regret. I can understand you think he's attractive. He's good-looking, even charming in his own way, and being in charge adds to his appeal. But we'll be gone again before you know it, and you've never been the type to fall into relationships that don't have a hope of going anywhere."

Meg fidgeted with the rolled-up sleeve of her shirt and watched one of the sea gulls arguing with a yellow-beaked crow of some sort over a bit of food someone had dropped in the grass. "Maybe a go-nowhere relationship is exactly what I need—not that I'm planning on having a relationship with Niall."

"I'm not blind, child. And he's an academic, for pity's sake." Ailsa frowned at her. "He can't make any money—certainly not enough to fly back and forth to see you—and he's Irish. Temperamental."

"Stop, Mom. Just stop." Meg raised her hand to ward her mother off as Ailsa opened her mouth again. "First, I'm going along for Adam's sake—because I like him. I like them both. But second, even if I was interested in Niall, that would be my business. There's nothing wrong with a holiday romance. You had one."

"Which is why I don't want you making the same

mistake."

"So you think that was the mistake—the relationship, not the pregnancy?" Meg said, feeling suddenly cold, as if a window had opened on her parents' marriage and an icy wind was blowing too hard to allow her to force it closed again.

Ailsa's head snapped back as if Meg had hit her, and Meg felt contrite but angry, too, on her father's behalf. Angry all over again. Normally she would have apologized for saying something like this, but she didn't.

"I don't know what's wrong with you lately," Ailsa said, "but you're being cruel—and heedless. You're trying to be kind to the boy, but consider it from his perspective. He's only just lost his mother. If you get involved now, what's he going to feel when you leave? He's vulnerable, and so are you. Don't you think I know seeing your sister about to have a baby must be hard for you? I saw you with Connal's daughter at their wedding. You've always been soft about children. But mothering Adam won't help either one of you."

The wind and waves filled the silence, and Meg looked across Dursey Sound to the ancient backdrop of green hills and checkerboard fields and pastures. She told herself that taking an interest in Adam wasn't about mothering him. It wasn't about anything except wanting to help. But she hated that her mother saw inside her to that vague incompleteness she thought she had hidden so well after her barren and short-lived marriage.

"It's dinner and a drive, that's all," she said, leaning forward to kiss her mother's cheek. "We'll still have plenty of time to celebrate together. I'll see you in the bar."

"Don't think I'll stand around here waiting for you," Ailsa called after her with such a mixture of anger and pleading in her voice that Meg nearly turned back out of guilt.

On the other hand, her mother excelled at guilt.

An hour later, Adam was in an almost manic mood as they sat in the cable car with a young couple from Boston who'd come to Ireland on their honeymoon and a middle-aged man who was taking his vacation to walk the Ring of Beara. The couple chatted to Adam about Dublin and Adam managed to sound relatively civil.

Niall seemed bemused by that at first, then he leaned close to Meg as they stood to climb out at the mainland station and whispered in her ear. "I don't know what you said to Adam, but thank you."

"Wait until we have an opportunity. There are things you need to know. Meanwhile, I think he's just happy to escape for a while."

Niall nodded, then caught up with Adam, who had walked a few feet ahead. "So what's it going to be? Restaurant or fish and chips?"

"Fish and chips. Then ice cream somewhere for afters?" Adam raised his eyebrows, and in that moment, to Meg, he looked absurdly, touchingly young.

Niall laughed and squeezed his shoulder. "Done and done. There's meant to be an ice cream and sweet shop in Castletownbere that's worth the trip. According to Gemma, anyway, and I wouldn't want to argue with her."

They queued up for fish and chips at Eamon's van, but there was a line seven customers deep to wait through. When they reached the counter, Eamon wiped his fingers on a rag and leaned across, beaming his Santa Claus smile at Meg. "You're back, then. Come to try the other half of my menu?"

"Absolutely. What's good?" Meg said, finding herself smiling, because it was impossible not to smile at Eamon.

"Your choices are fish or fish."

"I'd better have fish in that case."

"I've some nice haddock caught fresh in the bay this morning, or smoked cod if you like that better. It comes beer battered and served with homemade tartar sauce, and chips from my own fresh-grown potatoes."

"The cod sounds perfect." Meg stood back while Niall and Adam placed their own orders.

The hands Eamon had rested on the counter were peppered in scars, thin ones from cuts and rounder ones from hot splatters of grease, and Meg wondered how many years he'd spent in this van, peeling and cutting potatoes and working the fryers morning and night. "Have you always been here?" she asked. "Or did you do something else before?"

He leaned back and the usual smile faltered, making Meg wish she'd kept her curiosity to herself. "I was in the army a long while," he said. "But Dursey's where I was born."

Turning his back, he pulled out a stack of round chips wrapped in paper towels from the refrigerator and dropped them into the deep fryer behind him before dipping glistening pale shanks of haddock into a bowl of batter and then dropping them into a separate fryer. While the fish was cooking, as though he couldn't bear to be idle for even a moment, he began to slice potatoes that had been soaking in a bucket. His knife flew, steady and in perfect rhythm.

"I don't mean to be rude to you, you know." He glanced up at Meg. "It's not that I mind talking about the army, like. Only, for good or ill, it was hard being away from here, not being able to be here, so I don't much like thinking about those other years. It's nice being home again and having honest work—at least while it lasts."

Seeing Ireland now, Meg hadn't thought too much about how recently it had been very different. But Eamon must have lived through the Troubles and the economic problems of the eighties when people had left Ireland in droves, only to see the boom economy bring many home again, along with jobs and EU regulations and mounting debt that made the subsequent financial collapse even worse. With the internet and more tourism, there was opportunity again, but Meg could imagine that Eamon's generation might find it hard to believe anything good would last.

He finished the meals and wrapped them in foil, and they bought sodas to take along. Niall drove a short distance, then parked in the lay-by with the nose of the car facing the water, and he got out and patted the hood near the windshield. "Up you get," he said, holding his hand out to help Meg up. "Might as well enjoy the view."

"Up there?"

"Why not?" He had that look in his eyes again, half

amused, half serious, entirely too charming.

Meg gave Adam the bag of food and scrambled up onto the car. Minutes later, sitting between Niall and Adam, leaning back against the windshield and watching the water turn gunmetal gray beneath gathering clouds, she felt an unfamiliar sense of peace. The air was calmer than it had been, too, reduced to a breeze like a caress across her skin.

It wasn't quite the end of Ireland, the end of land, looking out this direction, but it was close. "I wonder if there's a psychological aspect to living beside the ocean," she said. "If it changes you."

Niall glanced at her as he tipped his head back to take his first bite of fish. "There's something called the blue-mind effect. I swear. A mild meditative state that makes you happier. That's provable through neuroscience."

"Maybe that's why Fergal is so happy. Music and water. A neurological whammy."

Niall chuckled, a deliciously low rumble of sound. He was an overhead fish-eater, Meg noted, rather than bringing the fish to his mouth from below, and she decided his option was somehow bolder, more adventurous, though she didn't know why she thought so.

Compromising, she broke off a piece and tipped her own head back to drop it between her lips. She savored the sweet, salty crunchiness of it, letting the batter dissolve on her tongue and melt into the flakiness of the fish before she looked over at Niall again. "Okay, the fish is as good as advertised, but I'm not sure I'm sold on your neuroscience. Given that Ireland's surrounded by water, you'd think the

Irish would be more even-tempered if the science was real."

"You've noticed a certain lack of calm in us, have you?" Niall broke off a bite of his own fish to dip into the container of tartar sauce.

"Just think if we were worse without the water," Adam said with a grin.

It was the closest thing to a joke Meg had heard him make, and her heart lifted. Niall, too, snuck a look at him, then nodded with a bemused half smile.

"Our whole history is tied to the sea, our livelihoods, invasion after invasion after invasion. And escape," Niall said. "When your island turns to hell on earth, it can seem a prison, too. But for all the people who've left, there are few I've ever met who wouldn't come back in a heartbeat if they had the chance. Right up through the eighties, people used to gather on the end of this peninsula to watch the ships sailing their loved ones away to America, and there were people on board the ships whose hearts were breaking."

Meg turned back to Adam. "Would you ever want to live anywhere else?"

He peeled the cone of paper away from his fries and reached for a packet of salt. "Don't know. Haven't done much living yet, have I?"

Niall laughed. "Fair enough."

"And you?" Meg asked Niall, watching the ocean carefully.

"Irish archaeology doesn't happen much outside of Ireland."

Adam swiveled until his drawn knee bumped against

Meg's outstretched leg, and he leaned toward Niall with his face intent and watchful. "Are you going to fire Kieran after what happened today?"

"Where'd that come from?" Niall asked, which Meg suspected was a rhetorical question to give himself time to think. She liked that thoughtfulness in him, the way he gave a conversation his full attention. "I don't know that I'd be able to—and firing wouldn't be the right word for it anyway. But I'd like him to find something to do that would be better for his temperament so I could bring someone else in who'd fit better with the team."

Adam stared back at him expressionlessly. Then his eyes slid away, and he said in a quiet voice, "Don't. He won't like it."

It wasn't the words as much as something about the way he said them that Meg found chilling, a note in Adam's voice that Meg couldn't place because it wasn't quite fear or anger or malice. Niall must have heard it, too. He had raised a chip to his mouth, and he paused, then lowered it again. "Did he say something to you about getting fired?"

"I thought you liked him, Adam," Meg said.

"He doesn't like being embarrassed, that's all," Adam said, flushing red. "And it's wrong that no one gives him a chance." He darted a look at Niall, then picked up a chip and broke it in half. "You and James and Liam, you've all worked together before. And Gemma and Liam are a pair. Kieran's the one stuck outside, and he's tired of being messed about."

"Everyone's tried to be friendly," Niall said. "He and Liam, James, and Gem were all here on their own with the volunteers for a while, remember. It's not just what you've seen since we got here."

"Maybe I see more than you do." Adam swung his legs off the hood and jumped down from the car, leaving the rest of his food sitting there. "I'm going down to the water."

Meg could almost feel Niall's muscles tensing with the strength of wanting to tell him not to go. But he stopped himself with a visible effort and sat eating while Adam darted across the narrow road and waded downhill through high grass and heather, startling a small, bright yellow bird that had been peaceably sitting somewhere into flight.

"I was afraid the improvement wouldn't last, but it was nice while we had it," Niall said. "Thanks for that, by the way. Did he tell you anything important?"

"A lot, actually. Not about Kieran—he's holding something back there, and I'm not sure why. But we talked about his mother and what happened. His father."

"His father?"

Meg decided the ugly story was better told Band-Aid style, torn away quickly so the wound could heal in the open air. "He called his father before the accident and told him Siobhan wasn't safe to be behind the wheel. His father accused her of being dramatic."

Niall sucked in a breath and his face went pale as he looked across the road to where Adam was walking through the field. "His father's a selfish idiot," he said. "Always was."

"It gets worse. After the accident, he told Adam he should have made it clearer something was wrong. Then while Adam was still reeling from that, he said he didn't have room for Adam to live with him, but Siobhan had wanted you to have him. I think all that got linked together in Adam's mind, the idea of not being able to save his mother and his father not wanting him, as if his father doesn't want him because he couldn't save Siobhan. And he thinks you only took him in because you didn't have a choice."

"Poor little eejit," Niall said, his voice full of heartache. "None of that's true."

"Doesn't have to be true for him to believe it," Meg said gently.

Niall sat up as though he couldn't bear sitting still, but on the hood of the car there wasn't anywhere to go. He set his half-eaten meal down beside him. "Fair point. Jesus, Mary, and Joseph, as if the boy didn't have it hard enough."

Across the road, Adam had descended to the shore line. Against the vastness of the ocean and the distant green hills across the bay, he looked impossibly small.

Niall watched him with a bleak expression, then turned back to Meg. "What can I do? What do I say to fix that?"

"Keep showing him that you do want him."

"How?"

"You're doing it now, just being here."

He cocked his head and looked at her, just looked, his eyes gone solemn and dark. "Do you have any idea how grateful I am that you're willing to help?"

"Of course I am. He needed to talk." Meg shifted her gaze over Niall's shoulder. "That might be the biggest part of his attraction to Kieran, too, you know. He recognizes Kieran's anger because he feels it himself, but Kieran's also treating him like an equal. Or so Adam thinks. Maybe it's true that Kieran doesn't have anyone else here to talk to—and Adam has enough compassion to recognize that. He's a good kid, deep down. A really good kid."

"I know that."

"The problem, from your viewpoint, is that Kieran represents both everything Adam wants and what he doesn't want, all rolled into a single package. That's endlessly fascinating to a teenage boy."

"Money, a flash car, and a nasty attitude, do you mean?"

"Something like that. But don't underestimate the allure of someone who can paint himself as a victim while justifying anger as 'standing up for himself'—which is the way Kieran has painted it, I think. Are you really going to try to fire him?"

"I would have a long time ago, if I could have. But getting physical with people, that far and away crossed the line, so I doubt I have much choice." Niall squinted up at the sun, his eyes the same pewter blue as the ocean fifty yards away.

He felt miles away, too, in that moment, for all that he was close enough for Meg to still feel the warmth of his body against her arm. Then he picked up her hand and folded it in his and turned back toward her. "Thank you. I mean it, Meg. I don't know what to say."

Their clasped hands looked oddly right together, his almost double the size of hers, but fitted, like cups or spoons meant to cradle within each other.

"Do you—" she began, then licked her lips and started over. "Could Kieran's father hurt your career? Do you suppose that's what Adam was implying?"

Niall pulled his hand away. "I doubt even Callum Stafford could have me fired, but there won't be much in the way of advancement if I lose the university a sizable amount of potential funding. Or get myself branded as a troublemaker. On the other hand, the staff and the dig are my responsibility. I have to put them before politics or position or Kieran's influence, so I'm going to have to fall on my sword and hope I come out all right. If I don't, well, I won't regret it. I should have done it sooner. Probably shouldn't have hired him in the first place, but it's a fine line, isn't it? I'd like to think I didn't let his connections influence me in that, but I know it crossed my mind. It gets muddy very quickly, and it's not hard to cover up reasons we're not proud of with other reasons that seem more valid."

Meg felt cold as the wind picked up. She lunged for a napkin that threatened to fly away.

Down by the beach, Adam stooped to pick up a rock, then drew back his hand and tried to skip it along the water. The angle was too steep, though, and it immediately sank. That was the problem—when you got in too deep, there was always the risk of drowning. Niall with Kieran. Herself with Ruben. Maybe even her mother and father when they'd first met. Who, in the end, was Meg to judge?

Adam's fish had gone cold by the time he wandered back, and he re-wrapped it in the original foil and they all walked together to the trash can near the road. Niall clapped him lightly on the shoulder as they returned to the car. "You don't need to worry about me, you know that, don't you,

Adam? You and I, we'll be all right, whatever comes."

"You talking about Kieran?" Adam asked, flashing a stormy look at Meg.

"Kieran, grief, misunderstandings. Doesn't matter. We're family, and family can get through anything life throws at us. Together."

RUINS

". . . until the last of them stands
humble and ashamed among the ruins . . . "

DAPHNE DU MAURIER
HUNGRY HILL

THERE WAS A FRESH DÉTENTE between Niall and Adam after that. By the time they'd finally pulled through the ruins of a pair of gatehouses off the R572 past Castletownbere, Adam was in a more cheerful mood. No sooner had Niall parked the car at the edge of the track, Adam spotted a sign ahead of them and took off at a run.

"Stay off the castle walls!" Niall called after him.

Adam waved his good arm and vanished up a trail into a curtain of ferns and trees.

"I hope you didn't mean that as a challenge," Meg said, following more slowly. "I'm not sure we need to spend more time in an emergency room."

Niall fell in beside her. "It's brilliant to have him running *to* something instead of running *away*. Makes for a pleasant change."

Dunboy revealed itself in stages, the way so much of Ireland did. The pair of ruined gatehouses they'd driven past at the entrance of the muddy track had looked both martial and imposing, their stonework and pointed gothic windows overgrown with ivy. Then there'd been a modern house off to the side, and now further down the road, a weathered sign gave a brief history of the Siege of Dunboy.

The English hadn't, it turned out, destroyed the castle as thoroughly as they'd razed the fort on Dursey Island. Bits of stonework and walls remained—not many, but enough to reveal there had at least been an imposing structure. The landscape and vegetation were different here, too, made lush by shade trees overhead and ferns and moss and grass growing between the stones. Seeing a flash of Adam's white T-shirt now and then between the foliage, Meg thought of the *bean sidhe* he'd described, and that conversation seemed, now, to have taken place a terribly long time ago, though it hadn't been long at all. She found herself half-expecting a specter among the ruins, and whether it was that preconception or something in the atmosphere, coming face to face with what little was left of the walls, goosebumps erupted on her arms.

"Cold?" Niall came up beside her.

She shook her head, wondering whether he had the same eerie sensation, and decided that he must feel it worse, since this had once belonged to his family. And she couldn't help remembering her own mixture of sadness and fury and pride when she'd first heard about her mother's ancestors in

Scotland who'd been persecuted by the English with such a vengeance that even the MacGregor name had been banned for centuries. Her mother's family had changed their surname to Murray and never changed it back.

This piece of haunted ground, here, was a place where the power of the O'Sullivan family had broken once and for all, and the clan had never been the same. Reading about it hadn't made it real the way it was now as she stood on the spot. She thought of the men, fighting, while the cannons bombarded the walls from ships in the bay and soldiers massed outside—4,000 men against 143. The O'Sullivans had sent out a messenger asking for terms of surrender, but the English commander had hanged him by way of answer. No surrender. No quarter. The O'Sullivan men had fought on, retreating to the cellar when the walls had been nothing more than rubble, and the English had shot the captain while—as his final act—he'd tried to blow up the gunpowder stores around them. Victorious, Carew's forces had hanged every last man who remained from a tree in the market square.

Niall shifted closer. "Is it only me, or can you sense the despair and blood? I often wonder if things like that are the product of too many stories from a father with a gift for tragedy."

"There should be rain falling and a piper playing," Meg said. "Places like this, there should always be rain."

He stilled, watching her, and though he didn't smile, there was a shift in his eyes that was as quiet as the clouds moving. Then he offered her his hand and helped her scramble up the bank. "Come on, I'll show you Puxley Manor before we go."

"Where's Adam?" Meg looked around, but he'd disappeared.

"He must have gone ahead. I hope he doesn't decide to climb the fence. What am I saying? Of course he will."

The ground was slick along what proved to be a shortcut, and they both slipped a couple times as they hurried. But nothing had prepared Meg for the view that opened up when they'd emerged from the trees, a gothic castle of pale stone, high gabled roofs, dozens of turrets and what must have been at least forty chimneys. The first glimpse was stunning, beautiful yet wrong, somehow. Awareness of the vacant windows, wild, overgrown grounds, and rusting security fence seeped in gradually, like a chill soaking into the bones. It was only then she realized that Niall still held her hand.

As though he'd just discovered it, too, he pulled away, but the warmth of his skin lingered against Meg's, leaving her more aware of his absence than she had been when her palm had been clasped in his. He moved to where Adam was already halfway up the chain-link fence, his useless right arm, awkward in its grimy cast, held close to his stomach where it made the climb still more dangerous.

"Come down from there, mate," Niall called. "We don't want the garda coming after us."

Adam rolled his eyes. "Like the guards have time for that."

"There are security cameras."

Glancing around as he hung there with his toes wedged into the links, Adam spotted a lens at the top of a post, staring straight at him. He hovered there a moment, although whether he was debating going on or merely saving face, Meg couldn't guess. At last, he kicked his feet out and dropped, stumbling a bit as he landed.

"Why's it empty anyway?" he asked.

Niall made no more comment about the climb. "Want the long story or the short one?"

Adam shrugged as if he didn't care, and Niall moved over and stood beside him. "I'll give you the compromise, then. You know about Owen O'Sullivan, right? After he'd betrayed Donal Cam at Dursey and Dunboy, not to mention fighting alongside the English before that, Owen expected George Carew to reward him. He hoped he'd get the land and title, but almost all the property in Ireland ended up in English hands sooner or later—or those the English selected—and this was no exception. The Puxleys eventually built the Beara copper mines and made themselves wealthy enough to build a home the size of this on O'Sullivan land. But there was a curse."

Meg grinned at the dramatic tone in his voice. "Of course there was."

Adam rolled his eyes. "An actual curse?"

Niall shook his head at him, as if in disappointment. "You can't be believing in *bean sidhe* and not in curses, mate. That's against the rules. Especially when it's an O'Sullivan curse. Or do you not know that story, either?"

"I love a good curse story." Meg raised her brows in

invitation.

Niall gave a soft laugh that rolled down Meg's spine. Then he continued, "Donal Cam didn't die at Dursey or at Dunboy. After Charles Wilmot swept in and laid waste to the whole of Beara and Bantry, slaughtering all the livestock and burning houses, fields, and storehouses, Donal led the survivors north to meet Hugh O'Neill—the Earl of Tyrone—in the dead of winter. They left New Year's Eve with a thousand men, women, and children, and arrived with only thirty-five. Then when the O'Neill surrendered, Donal Cam was one of the few rebels the English refused to pardon. He fled to Spain, where he was murdered as he came out of church, probably by an English spy."

"What about the curse?" Adam said, impatiently.

"I'm coming to that. The point is, Donal Cam wasn't the last of the O'Sullivan Beares. A century and a half later, the chief was one Morty Óg, a smuggler and notorious recruiter for the Wild Geese, the Irish exiles who made a living by hiring themselves out as mercenaries to the French. Morty Óg had fought with them himself, and there were some who claimed he'd been beside Bonnie Prince Charlie at Culloden, then helped the prince escape. He lived here, in the shadow of the old O'Sullivan castle with the land owned by Puxleys. And because he was a thorn in the side of the English, they ordered John Puxley, who was the local revenue officer, to catch him. Morty Óg didn't go quietly, though. He had the loyalty of every man and woman in Beara, and he outsmarted and out-sailed Puxley and made him look ridiculous. In retaliation, Puxley killed a young

O'Sullivan lad, then he and his men kicked the body all the way down the road to the boy's mother's house."

His face was grim as he said that, as though he felt the horror of the story as much as Meg did, and she loved that these things still mattered to him, that he could feel the pain of them down through the centuries.

"That's awful," she said, shuddering.

"It was one indignity too many. The woman hobbled straight to Puxley Manor and cursed John Puxley, the whole Puxley family, and the land they'd stolen. Then John Puxley had her burned alive in her cottage and, in turn, Morty Óg shot Puxley dead on his way to church for the Easter service."

"Well, there's poetic justice for you," Meg said.

Adam threw Niall a quick, appraising glance. "It's still murder, isn't it?"

"Of course," Niall said.

"Kieran said you'd try to make Morty Óg out to be a hero like you do with Donal Cam, but he killed other Irishmen. And kidnapped them to send to fight in France."

Niall's shoulders went rigid. "Kieran told you about Morty Óg?"

"He says you want to make the dig all about English villains versus Irish heroes when it wasn't."

"No one's ever only one thing, hero or villain. Not when they're fighting to survive." Niall pushed his hands into the pockets of his khaki outdoor pants and rested a boot against the fence. "And whatever Kieran claims, any story we tell is about feelings anyway, otherwise it's nothing more than dates and dust on a page. You're an O'Sullivan, Adam. That feeling in your gut when you imagine the boy's body being kicked, the woman being burned alive? That's your own history. We Irish have told stories for thousands of years because life's a circle, and we want to avoid making the same mistakes again. But unlike some people, we don't write the fact that Morty Óg was a smuggler out of the story, either. Or that he murdered a man. Did Kieran tell you the rest of it?"

"Rest of what?" Adam asked, not looking at him.

"Yes, there were men who Morty Óg took by force to join the Irish Brigades, but they'd given their word to join and then changed their minds. Morty was the sort of man who had a moral code—a harsh one, but he lived by it. That's the real curse, the way I see it. Puxley's wife stood screaming beside her husband's corpse, and Morty could have killed her, too. But he refused to murder a woman, even when he knew he'd pay the price for that with his own life. If he'd killed her, there would have been no one to point the finger at him."

"Are you saying he should have murdered her?" Meg leaned her shoulder against the fence.

"Not at all. Only that he knew leaving her alive meant he would hang. He made a choice, and knowing what a choice will cost you is in itself a curse."

Adam turned back to the manor and curled his fingers through the diamond-shaped links in the fence. "I thought you meant the magic sort of curse."

"We all curse ourselves in different ways." Niall

gestured at the ruins in front of them. "Puxley Manor is the perfect example. Maybe if the Puxleys hadn't felt they needed to prove themselves, they wouldn't have spent every penny they had trying to build the grandest house in Ireland. When the mines ran out, they had to scurry back to England, and the place stood empty until the IRA finished it off in 1921. It was a wound on the landscape after that. Cows grazing in the Italian marble halls, bats in all fifty-four of the chimneys. Investors bought it in the nineties, fancying it for a grand hotel. No expense was spared, but the money ran out again. You might say it was a coincidence more than a curse, so, but it depends what you want to believe. Who or what you want to blame."

Adam worked the tip of his sneaker into the fence, making the metal rattle. Niall watched the boy with his own expression both fierce and tender. Fiercely tender. It made Meg feel she was intruding on something between the two of them, but she was afraid to move and break the spell.

Niall turned back toward Puxley Manor. "To my mind, it's human nature to want to assign blame when disaster strikes," he said. "We blame ourselves, or a curse, an enemy, injustice, bad luck. Having somewhere else to point the finger keeps us from having to blame the people we love or just accept that sometimes, tragedy is random and there's nothing we can do to prevent it."

Adam's head was bowed, the stretched-out neck of his T-shirt too big so that his collar bone jutted through. Still two feet apart but closer than when they'd started, he and Niall both studied the carcass of recent Puxley history that

THE BONNIE PRINCE

"The song from the glen, so sweet before,
Is hush'd since our Charles has left our shore."

ROBERT BURNS
"THE WHITE COCKADE"

AILSA CAMERON'S GLARE WAS COLD enough that it
should have chilled the entire bar. But as one of the
main subjects of her scrutiny, Niall only felt hot and
stifled in the close room that did a creditable job of
mimicking the feel of an old pub, a place for friends to gather
around a smoky turf fire with a pint of ale or a glass of aged
Irish whiskey. Tired of feeling under the microscope, he
extricated himself from the two young American women
who'd been trying to flirt with him and slid further down the
bar where he had a better view of the front where Fergal had
kidnapped Meg and Adam and nudged them onto stools
near the fireplace.

Adam looked dubious but also flushed with heat and
excitement as he took the guitar Fergal handed him and

settled it awkwardly on his lap, his cast-encased right arm draped over it.

One of the women who'd been talking to Niall drifted closer again. "So do you live nearby?" she asked. "You're Irish, aren't you? I love the accent."

She was attractive and nice enough, but Niall had no interest at all. His eyes slid back to Meg and Adam. "That's my nephew up there," he said. "He's about to play."

"He looks a bit like you," the woman said. "And is that your sister?"

The word stabbed into Niall, the pain of it cold and sharp, a double hit that brought both the realization he no longer had a sister and the awareness that his feelings about Meg were anything but brotherly. Still, he couldn't define what she was, so all he said was "No."

The woman hovered as though she was trying to decide whether to drift away or try again to engage him in conversation. Between her and Meg, the contrast was stark. Where the woman wore a slithery blouse unbuttoned far enough to reveal the lace edge of a bra and ample cleavage, Meg had changed into dark jeans and a thin, pale blue sweater that hugged her slender curves, called attention to her elegance, and added a wash of color to eyes as changeable as the sea.

Niall had never been averse to a bit of fun, but he preferred friendships that had the possibility of going deeper. Most of the time, if he wasn't interested, he had only to be politely friendly and women got the hint. With Ailsa Cameron glaring at him, he found himself wishing the

American woman wasn't quite so slow to catch on. He didn't want Meg to get the wrong idea.

Or her mother.

Ailsa, looking sharply attractive in a black silk blouse and more of her heavy silver jewelry, stood with the same group of volunteers from the dig she'd been with since Niall and Meg and Adam had returned from Dunboy, and although Meg had gone over and tried to draw her into conversation, Ailsa had seemed intent on freezing her out. Punitive, that was the word for her attitude. She'd given Niall and Adam a frosty smile, exchanged a few polite questions with Meg, then turned back to the handful of women who'd clustered around Brian Sheehan. Brian, who Niall was used to seeing in wellies and overalls, looked unaccustomedly tidy with his lion's mane of white hair tamed and a dark jumper over a collared shirt. And he was enjoying Ailsa's attention, spreading his own charm and brand of Irish blarney with a liberal hand.

Meg, both hurt and worried by the attitude, directed small, appraising glances at her mother even now. Mostly, though, she concentrated on Adam as he tried to move his fingers over the guitar strings. A shimmer of sweat had pricked out on Adam's forehead, and Niall couldn't tell whether that was from the pain of his broken forearm, from the heat of the fire and the lights and the crowd, or from anxiety about performing. But just as he was about to walk over and check, Fergal handed Adam a guitar pick.

"Here, try that," Fergal said. "You won't need to move your fingers as much."

Adam's nod was stiff with determination. "I can do it."

He played a few random chords with the pick, then plucked out the first notes of "When Irish Eyes Are Smiling." Niall winced at the memory that conjured: Siobhan singing the same song to Adam, holding her face a few inches from Adam's and singing as loud as she could until, no matter how dark a mood he was in, Adam gave in and smiled back at her. Adam'd had dark moods even before the accident, Niall realized. Funny how he hadn't remembered that.

"Good lad. That's grand, now." Fergal gave Adam's shoulder an approving pat, then looked up at Meg. "You know this one?"

Meg had found it in the book, and she tapped the page and nodded.

The sheet music as much as anything else was a reminder of Fergal and Ari's skill in putting together a thriving tourist trade. Authentic music nights in Ireland were mainly locals who already knew the songs, or they picked them up and passed them along by playing, something akin to an insurgent remnant of a time when the bards were banned by the English and stories went underground.

Adam plucked the guitar strings and Fergal settled the *bodhrán* drum on his thigh, and with the beater flying against the skin, he paced out the beat. Niall checked his phone, still waiting for Graeme to ring him back, but there was nothing, and he put it away again, feeling both surprised and pleased that Adam had been willing to try to play.

Adam was hesitant at first, the notes slow and careful,

reminding Niall of Siobhan sitting cross-legged on the floor in her flat. Neither she nor Adam'd had much inborn patience, and she'd chided him while she taught him to pluck out chords, her long hair tied back into a messy knot pierced by a pencil or whatever she had lying around, her smile as wide and quick as her temper. She'd loved singing, had Siobhan, but more than that, she'd loved having people watch her sing. Having them admire her music.

Meg had none of that. She kept an eye on Adam as she sang, studied his fingers and his face, her concern to protect him from hurting himself obvious.

But she could sing. Really sing.

Even as others in the room joined in, her voice rose pure and clear through the microphone, its power growing along with Adam's confidence as they finished "Irish Eyes" and slipped into "Star of the County Down," and "The Wearing of the Green," and "The Rising of the Moon." Seeing the two of them, watching Meg, Niall felt something warm uncurl in his chest, spreading like the heat of good whiskey that left a fine complication of flavors on the tongue.

"Can I buy you another of whatever you're drinking?" The American woman beside him put a hand on his shoulder and raised her own empty glass as she spoke into a momentary lull while Meg and Adam took a break to sip some water and choose another song.

Niall had forgotten the woman was there, and his attention shifted back to Meg and brought him a vague sense of guilt. She looked over just then and their eyes caught. She smiled, a generous, open smile, and that generosity—all of her—caught him in the solar plexus with an unfamiliar kick of happiness. He couldn't help smiling back.

"Oh," the woman beside him said, her eyes moving from him to Meg and back again. "I see. Sorry, I didn't realize."

She turned to drift away and, feeling apologetic but oddly buoyant, Niall stopped her. "No, I didn't mean to be rude. Let me buy you and your friend a drink instead? It's my country, after all. My duty as host."

"Sure. Why not?"

Ignoring the unmissable fact that Ailsa Cameron was frowning at him again, Niall gestured for Sean, a distant cousin of Fergal's from Allihies who tended bar in the evenings, to come over. After ordering whatever the two American women were having, he added another glass of wine for Ailsa.

"Did you run over her dog or something?" Sean asked. "She's been glaring daggers at you all night, and she'd proper scare me if she was looking at me like that."

Niall's phone vibrated in his pocket, saving him from having to come up with an answer. Since it was Graeme O'Neill at last, he dropped a banknote on the bar to cover the drinks and excused himself to slip out into the corridor where it was quieter.

Graeme barely gave him the chance to say hello.

"We've been over this, Niall," Graeme said. "Leaving me more messages about getting rid of Kieran won't change the situation."

"Did you hear where I told you he pushed three of the

staff today? Nearly knocked both Gemma and James over in front of the volunteers and hit Liam on purpose."

"It's awkward, but you'll need to find a way to make it go away."

Niall walked through an empty sitting room to stand looking out the window. The clouds were gathering, gray darkness painting itself over gaps of deeper black scattered with fistfuls of stars. "The fact that Kieran knows my hands are tied—the fact he thinks he's above having to play by the same rules as the rest of us—made it impossible for him to be part of the team on any functional basis. Forcing me to keep him on has been unfair to the others and to him, and it's making the problem dangerous. We're leaving ourselves open to liability, Graeme, and I won't stand by and wait for someone to get seriously hurt."

"I doubt it's as bad as all that," Graeme blustered. "You can talk to them all. Smooth things over."

"And if they file reports with Human Resources?"

"Then for God's sake, stop them. That would be a disaster if it leaked to the press."

"Wouldn't it just," Niall said. "Seems to me it would be much safer all around if there was a different project that required Kieran's attention. Preferably in an empty office somewhere until he can re-learn to play well with others. He's got a good brain in his head, and we're letting it go to waste because we're not able—or willing—to hold him to the same standards as everyone else."

The phone went silent, but Niall had said what he needed to say, and all he could do now was wait. Going to

Kieran with the reports was the next step, and without Graeme's backing that could get ugly fast.

Graeme released a sigh. "You're a proper pain in my backside, you know that? Don't do anything until I've had a chance to think. And I'm not happy. Not at all."

"Neither am I, believe me." But heading back into the bar, the sense of having failed the team he'd been living with gave way to a deep relief, and, mingled with a sliver of hope for Adam, he felt lighter than he had in weeks.

The mood in the bar had changed as well. Where before while Meg had been singing, others had sung along or, if they didn't know the words, had continued drinking or chatting, now everyone was silent, their attention focused on the front of the room. Meg's voice swirled like smoke, clear highs dropping to surprising lows, accompanied by Adam and the beat of Fergal's drum. Niall couldn't place the song until she repeated the haunting chorus of "I Dreamt that I Lived in Marble Halls," but she conjured up the feeling of Puxley Manor, its gilded, ghostly emptiness. The other songs they'd done so far hadn't used half of the power of her voice, the sort of power that came from emotion that wasn't exaggerated or filtered or muffled. The sort that came when someone cut their heart open and offered its contents honestly, letting longing and love, fear and heartache, all become a gift they gave the audience.

The guitar chords were simple, but they were unfamiliar. Partway through, Adam fumbled. Instead of picking up right away, he stopped, and Niall held his breath, hoping he wouldn't stop and suddenly storm off. Meg shifted over and put her hand on Adam's shoulder, but she kept singing without the accompaniment, and an instant later, Adam picked the tune back up.

What made Niall glance down the bar at Ailsa Cameron just then, he couldn't have said. But if he'd expected to find Ailsa watching her daughter with pride, he'd been mistaken. Ailsa's expression was tense, her profile set tight by anger and more than a little plastic surgery. Even when Meg finished and the audience erupted in applause, she stood motionless until Brian Sheehan clapped her on the shoulder and whispered something obviously congratulatory in her ear. She came alive then, with a nod and a wide, practiced smile.

Niall wandered over to stand beside her. "You must be very proud of Meg. I'd no idea she could sing like that."

Ailsa took a long sip of wine. "Why should you? You hardly know her."

"Niall makes it his business to learn about people," Brian said, setting his usual bottle of water on the bar. "He's a good man. The sort who doesn't come around too often. Meg could do a sight worse, if you ask me."

"I didn't realize you two knew each other so well." Ailsa swirled the clear amber liquid in her glass with a sour smile.

Niall decided there was no accounting for taste. "Brian's my landlord in the village."

"I only stay the night on the island now and then, but I'm out there working the sheep and cows most days." Brian turned back to Niall. "It's grand to be seeing Adam having fun for a change instead of moping. Good idea having him here to play. Been hard on him, hasn't it?"

"It'll be a long road yet," Niall responded affably. "I'm not sure you ever get over losing a parent. And that said, I'd better make certain he's not doing his arm any damage with all this playing."

Ailsa grasped his elbow before he could get away. "You know Meg will be going back to her life in a few short weeks, don't you? You could save her some pain by staying away."

Niall looked down at the hand that had caught his sleeve, and he shook off her hold. "The last thing I want to do is hurt her," he said, "but I think it's up to her if she wants to run the risk."

Brian had been watching Ailsa with an odd expression, and he nodded. "You'll be leaving, too, won't you? Life isn't getting any longer, *acushla*. In the end, you measure it in laughter and not in years."

Ailsa's expression locked into a steely smile, and Niall turned his back on her and took a few steps toward Meg. But she had been laughing and shaking her head at whatever song Adam and Fergal were trying to convince her to sing, and they had finally won. Adam set down the toe-tapping intro to "Mairi's Wedding" on the guitar, and Fergal joined in on the drum. Around the room, people began to clap their hands. Fergal, the *bodhrán* braced on his thigh, the beater flying in his hand, rocked his entire body to the beat.

The song was too fast to manage without practice—Meg had been right to protest—but she laughed through her own mistakes. When the music ended, she tapped her chest as though she had no breath left, and she shook her head when Fergal flipped the book to a different page. Instead she leaned over to speak to Adam, who wiggled his fingers and seemed to assure her he was fine. She insisted, and before Niall could go and help her, Adam slid out of his chair with only a faintly truculent expression, and they both eased through the small crowd toward the bar. A few people stopped to speak with them, and Meg nodded or smiled, or listened. Mostly she listened or asked a question to get Adam into the conversation.

Niall thought how rare it was, these days, to find someone with a gift for hearing what people had to say. Maybe it was her profession, but he tended to think more in terms of journalists talking, writing, expressing themselves, when what they were meant to do was find the stories. Find the truth. In a way, the two of them had that in common, too.

Adam came and stood beside him, and Niall thumped him on the back. "That was brilliant. We'll have to go get your guitar out of storage," Niall said. "I should have thought to bring it with us."

"Didn't feel like playing then," Adam said with a shrug.

"Well, it'll be an excuse to drive up to Dublin anyway, maybe next weekend. What do you say? We can pick up anything else you want now we've settled in here. Get some more DVDs, too, since you've watched everything we brought a hundred times. You want a soda? Some tea?"

"A beer?" Adam raised his chin in challenge and pulled the ever-present pack of cigarettes from his pocket.

"Nice try," Niall said, suppressing a smile, "but no, and

away outside with you, if you're going to smoke. Or you could stay here and keep singing. Your choice."

Adam's lip curled faintly, but he stuffed the cigarettes back into his pocket. Niall took that as a victory. Those came few and far between.

Then Adam looked down at the scuffed tips of his trainers, moving from rebel to small boy with another of the lightning shifts that had kept Niall so off balance all these weeks. "I did all right, didn't I, Uncle Niall?"

"You did, yeah." Niall wanted to pull him close and hold him. But he needed to be so careful, so he added only, "It sounded grand."

"Had to fake my way through some of it. Didn't know the Enya song."

"No one minded."

Meg arrived then and, placing both hands on Adam's shoulders, she bent and kissed him on the forehead with none of Niall's compunction. "That was fantastic! It would have been great for anyone, much less when you're playing with a cast on your arm."

Adam shrugged, but he looked pleased. Fergal had picked up the guitar again, and behind the bar Ari slid down a glass of wine for Meg along with a Coke for Adam. "Good job, the both of you," she said, looking from Meg to Adam. "Sure you don't want to go back and do some more? It'll be my turn otherwise."

"I think I'm about sung out for the night," Meg said.

"Well, that was a rare treat, so more tomorrow, I hope." Ari's dark skin glowed beneath the painted chandelier, catching the light in droplets. She carried her fiddle over to join her husband, eased it from the case, and positioned it underneath her chin. Fergal then beckoned Brian Sheehan over, and Brian picked up the beater and the *bodhrán* and settled down with them on his knee.

Fergal raised the microphone a few inches and surveyed the room. "Those of you who speak Irish may know the words to '*Mo Ghile Mear*'—'Our Gallant Hero'—and the rest of you can sing along phonetically to the chorus and feel like you've learned the language. It's an old Jacobite tune, the goddess Éire mourning for the rightful king in exile and for the fate of Ireland without our Bonnie Prince who'd gone back over the water after the defeat at Culloden. You might not know how many Irish fought with Charlie on that day, but there's a school of thought that claims he spent the night right here on Dursey Island before our very own Morty Óg O'Sullivan Beare smuggled him away to France on his frigate. And why not, so? It's known Morty Óg smuggled everything else." There was a round of laughter, which Fergal waited out before straightening his long, lean frame.

Drawing gravitas around himself like a mantle, Fergal sang in a rich tenor, the words slow and dignified. Then Ari came in on the verse, her fiddle beautifully mournful, and Brian added the beat of the *bodhrán* that was somehow a lament, a wake, and a battle cry all rolled into one.

It had never seemed odd to Niall that moments of song could sweep time away. In Ireland, so many things did that. Old sorrows and grievances were passed down, millennium by millennium, along with ideas and traditions and beliefs. It didn't matter that he knew the history himself, knew the mistakes that had caused the bitter loss at Culloden or the tragic aftermath. Irish songs were always about far more than their words. And the fear of how a Catholic country would fare under brutal English—Protestant—rulers had more than come to pass. Not that the Catholics or even the Irish in general had been saints. The more time Niall spent pulling artifacts from bloody ground, the more he realized hell on earth had been created too many times by men who claimed to act in the name of God.

Fergal and Brian and Ari shifted straight from "*Mo Ghile Mear*" to the call to war of "*Óró Sé do Bheatha 'Bhaile*," and the beat of Brian's drum coursed through Niall long after Ari had sung "The Parting Glass" to bring the evening to a close. Even Meg's mother sang along with that one, though whatever had her angry with Meg didn't seem to have diminished.

She swept down the hall ahead of them on the way back to the bedrooms a few minutes later, her back as steel-straight as a queen in a corset and only a slightly unsteady gait giving away how much she'd had to drink.

"Good night, Ailsa," Niall called. "Thanks again for the accommodation."

"Good night." She moved on to the next door over without a backward glance.

Meg started to follow her, but Niall caught her by the hand. "Hold on a minute."

Her eyes were like water, clear and endless, and Niall felt a little drunk himself as he unlocked Meg's room and held it

216

open. "I'll be in momentarily, Adam," he said. Then he eased the door shut again and turned back to Meg. "I wanted to say a proper thank-you."

She looked down at the long narrow expanse of blue patterned carpet. "It was a great day—I enjoyed it."

"Did you, now?"

Her blush deepened, and he loved seeing it, loved the way her eyes wouldn't quite meet his. "Fish and chips and ruins," she said. "What was not to like?"

"My sentiments exactly. And the company couldn't have been better."

"Adam was fun, wasn't he?"

"You know that's not who I meant."

She laughed. "Maybe, but why should I let you off that easy?"

He pressed back against the wall, snaking an arm around her waist to pull her with him as a couple of guests squeezed passed en route to their own rooms further down. She felt good in his arms, as familiar as a well-fitted glove, but she brought every nerve ending roaring into life.

"I'm getting the feeling you'd be worth any amount of effort," he said quietly.

"I meant effort—not flattery." Her voice was throaty with a hint of laughter.

"It isn't flattery when it's true, and here's a bit more while I'm in the mood for confession: I've been wanting to kiss you since the doughnuts this morning. Would you mind very much if I did?"

She smiled, another of those quick flashes that lit her

ECHOES

HER LIPS STILL TINGLING FROM Niall's kiss, Meg gave herself a minute of solitude by returning to the bar to get her mother a bottle of water. There were kisses, and then there were the kind of kisses that required recovery before you had to face a disapproving parent. The kind of deliciously decadent, all-encompassing kisses that made you remember why a kiss was something that could make people forget themselves, make you feel bigger than yourself. Every nerve in Meg's body had sizzled when Niall had kissed her, and they'd both stood back breathing hard, looking at each other in a silence filled with wordless things. It had been the kind of kiss that made Meg realize she'd been sleepwalking through her life.

Hurrying past his room—her own room—she imagined

him lying in her bed, and she wondered if he was thinking of her. Wondered what he was thinking.

She stopped outside her mother's door and shifted the glass and the bottle of water into one hand to reach for the key in her pocket, but she took another minute, just standing there. Remembering. Recovering.

When she'd given herself enough time to look normal again, she let herself inside and went to set the water on the nightstand for her mother. The room was tastefully decorated in pale wood and white fabrics with deep touches of red. While the bed was a double, her mother had settled herself resolutely in the center of it, arms folded and covers pulled to her chest as she sat propped against the pillows, making it clear she wasn't going to share. She hadn't even taken the time to remove her makeup or the heavy necklace at her throat.

"You certainly took your time saying good night," she said.

Meg responded coolly, "I thought you might wake up thirsty."

"Convenient excuse."

"What is it with you tonight?" Meg turned around and stared at her. "You've been awful since the minute we got back."

"Because I don't want to see you getting hurt—and it's clear you're going to be. That's the only outcome to this."

"You can't know that."

"I see how the two of you are looking at each other."

Meg pulled her pajamas from the overnight bag she'd

brought in earlier and retreated toward the bathroom to slip them on. "I don't want to argue with you, Mom. Not tonight. Did you have a good dinner? That Brian Sheehan seems nice."

"He was there with the group, that's all. Nothing to do with me."

"He seemed to be flirting with you especially."

"He's a farmer. And I didn't come to Ireland for a flirtation."

Meg balanced on one leg to pull on the shorts of the soft blue pajama set. "Then why did you come?" she called through the half-open door. "I could have sworn you wanted an adventure."

"Why is that so wrong? Tell me that. I haven't had fun in years. Nothing is fun anymore. I hate that you and Anna hate me now. Your father hates me. Even Elspeth."

Meg emerged from the bathroom and leaned against the jamb. "I don't hate you."

"You're disappointed in me. But what did I do that was so very bad? I made a better life for myself. For my children." Ailsa's voice was petulant and a little slurred, worse enough off for drink that Meg wasn't sure she wanted to have this conversation with her.

On the other hand, maybe it was exactly the time to have it.

She went and sat beside Ailsa on the edge of the bed. "Imagine if I came and told you I had done what you did. Threw away love for money and got myself pregnant on purpose to trap someone into marriage because he had better prospects. And he was meant for my sister. What would you say to me?"

"How was I supposed to know he was meant for Elspeth?"

Meg couldn't allow herself to be deflected. "And what about Daddy? You took his choices away, you pretended you loved him, and I'm sorry, Mom, but yes, finding out all that was a little disappointing. I'm trying to understand, I honestly am. I get that things were different then, but—"

"See? You hate me. Everyone hates me," her mother said, "and it isn't fair. I did everything for you girls—I've spent my entire life making sure you could have whatever you wanted."

"Do you think we want things at the expense of Daddy's happiness? Your happiness?" Meg stared at her mother, wondering if she'd ever seen her, really seen her before. All Meg's life Ailsa had loomed large, a force of nature that blew away everything in its path. Now she just looked small and spent, like the remnant of wind after a hurricane has blown itself out.

"Be honest with me," Meg said. "Knowing what you know now, would you make different choices, if you had the chance?"

Her mother stared at her, her lip trembling and her fingers tight against the coverlet. Meg held her breath, hoping that something real would come out, something . . . just something. But Ailsa rolled over onto her side, reached for the lamp and switched it off before moving back to the center of the bed.

Meg thought that was the end of the conversation, but a moment later, Ailsa spoke into the darkness. "If I'd made different choices, you wouldn't be here, Margaret. Or your sisters. God punished me anyway, taking that baby away from me, and don't think I haven't spent every day of my life knowing that was the case. You can't ask me what I'd think of myself, because I'm not that girl of eighteen anymore. I'm not sure who I am, or even who I was. I only know who I didn't want to be. I couldn't stay in the glen for the rest of my life and marry a farmer, a MacLaren, and I couldn't have stayed in Scotland or even moved to London without having been sucked straight back to Balwhither. You've only been there the once for the wedding. You saw how beautiful it can be, how peaceful. You didn't see the bleakness, how you fight to get through every winter, and how the past sinks its claws in and doesn't let go until it has strangled the life right out of you. All that expectation. All those ghosts."

Stunned, Meg sat where she was, frozen in the same patterns of love and rejection that had always characterized her relationship with her mother. Maybe part of that was her own doing, she realized. Ailsa had always been ruthless and a little vindictive, single-minded in everything she did. Odd that it had taken coming here to Ireland, even more than the trip they'd made to the Highlands where Ailsa had grown up, to reveal that all those qualities stemmed from her mother's childhood fears.

And it wasn't as though Ailsa had given them a future free of expectation. Growing up in Cincinnati, she'd constantly reminded her daughters of their position in the community, but it had been a position her husband had built with his law practice, centered on his law partners and the people he and Ailsa had met at the country club. Meg and Katharine and Anna had gone to a private school, and their friends had all been the same, the children of lawyers, and doctors, and businessmen, but Ailsa had always made certain her girls had the best of everything.

In Scotland, her own life would have been very different. Yes, the old Murray house was still one of the biggest in Balwhither, but the money to go with it had long since been spent. Ailsa and Elspeth had grown up with a father who'd scrabbled, year by year, not to lose what had been passed down through generations.

He hadn't, though, and after he was gone, Meg's aunt had stayed in the Murray house and opened a museum for the English tourists. Aunt Elspeth, even more than Ailsa herself, had always been a bit creative with the truth and if the "artifacts" she displayed—old claymores, daggers, golden rings, and fairy thimbles she bought in junk shops and online auctions—hadn't strictly belonged to the people to whom she attributed them, she put that down to the necessity of paying the bills. A small act of rebellion and survival. Maybe it wasn't so very different, Meg thought, from what Morty Óg O'Sullivan had done. Maybe truth, in the desolate places, the beautiful struggling places that had evolved into what they were on the edges of English prosperity, was all a little relative.

With a sigh, Meg drifted back to the bathroom. After brushing her teeth, she washed her face, paying extra attention to the area around the stitches where the skin on her cheek was beginning to itch as it knitted. Then she pulled a spare blanket and pillow from the bottom of the wardrobe cupboard and settled herself on the narrow chaise lounge beneath the window. It was impossible to sleep, though, with too many things running circles in her mind. She would have liked to dream about kisses, or at least to have the luxury of being afraid of what wanting to dream about kisses meant. But her mother's anger and her own disappointment intruded.

Her mother's breathing grew steadier and slower, and the room felt like it was closing in on Meg. Levering herself up, she twitched the curtains open to reveal the view. Water, after all, was supposed to be soothing.

Moonlight had bathed the ocean in gold dust, but across Dursey Sound wraiths of fog were rising from the green fields on Dursey Island, spilling along the cliffs and toward the sea. The whole island looked like it was brewing from a witch's cauldron, new and ancient all at once. Incredible and breathtakingly beautiful. Gathering the blanket around herself, Meg grabbed her phone to use as a camera and slipped outside through the sliding door.

Her toes curled on the cold flagstones as she made her way down the rise toward the cliff, and she didn't stop until she reached the edge of the patio. The fog was swelling by the moment. Lit by the moon, it writhed like a living thing, a gray gold specter, rolling over and over itself as it dropped along the cliffs to meet the white spray of water breaking on the shore. Meg raised her phone to capture it in a photograph, wishing she had a real camera with her. But she had video, and she switched to that, hoping to catch a fraction of the moment's power. Then a small movement, a spot of luminous silver drifting amid the fog, caught her eye.

Gliding from Oileán Beag to the main island, the slender shape radiated light and gave the impression of a figure cloaked in mist, or a woman in a long gray dress. Whoever it was, if it was anyone at all, was only visible a moment, but the glow remained, weaker and more dispersed than a flashlight, growing smaller and dimmer until it was entirely lost within the fog.

Intent on spotting it again if she could, Meg ignored her cold feet and stepped over the low stone wall at the edge of the patio to run through the damp grass that descended to the cliff. Even in that short time, the fog had thickened, overflowing the island to collect just above the surface of the ocean as if the water was fighting to push it back.

Meg stood motionless, watching, her heart drumming like the beat of Brian Sheehan's *bodhrán* that still echoed in her mind. Finally, realizing that her teeth were chattering, she huddled deeper into her blanket and crept back to her mother's room. She eased the door shut, the way she had as a teenager the few times she'd dared to challenge Ailsa's iron rules. But if her mother heard her, she said nothing, and there was no movement from the bed.

For a long time after she had settled herself on the chaise beneath the window, Meg lay shivering, thinking. Eventually, though, she slept.

NIALL WOKE, DISORIENTED IN THE unfamiliar bed, to the sound of Adam breathing and the mobile phone vibrating on the nightstand. It was scarcely five o'clock, and Niall's heart thudded as he groped to answer. No good news ever came this early in the morning.

"I've been thinking over what you said," Graeme O'Neill told him without preamble.

"You must have been if you're phoning at this hour."

"It usually takes seven calls to connect, so," Graeme snapped, and then he sighed. "Go ahead and speak to Kieran if you feel you must, but make sure you have those reports in your hand before you do."

Niall sat up, thoroughly awake now. "I'd planned on that, but I'd prefer to have a face-saving alternative to offer him. Carrot and stick. It's the only way we're likely to avoid a nasty fight."

"I couldn't think of anything, but if I know you, you wouldn't have suggested it unless you already had something in mind."

"I do, but hold on a moment." Glancing over at Adam beside him in the bed, Niall padded to the sliding door, let himself out onto the patio, and stood shivering in the wind. "It occurred to me that you might be willing to teach a course on the modern reinterpretation of the *Pacata Hibernia*. If, that is, you had someone like Kieran who could prepare the material for you."

"Are you mad? If his father is made *taoiseach*—and now that he's head of the party nothing short of a miracle will stop it—the last thing he'd want is some reporter dredging up the atrocities and decisions from the *Pacification of Ireland*. If you think Kieran's delaying the excavation of the massacre to save his father embarrassment, imagine what he'd do to explain all that away. The *Pacata* is only starting to be reexamined, and I won't put my name to biased research."

"You wouldn't need to." Niall tipped back his head and looked out toward Dursey Island. "You could present the Irish perspective against the English, and if that doesn't work, you could delay publication—indefinitely. One way or the other, you'd also need to find a course or two he could teach."

"*Can* he teach?"

"He can be charming when he likes. He's good, Graeme. On paper, he's excellent or I'd never have hired him. I think he could benefit from your guidance."

"Bollocks." Graeme paused, then something scraped on the other end of the line, and he swallowed audibly as though he'd taken a large sip of coffee. "And where am I meant to find the budget?"

"I have it on good authority his father wrote the university a rather large check recently. Maybe you could get some of that."

The fog that had come in thick the night before had dissipated, leaving behind wisps of mist that clung to edges around the cliffs, pale pink and gold in the imminent sunrise like the interior shells of muscles from Bantry Bay. A strong wind set the tide racing in the sound, sending plumes of white froth high against the cliffs, and further out, something dark bobbed in the water, some bit of jetsam from one of the several passing fishing vessels that were churning their way out into deeper water.

"All right," said Graeme eventually. "But you'll need to get him to agree, and don't be surprised if you find yourself with less funding before all this is over. Or out of a job altogether."

He disconnected and Niall leaned back against the sliding glass door, waiting for the hushed moment when the sun would break the horizon, the moment when the world paused to take a breath and the secrets carried on the wind echoed back from far away. A gull cried, soaring in the distance, and as the morning lightened and the sky and sea caught fire, Niall would have loved to knock on Meg's window and pull her out, to have that moment of peace and possibility of daybreak with her beside him. He would have liked to kiss her again and see if a second kiss between them could be as good, or whether it had been some alchemy of relief and happiness and music that had made it feel different from other kisses.

But even at breakfast, between Adam and her mother's disapproving presence, being alone for so much as a minute or two wasn't possible. Then there was a spate of finds throughout the morning that kept him scrambling, finds ranging from the carcass of a seventeenth-century sheep to a hammer from a broken musket.

In between, he spoke to Gemma, Liam, and James and

got them each to write out a statement—though not an official complaint, not yet—and with those in hand, he waited for Kieran to show his face. Kieran was sulking, though, and by lunch when he still hadn't appeared, Niall decided not to bother trying to phone him. Mobile reception being what it was, he left Adam with Gemma cleaning sheep bones, and he walked to the cottage that Kieran was sharing with James, Liam, and Gemma on the far end of the village. Getting no answer when he'd knocked several times, he wandered around to the back, but Kieran wasn't on the patio, either, so he opened the kitchen door and poked his head inside.

"Kieran? You here?"

He edged inside and stood listening, but the cottage had the empty feeling that houses took on when there was nothing living within. Niall walked through, calling out again as he reached the bottom of the stairs, then climbed to the loft that Kieran and James shared.

He had no trouble discerning which side was which. James' half was compulsively neat—the bed made without a wrinkle, the nightstand next to it devoid of anything but a lamp and a copy of Donal Ryan's *All We Shall Know* marked by an actual bookmark instead of the scraps of paper or ticket stubs Niall tended toward himself. The other part of the room looked as though a suitcase had exploded, or rather two suitcases, because both were propped, half-empty, open on the floor, their contents stirred around and spilling over onto the unmade bed, the back of the desk chair, and in piles along the floor. In the bathroom, a used towel hung over the sink beside a toothbrush and a tube of toothpaste with the cap left unscrewed. The bathmat, still damp, lay crumpled in the corner.

Irritated, Niall descended the stairs and exited, and as he was walking back to the dig site, Brian Sheehan emerged from a shed near the road. "You all right there, Niall?" Brian asked. "You look like you've the cares of the world pressing on you."

"You didn't happen to see Kieran around anywhere, did you?" Niall asked.

"Is he the surly one?"

Niall allowed himself a grin. "Most of the time."

"Not today. But then I was late coming in this morning."

Niall's grin widened. "I saw you were busy last night. Good job, too."

"I hope you're meaning the drum."

"What else?"

They smiled at each other, and if Niall was thinking he couldn't begin to see what there was in Ailsa Cameron to interest Brian, he didn't say so. Odd taste in women aside, he liked Brian, and he wondered if he'd have had the courage himself to leave teaching primary school after a lifetime in Galway to start farming on Dursey at the age of sixty-two.

Heading back to the dig, he found his irritation with Kieran had only grown, and since Gemma was still working with the sheep bones in the lab, he asked Liam and James to the tent as well. "Did Kieran say anything about going to the university today?" he queried. "Or when he's expected back?"

"Didn't know he'd gone anywhere," Gemma said, looking up from where she was working dirt away from the bones with a chopstick that she'd whittled down into a point. "I assumed he was sulking at the house all day."

"Good riddance, too," James said, then his features, always sharp as a fox's, sharpened even further. "Will you be speaking to him about the reports?"

He'd looked pale since writing out his statement, and Niall imagined it had to be hard for a grown man to admit—in writing, no less—to being bullied and almost knocked over. But James had always been a prodigy, young going to university and graduate school, inevitably a bit too smart for his own good. He'd probably been a target his entire life. The thought made Niall furious with Kieran all over again, and he wondered if he was being soft talking Graeme into giving him another chance, kicking the can farther down the road, or whether he was only being pragmatic and doing the logical thing.

"We'll have to see what happens," he said in response to James' question. "In the meantime, send him my way when you do see him. I'd like to get all this settled today so I can try to find someone else in case Kieran decides he'd rather not stay on."

Liam, who'd been staring at the yellowed grass inside the tent, looked up. "I was thinking about that. Aileen Donovan might be free. Remember her from two years ago? She's still working on her doctorate at Trinity, but she had a broken leg that won't be coming out of the cast until next week. She didn't have any work lined up for the summer because of it, and she's like a dog with a bone tracking down research, if you're wanting someone to follow up on things like the pendant, household accounts, and so on. And she's good with volunteers."

"Brilliant," Niall said, his mood lifting. "We can try to get in touch once Kieran and I have had a chance to speak."

The day wore on, however, and Kieran never came back to the dig. Niall sought out the rare spots of mobile coverage now and then to leave more messages, but if Kieran had, in turn, left voicemail for him, it didn't come through. Toward the end of the day, Niall checked the rental cottage again, but it was still quiet and empty.

He decided, by the time Meg and her mother were preparing to head back to the bed-and-breakfast, to go across with them. Apart from the fact that he'd barely had a chance to see Meg the entire day, he didn't like the idea of having to offer Kieran an ultimatum based on the reports by his coworkers and then send him straight to the house with the others with no chance to cool off in between. Altogether, it would be far safer for everyone concerned if he caught Kieran on the mainland and offered to gather up Kieran's things himself or at least made sure he was with Kieran when he went back to the cottage.

ADMISSIONS

T HE WIND SNARLED, LASHING AT the cable car as it
swayed above Dursey Sound. It was worse than any
crossing they'd made before, and Meg's mother was
pale as she stared down at the hands clasped in her lap.
Pressed tightly together, those hands seemed vulnerable and
weak to Meg, in a way that her mother had never seemed.
They were soft hands, crossed with blue veins across the
backs, the careful manicure of her French-polished nails
preserved by the gloves she wore when she worked in the
trench. It struck Meg in that moment that preservation of
appearances was her mother's lodestar, and the tragedy of
her life. Instead of striving for happiness, Ailsa had settled
for the appearance of it. And she'd wanted nothing more
than to have her daughters validate her choices. Maybe all

parents wanted that.

Meg leaned forward and clasped Ailsa's fingers. "We're almost there."

"Don't start worrying about me," her mother said, flinching away.

With a small, hollow ache, Meg pulled back. She glanced at Niall, but he was squinting out the window at the sky. Where, earlier, the wind had scoured even the smallest clouds away, now it was ushering in a dark, roiling bank of thunderheads that advanced from the horizon like an army gathering.

"It'll be a hard storm, this," he said.

Meg told herself it was absurd to feel happy about that. "So no boats crossing over later, I guess? Does that mean you'll want to stay here again tonight?"

His gaze drifted toward Ailsa, who had gone even stiffer in her seat. "Probably better to eat our fish and chips and head back on the last cable car. I'd hate to put you out two nights in a row."

"I wouldn't mind. If you want to," Adam said from beside him.

Ailsa gave a soft huff, barely audible above the wind, and pursed her lips.

"Maybe not tonight, Adam," Niall responded. "You were up half the night getting your fix of mindless television, and Meg might not be thrilled if we turf her out of her room again."

Another glance at her mother decided Meg against repeating the invitation, and as soon as the cable car had disgorged them, along with the three German tourists who'd shared it with them on the way over, Ailsa pulled her aside.

Slinging the lavender daypack across her narrow shoulders, Ailsa braced herself against the wind and clutched her windbreaker around herself. "What's this about fish and chips?" she asked Meg, her voice petulant. "I thought you were coming back with me for dinner."

"Why don't you come with us? Eamon's fish is worth trying, and Niall wants to talk to Kieran as soon as he gets here. I'd like to keep him company."

"Fergal told me this morning they were making a special spiced beef and more of that soda bread you loved. And rhubarb tart for dessert. You love rhubarb."

Meg hated rhubarb—it was Katharine who loved it—but her mouth did water at the memory of the warm brown soda bread that had tasted of buttermilk, slathered with fresh, salted butter as thick as cheese. She glanced over at Niall, who was frowning down at his phone. His dark hair was wild in the wind and a score of lines etched out his irritation between his brows. And then Adam, who'd walked on ahead of them all, stopped abruptly.

"I thought Kieran had gone to the university or somewhere, Uncle Niall."

"I assumed he did."

"He can't have if his car's still here."

Niall peered across the parking lot to where a screaming red Porsche 911 stood beside his own white Peugeot that had been washed clean by the recent rains. Frowning, he said to Meg, "Will you wait here a minute?"

"Of course," Meg said.

He strode toward the Porsche, tucking his phone into his pocket, with Adam jogging along beside him.

"You do realize you're being stupid?" Ailsa asked as Meg watch them go. "But it's not only your heart I'm worried about. That boy's not stable—the way he's always staring at people. The way he's angry one minute and normal the next. He's hurt you once already."

"He's a child."

"He's a teenage boy. You don't know what they're like or what they're capable of doing. They can hurt you in ways you can't imagine."

Something in her voice, a small tremble, made Meg's attention sharpen, and the rest of the world fell away. "Did someone hurt you?"

Ailsa's shoulders stiffened. "Why would you ask me that?"

But Meg knew her, and even before her mother's hand rose to pull at the thick silver necklace she wore as if it was strangling her, she recognized the tension. "I'm right, aren't I?" Meg asked. "Is that why you needed to get away from Balwhither?"

Ailsa shook her head. "Of course not. Don't be so melodramatic. I meant in general."

Meg studied her mother's face, the eyes that had darkened with worry and the lines around them that had deepened. It was fear, she realized, that expression her mother wore, but she couldn't tell if it was the memory of fear—or fear that Meg would ask more questions.

There were two types of people in the world, Meg had decided long since: those for whom a secret lost its power over time and those for whom secrets only loomed larger and more dangerous with every passing day. She'd thought her mother's vault of deceit had finally been emptied with the revelation of the pregnancy, with the slip of Ailsa's tongue made in the heat of an argument in which she'd admitted getting pregnant on purpose during that excavation in the Hebrides. Now Meg realized there was more.

"Did John MacLaren hurt you?" she asked Ailsa quietly. "Is that why you wanted to get away from him?"

Ailsa clutched the windbreaker tighter around herself as the wind battered them both. "Stop it, Margaret. You're my daughter. Just because you think of a question doesn't give you the right to ask it. You're not entitled to know everything."

"Don't you think knowing that would make a difference?"

"Well, it shouldn't. What do you care about my reasons? What right do you have to judge? All I did was build a better life for myself. For you and Katharine and Anna. For your father. And maybe it wasn't the love of a lifetime between us—but not everyone has that."

That was hopeless and sad, and Meg felt for her mother, but it was also an excuse. Yet another excuse. "Aunt Elspeth could have, though," she said. "She and Daddy could have had it."

"You don't know that! They don't know that!" Ailsa's face grew molten beneath the smooth skin, her eyes threatening to boil over. "We all want what we can't have. That's all it was. Do you honestly believe I never noticed how they avoided looking at each other all these years? How different he was whenever she came to visit? You don't think that hurt me, too? You all assume it was easy for me, growing up in Breagh House, looking the way I did. You think my whole life was cake and roses, but there are people who'll punish you for being beautiful. For having the wrong address and the wrong blood running through your veins. I had to get away."

Her eyes grew hard, as if the admission had touched a core point of weakness.

"Are you saying this was about the family?" Meg asked quietly. "That's why you didn't want John MacLaren? Because five hundred years ago some MacGregors killed a few MacLarens?"

"I'm saying John MacLaren was an angry man who liked to punish people. So, yes, all right. He hurt me. He hit me once, because that's the kind of man he was, and if hadn't left, he would have kept hitting me between apologies. A man who hits once doesn't stop. I would have become weak if I stayed. I'd have become one of those women who justifies and excuses and finds a way to separate the ugly part of a man from the part she finds attractive. The part she needs. I got out because I needed to get out. Does it make you any happier knowing that?"

Her body had started to shake, and she suddenly looked small and frail and old, as if the wind that was steadily gaining force had blown through her and left her too dry to even shed the tears that should have gone along with her words, with the tightness in her voice. Meg stepped in and drew her close, felt her body trembling.

"Oh, Mom. I'm sorry."

"Don't you pity me. I decided to change my fate before it trapped me, that's all," Ailsa said against her shoulder. "Don't."

"I won't," Meg lied, her heart breaking.

"And you can't tell anyone else—no one. Not Anna, not your father. Certainly not Elspeth. Promise me."

It was a promise Meg had no intention of making, because it changed everything.

Some things.

Not that two wrongs made a right.

With her own parents and her sister and her family roots in the glen, Ailsa would have found it impossible to avoid going home for holidays and weekends no matter where she moved for work—anywhere except America. And every time she returned to Balwhither, she would have seen John MacLaren, been drawn to him. Even if she'd gone to the police, that had been a different era. Just as airplanes had been prohibitively expensive and telephone calls between continents had been a luxury, the understanding of violence against women had barely been a blip on the radar.

Meg thought about Ruben, about her own stupidity in seeing him. About how much she blamed herself, and how she'd walked away rather than fighting for her job because she had doubted her own role in what had happened.

No, two wrongs never made things right. But Meg was

the last person who could judge her mother.

"Problem?" Niall's voice startled her as he spoke from near her shoulder. "You look upset."

She hadn't heard him approach.

Ailsa stepped back. "We're perfectly fine," she said, sounding calm and brisk and businesslike. Then, with an impatient *tsk* of her tongue, she wiped the skin beneath Meg's eyes with the pads of her thumbs, brushing aside tears Meg hadn't known were there. "Well, I don't know about you," she added, "but I'm going to call it an early night. I've a bit of a migraine coming on, so I'll ask Fergal if I can have a bowl of soup in my room."

Meg wanted to shake her, because it was the same thing her mother had done all her life—pushed everyone away the moment they got genuinely close, the moment they could see a crack in Ailsa's carefully constructed facade. It had to be so lonely for her beneath that armored shell.

"Are you sure, Mom?" she asked.

"For heaven's sake, Margaret. Do you think I want to keep talking about this? Go. Do whatever you were going to do. You will anyway."

She turned without waiting for Meg to reply, and Meg couldn't decide whether to go after her or stay.

"Are you certain you're all right?" Niall asked, studying Meg.

"No, but that wasn't about me."

"Go take care of your mother. Don't worry about us. I think dinner's off anyway. The engine on Kieran's car is stone cold, so if he left the island at all today, he's been back for a while. And I know he didn't go to either the house or the dig site. I'll need to ask Pete in the control room if he's seen him."

Meg took a deep breath and tried to get her mind refocused from one problem to the other. "And if he hasn't? He could have simply gone to work somewhere else on the island, couldn't he? After his behavior yesterday, he might not have wanted to face the volunteers."

"He's not the take-solace-in-nature sort," Niall said. "But let's not get ahead of ourselves, shall we? I'll go have a word with Pete."

Looking from Adam's pinched expression to the tension in Niall's jaw to her mother's retreating figure just climbing the path up to the bed-and-breakfast, Meg was even more torn about what to do. But she couldn't help her mother—she knew that from experience. The more she tried, the more Ailsa would push her away. She could do something for Adam, though. And maybe for Niall.

"In that case, why don't Adam and I get the fish and chips while you're off doing that?" she suggested.

The gratitude in the look Niall sent her told her how worried he was. She wasn't sure why, but evidently, there was more to the story than she knew.

There was a line at the caravan, and by the time they had waited through it and stood at the counter while Eamon cooked their food, Niall was back. A shake of his head was all the answer he needed to give, and Adam went pale as a ghost and quiet.

"Maybe he did just decide to go take a look at some

potential sites on his own," Meg said.

Adam shook his head. "He wouldn't. He—"

Niall waited for him to finish whatever he'd meant to say, but Adam stared down at the ground. "He what, Adam?" Niall finally asked. "If you know something, now's the time to tell us."

"Nothing."

"It doesn't quite seem like nothing."

"But it is! It's stupid."

"What is?"

"Forget it, will you? Just never mind."

Niall raised his eyes to Meg's as Eamon handed them their meals, and he was so clearly divided between desperation and exasperation that Meg imagined him and Adam snapping at each other again, not communicating, all the way back to the island and however long it took to figure things out. They'd made progress—she was sure they had—and she hated to think of that falling away again. She knew, too, how it felt not to be able to communicate, to feel like you were battering at a wall you couldn't break through.

"If you'll let me run by the Bay Point and grab some clothes, I'll come back to the island with you. I can give you a hand looking for him—if you don't mind letting me sleep on your couch afterward."

"Or maybe you could keep Adam here?" Niall asked. "I hate to ask, but—"

"No!" Adam cried. "If you're going to look for Kieran, I'm coming with you."

"We've no idea what we're dealing with, mate. More

than likely, there's nothing to it at all, and he's back at the house already or soon will be. He knows better than to stay out with a storm like this approaching."

If he'd meant to reassure anyone, he failed, and he knew it. But it helped Meg reach a decision. "Grab my dinner for me, would you?" she said to Adam. "I'll see you in a couple minutes."

She started back across the parking lot toward the Bay Point and Niall hurried after her and stopped her when they'd gotten out of Adam's earshot. "Are you sure you don't mind doing this?" he asked. "I don't want to keep dragging you into our sordid mess."

He rubbed his temple as if his head ached and his jaw was set. Studying him, Meg couldn't help asking, "How worried are you, Niall? On a scale of one to ten."

Niall rocked back on his heels. "I'd be less concerned if I didn't have the sense that Adam was withholding something important. The worst of it is, if it turns out there is a real reason for worry, we may not be able to reach anyone who could help us until morning. So if you really wouldn't mind coming back over to give me a hand with Adam, I'd be grateful."

There had been so many moments of late where Meg had wanted to offer physical comfort to someone, to pull someone into her arms and just hold them. Although words were her stock in trade, they so often didn't seem to be enough. Still, the power of human touch, so desperately needed, could too easily be devalued or mistaken. Standing in a parking lot, in view of Adam and everyone in the world, wasn't the right moment anyway.

As if he'd felt some of what she felt, Niall reached out and caught her hand. Just that. Lacing his fingers through hers, he lifted her hand to his lips then held it there a moment, wordlessly, before letting go.

Sometimes, Meg thought, a gesture was worth a thousand words.

REVISIONS

"The curves of your lips rewrite history."

OSCAR WILDE
THE PICTURE OF DORIAN GRAY

AILSA FELT LIKE A FOOL talking through the door when Meg knocked. But she couldn't bear having her daughter look at her. Pity was the cruelest of emotions. In its name, the recipient was stripped of all respect and human dignity and expected to be grateful for being shown kindness. Hatred, anger, jealousy—those were at least honest feelings when you met them face to face, and they were bearable.

Ailsa leaned back against the door. "Go away, Margaret. I told you I don't want to talk. You can't browbeat me into it."

"Please let me in, Mom."

"No. I'm going to bed with a book to forget how rude you've been."

There was a pause outside, and Ailsa held her breath,

hoping that, for once, Meg would accept words at face value and leave well enough alone. Leave her alone.

"I came to tell you that I'll stay if you want me," Meg said after a moment, "but if you don't, if you really don't, then I'm going back across with Niall. Kieran's taken off somewhere, and Niall may need help with Adam. With the storm coming in, that means I won't be able to get back until tomorrow. Will you mind?"

Ailsa shouldn't have minded. She tried to tell herself she didn't. That was the thing about choices, though: sometimes Ailsa felt as if she'd spent her entire life second-guessing every one she had ever made.

"Do whatever you like," she said, "but just remember I told you not to get involved."

"That's great, Mom. An I-told-you-so before the fact." Meg sighed. "Look, I'm asking what you *need*. What can I do for you?"

"I don't need anything. Did I say I did? Go do whatever you're going to do, and don't give me another thought," Ailsa said, looking at the wide stretch of blue carpet in the empty room and the neatly made double bed.

"You could come with us. Give us a hand." Meg's voice was hesitant.

"Why would I do that?" Ailsa's fingernails curled into her palms. "I've already told you I'm getting a headache and want an early night."

There was another brief silence. "Can I get you some water? A glass of wine? Something to eat?"

Ailsa tipped her head against the flat plane of the door

and closed her eyes. "A bit less back and forth would be welcome."

Meg was silent so long this time that Ailsa began to wonder if she had left. But eventually Meg said, "Fine. Good. Good night, Mom. I hope you feel better."

Ailsa opened her eyes, and the etched glass globe of the overhead fixture fractured into damp rays of yellow light. "I love you," she whispered. Then she made herself repeat it louder: "Good night, Margaret. I love you."

But Meg had already gone, and Ailsa stood at the door for a long time, hating the silence and the filter in her brain that somehow always made it impossible to say what needed to be said.

Maybe she should have paid more attention in church when she was younger, she decided. Or maybe someone should have mentioned that the conscience lived in the silences of a life, filling them with memories and regrets until one became desperate to drown them out.

Without silence, Ailsa could always pretend that things were fine. Good, even. Then without warning, in the silence when she was alone, her choices all swept in to haunt her, and she became afraid that she would always be alone, that the silence would grow louder and louder and louder every empty day.

Briefly, she considered opening the door and running after Meg, saying she'd go with her. But if she couldn't bear pity from strangers, the thought of having to see it in her own daughter's eyes was more than she could bear.

Pushing herself away from the door, she strode to the

closet and threw it open. She'd over-packed as usual, but that, too, was good. She found what she was looking for: the royal blue dress with a gathered waist and a deep V-neck— the one that showed off all her best features and hid what needed to be hidden. She laid it down on the bed and went into the bathroom to start her shower.

If Meg didn't want her company, there were other people who did. She'd go have a good time with the other volunteers. Dinner and some wine and a bit of music. She'd soon feel better.

She'd feel great, and she'd forget.

ILLUMINATION

*"The light of lights looks always
on the motive, not the deed."*

W.B. YEATS

K IERAN STILL WASN'T AT THE house, or the cottage lab
in the village, or the dig site, or Kilmichael. Having
fanned out to search, Meg, Niall, Adam, and the dig
staff eventually gathered back in Niall's kitchen. Adam curled
himself into his usual chair by the window, and Meg,
concerned about how quiet he'd gotten, sat down beside
him.

Outside, the rain at the front edge of the storm was
already coming down, driven almost sideways by the
shearing wind. It was a warm rain, though, not unpleasant,
and they'd all brought the scent of it in on their clothes as
Gemma, obviously in need of something to do with her
hands, bustled around making tea. James and Liam opted for
whiskey instead, and while Liam took slow sips, James
knocked his back in a single gulp and poured himself another

shot from the bottle Niall had set down on the table.

"All right. Let's approach this with a bit of logic. When was the last time anyone saw him?" Standing beside the door, Niall leaned back against the wall.

Gemma and Liam exchanged a glance, then Liam shrugged and left Gemma to answer. "This morning." She turned with the kettle in her hand and poured hot water into the chipped ceramic pot she'd already prepared with bags of Twinings tea. "Liam and I left about eight o'clock for the dig site. James was just ahead of us on the road."

"Did Kieran say anything in particular?"

"I wasn't in the mood to be friendly, to be honest," Gemma said.

"So you didn't have any meaningful conversation?" Niall asked.

"Well, we didn't talk to him as such," Liam said. "He was still in the shower when we left the house. Maybe I should have shouted out we were leaving."

"Why?" Gemma spun toward him, red curls and temper swirling around her face. "No point feeling guilty just because he's gone off sulking somewhere."

"Talking to him, or trying to anyway, would have been the civil thing."

"Revisionist," Gemma snorted.

Niall turned to James. "What about you?"

"Me?" James had settled himself in the chair by the window and sat hunched over his half-empty glass like a hen brooding over a secret egg. He threw Niall a look through narrowed eyes and quickly looked away again. "Kieran woke me up with all his stomping around, and I saw I'd overslept so I legged it into the bath while he was getting his coffee— I'd have had to wait twenty minutes otherwise, and he'd have used up all the hot water as usual. But he never said a word when he came back upstairs. I was making the bed, and he went in to get his shower. Then I grabbed a protein bar and left."

"So you didn't see how he was dressed?" Niall asked. "None of you? Could you tell what clothes might be missing if we had a peek through his things?"

"He'd skin us alive if we tried," Liam said.

"Not that it would help. He lives like a pig and expects everyone to clean up after him." James frowned down into the amber whiskey, his cheeks flushed and his eyes as clouded as the storm beyond the window. His voice had a ragged edge, and Meg decided that her mother's assessment of James must have been wrong after all. There were iceberg levels to him below the surface, the deep reserves of emotion that made people fascinating and unpredictable. "It'll be what Gemma says anyway," he continued more evenly. "He'll have gone off to sulk somewhere hoping we'll get worried. His way of punishing us for the fact that he embarrassed himself."

"You didn't talk all that through last night?" Meg asked.

"With Kieran? You're joking?" Gemma snorted. "His highness never bothered coming down. Just stomped around upstairs, drunk and ranting."

Meg turned to James. "What about you? You must have said something to each other."

"Not really." James gave her a one-shouldered shrug. "He tried to bite my head off when I went up, so I took a walk until I was tired. And of course he didn't apologize."

"Well, he wouldn't," Gemma said. "Never does."

"Do you even hear yourselves? The lot of you?" Adam jumped up and his chair fell back against the wall. "None of you ever gave him half a chance."

Niall shook his head in warning. "Adam—"

"No, hold on." Meg caught Adam's arm before he could stomp out of the kitchen. "Adam, what did you mean by that?"

Adam's face went red, and he glared down at the gray tiles on the kitchen floor. "No one ever listened to him. He tried to tell you things—he kept trying to tell you—and no one listened."

His voice had gone hollow and quiet, and even before he'd finished speaking Gemma and James had started grumbling again, but over Adam's head, Niall's eyes met Meg's. She saw the understanding hit him, sink in, and leave him shaken. But the kitchen full of people wasn't the place for words, and Niall seemed to know that, too. He peeled himself off the wall, ruffled Adam's hair, and then pulled him into a one-armed embrace, a fierce one, and dropped a kiss into Adam's hair.

Adam stood stiff, breathing hard.

He was so young, Meg thought, and so powerless—and so aware of his own lack of power. "Why don't Adam and I go back up to the cottage and look around in Kieran's room?" she suggested. "Adam knows him as well as anyone, and there might be something there to tell us where he's gone."

"Good." Niall released Adam and stepped back, visibly shaken. "Yeah, good. Maybe Liam and I should take the car and drive the length of the island meanwhile. If Kieran's holed up somewhere, that's one thing, but if he stepped wrong and twisted an ankle, I don't want him out in the storm all night. We can start at the far end and work our way back here."

"Brian keeps the keys to his Jeep in the kitchen," Gemma said. "I could take that and drive the upper route to the signal tower."

"And I can recheck the buildings at Kilmichael," James offered tentatively. "In case we missed anything earlier."

Liam was studying him thoughtfully, but also absently, as if his eyes had fallen on James without really seeing him. Then he seemed to give himself a mental shake. "I had better go with Gem," he said to Niall. "She's more likely to need me than you are."

Gemma rounded on him, bristling. "Why would I need you, you great, fat lump?"

"Because the terrain is rougher at the top, so it's harder to search and drive." He grinned at her, and with his dreadlocks still wet from the rain and his damp shirt plastered against his chest, he looked more than ever like a Viking raider.

Gemma just pressed her lips tight and pushed past him.

As if the decision to do something—anything—was a relief to everyone, they all scattered to pull on their rain gear.

Adam had clambered up the stairs and while Meg waited for him to come down again, Niall paused beside her. "Look, I'm sorry about all this," he said. "I keep dragging you into my messes, and I've no right at all to ask you for help."

Meg waved that aside. "You need to stop apologizing. I want to be here. And you heard what Adam said."

"You think that's what's made him give Kieran a pass all this time?" Niall asked, frowning.

"One of many things, probably. He's been through a lot. But then, I don't know Kieran. I can't begin to judge whether he was conscious of saying all the things Adam was processing himself or if that was just a vicious coincidence."

"I wish I knew that myself," Niall said.

Meg fell silent, and in her mind she could imagine Adam in a hospital waiting room, his gangly forearms splayed across his knees and his head hung low while his own father accused him of not making himself clear about his mother's condition before she'd gotten into the car. As if it had been Adam's responsibility to speak for her. As if it was Adam's silence that had made her die. No wonder he'd tried to speak up for Kieran even when he didn't know what needed to be said.

"I'd love to get Adam's father into a room alone for a few minutes," she said. "How is it that you need a license to own a dog, but any idiot is allowed to become a parent?"

Niall brushed a strand of hair off Meg's cheek and tucked it behind her ear, then he lightly brushed the skin below her itchy stitches and gave her a long, slow smile. "You're fierce when you're riled up, aren't you? Just one more reason I can't seem to make myself stop thinking about you."

Meg's breath hitched, and she wondered how a smile, only a smile, could change her mood completely. "Thinking is all well and good," she said, reaching up to cup his cheek, "but what else have you got?"

He grinned, and his eyes lightened, the worry in them momentarily pushed aside. Stepping closer, he bent his head slowly enough that her heart had time to stop and then take off again at an undignified gallop. When their lips had almost touched, he paused, letting the current arcing between them build. She found herself debating between anticipation and gratification, wanting the deliciousness of wanting him almost as much as the kiss itself. Then his lips were there, soft and hard and certain against her own, and gone again.

"We'll have to continue this later," Niall whispered, barely raising his head so that the warm breath of every syllable spilled across Meg's lips. "Whenever Kieran's turned up again, I'd like to take you for a quiet dinner somewhere, just the two of us, and say a proper thank-you."

"I'll settle for the quiet and the thank-you. Dinner optional," she whispered back, and she spun away as Adam galloped down the stairs carrying a couple of small rechargeable lanterns.

Clearing his throat, Niall turned toward the door. "Well, I'd better get a move on, too, since James is waiting for me to give him a lift. No point in trying to ring me with this storm if you find something, but I'll have my phone anyway—or there's a public box in Kilmichael, in the garden of the first house after the village boundary, in case there's an emergency. With luck, I won't be long. I want to check with the writer and that couple who live down in Tilickafinna. With any luck, Kieran's holed himself up with one of them to wait out the storm."

Adam's expression turned mulish and distant as they said their goodbyes, and he stood frozen a moment after Niall had gone. Meg slipped back into her jacket and pulled the hood close around her face. "Kieran will be all right, Adam," she said. "Even if he is out in the storm, it's just a little wind and rain."

Adam flicked her a look she couldn't read. Then he bent to pull on his boots.

The wind was blasting as they let themselves outside, and the two cars were already heading in opposite directions, Niall down the lower route and Gemma and Liam up toward the island's spine. Their headlights turned the rain to crystal in front of them and reflected off the puddles in the road. Meg drew the hood of her jacket closer and then splashed toward the house where Liam, James, and Kieran had been staying, and it was only after she'd taken a few steps in that direction that she realized Adam was still standing in the road watching Niall's car driving toward Kilmichael.

"You coming?" she called.

Adam didn't answer, and she walked back toward him. But a moment later, she stopped and shielded her eyes with her hand, sending the water streaming in cold rivulets down her sleeve.

About where Adam was looking, a gray figure was

moving through a field, a luminous silver shape that made the rain around it shimmer. Meg blinked and whatever she had seen was gone, but in the howl of the wind there was an echo of sorrow so bottomless it caught in her throat and rooted her feet into the ground. "Did you see something?" she asked Adam. "Just now?"

He didn't answer, but he switched off his portable lantern and took off running—not back to the house but in the direction of the field, the same direction the headlights of the rusting Toyota were still bobbing along the road.

"Adam, wait for me." Meg hesitated, then switched her own lantern off and hurried to catch up. "Where are we going? Why don't you want your light?"

In the darkness and the rain, she couldn't see his face, so the sense that he was looking at her, weighing her, was more instinct than anything else. "I want to see what James is going to do, but you don't have to come."

"Why James?" Meg asked, feeling disoriented.

Adam's coat rustled as he turned his head. "You wouldn't believe me."

"Give me a chance."

Instead of answering, Adam increased his pace, and she hurried uphill in his wake. The wind drove the rain like needles into her face, and in the fields between them and the cliffs as they left the village, the white forms of miserable sheep huddled together, or occasionally the disjointed white markings of cows floated in the darkness, tricking her brain into seeing shapes that weren't there. A lichen-flecked standing stone in the field below them, too, seemed to hover like a ghost, changing position when she took her eye off it briefly.

The distance between the two villages wasn't great, and they'd soon reached the earthen fence that traversed the width of the island to separate Ballynacallagh township from Kilmichael. Ahead of them, the lemon glow of Niall's headlights stopped moving. Adam quickened his steps into a jog.

Then Niall's car eased away up the track again between the sparse houses that sat derelict or with their windows boarded up alongside the road. A flashlight switched on in the village, the beam weak through the rain and distance, and Meg could just make out the figure of James behind it in his orange raincoat. The light remained stationary until the car's lights had vanished, and then it finally moved forward, past the first of the houses and straight down the road, not as if James was looking for Kieran, but quickly, purposefully. As if James wasn't engaged in a search at all but moving instead toward a specific destination.

Meg caught Adam's sleeve and tugged him to a stop. "What's out in that direction?"

"Tilickafinna village and Dursey Head, but those are miles off. There's Corr Áit a few fields over and an old holy well somewhere," Adam said, then he turned toward her. "You're starting to believe me, aren't you? Everyone thinks because James is small and weak and acts like the victim we should all feel sorry for him—but he hates Kieran. Hates him. So why would he volunteer to look for him?"

"It's what anybody would do."

"Not James." Adam shook his head. "You don't know him, and he's walked straight past the buildings he's supposed to be checking, hasn't he? So where's he going?"

James passed a second structure without stopping. Cold from more than the rain, Meg wanted to protest that Adam was only imagining something sinister, worrying for no reason, but she couldn't—wouldn't—say that. Yes, there might still be a dozen rational explanations for James' behavior, but what if Adam wasn't wrong? What if there had been more than they knew between James and Kieran, something else that was pulling James to Kilmichael? If James suspected where Kieran was and hadn't said anything, then . . . Well, Meg hated to even speculate, but it prompted questions she wanted answered.

Her stride lengthened until it was faster than a jog, and Adam kept pace beside her.

She slowed to get her bearings when they reached Kilmichael. The village wasn't large. The first house stood on the right, with a white phone box in the garden and an electrical pole beside a picnic table at the base of the drystone wall. Beyond it, the old post office was boarded up, and apart from the structures that stood alongside the road, there was little more than an empty area with a cluster of buildings around it. n the near darkness, it was often hard to distinguish livestock sheds from houses, bare stone walls falling apart as though they hadn't been used in hundreds of years on some, while others had the general dilapidated look of recently abandoned dwellings. Still more had curtains on dead-dark windows and empty broken flowerpots on the doorsteps.

"Where's the church?" Meg asked.

Adam pointed to the open space. "That green area used to be the burial ground, but either Carew's men or Wilmot's destroyed the church in the massacre. They killed everyone inside, then burned it. They've reused most of the stone since to build more houses. But you see how far it is to the cliff. You wouldn't want to carry burnt corpses all that distance."

He said it matter-of-factly, and Meg couldn't help shuddering at his easy acceptance of such gruesome deaths. It had been one thing when he'd described the massacre— she had dismissed that as the lurid fascination of a teenage boy. Even Niall's story about Puxleys kicking a body down the road had been different in a way Meg couldn't quite explain to herself. Somehow, it didn't conjure the same visceral visual, the same depth of horror. She tried to imagine Kieran discussing the mechanics of carrying burnt corpses with Adam, and the coldness of that discussion left her stomach churning.

Ahead of them, the last building in the village was approached by a short, separate track barely discernible in the grass. James' flashlight cut toward it, reached it, and then went dark. The roar of the ocean and the wind was louder without the light to focus Meg's attention, and the water dripping down her neck felt colder, as though the temperature had dropped. Then citron glow reappeared, bobbing away on the other side of the house and veering off into the quilt of stone-walled fields and the cliffs beyond.

"Told you," Adam said, and he broke into a sprint.

It was that moment, seeing him racing ahead, that brought Meg to her senses. What was she doing? This wasn't a story, it was a dark night that was no place for Adam, and letting him indulge his suspicion of James was probably the very last thing she should be doing. What had she been thinking?

Kicking herself into a flat-out run, she raced after Adam, but he was moving fast and some instinct she was afraid to examine kept her voice low and soft as she called after him, "Adam, don't! Come back here."

He vanished inside the old shed and ducked through the other side, hopping over the attached fence to avoid the barbed wire atop the wall along the road. By the time Meg had jumped over herself and landed ankle deep in the wet, muddy pasture on the other side, James' flashlight was already two fields over and still moving toward the cliffs. Adam followed him, bent almost double as he ran, and after crossing a third drystone wall, James finally stopped and swept the yellow beam systematically over the grass and rocks and low-growing bushes.

Adam kept running. Once he'd slipped over the final wall, there was no cover to hide behind. Sending up a curse for her own stupidity, Meg swung herself over into the field, too, digging deep to find a gear she'd never bothered to use on the treadmill and had almost forgotten existed. "Adam," she called quietly, without much hope of being heard above the wind. "Stop! I mean it!"

EMPTY FIELDS

"No more to her maidens
The light dance is dear,
Since the death of our darling
O'Sullivan Beare."

ANONYMOUS
"LAMENT FOR O'SULLIVAN BEARE"

J AMES STOOD IN THE CENTER of the field, his back to them as the flashlight searched the ground. Adam approached him like a poacher stalking prey downwind, closing the distance to twenty feet, then ten, then eight. James was too focused on his task to notice, or maybe any sound was lost in the fury of the ocean closer to the cliffs along with the wind and rain. He didn't turn, and Meg was torn what to do. Follow Adam and brazen it out, or be more cautious and approach from a different direction just in case . . .

In case of what?

She found it hard to wrap her mind around the possibilities, but she couldn't discount what instinct and

Adam's certainty told her. Instead of following Adam directly, she cut across the field at an angle that would put her a little ahead of James and she pushed herself even faster.

Racing through the tall grass studded with rocks and yellow furze, she had almost reached them when James suddenly swung around and shone the flashlight at Adam's face. "Adam?" His voice was raw over the roar of the wind and the crash of the waves pummeling the cliffs as he shouted. "What are you doing here?"

He seemed more puzzled than alarmed, and he let the light drop a few inches. But there was something about his words, the way he stood, the way he moved, that made Meg freeze in her tracks.

"What do you want, Adam? Are you following me?" Behind the light his features were swallowed within the hood of his orange jacket, leaving darkness where his eyes should have been.

Adam backed a step. "You said you were coming to look for Kieran."

"I am. I saw something moving out here. Some*one* moving."

"On the ground?"

"I thought maybe Kieran might have fallen, but I don't see him. It must have been a trick of the storm." James shrugged and stepped closer again and waved his flashlight back toward the village. "Since you're here, you may as well help me check the buildings. Come on."

Again it was nothing concrete, but a sense of wrongness sent Meg into motion, and James' own sixth sense must have tingled because he swung around. Something glittered in the grass between him and Meg as the flashlight rocked past it, and they all saw it at the same time. Adam and James both dove at it, but Adam reached it a second sooner. Keeping a hard grip on whatever it was, he wrestled it away from James and ran to stand at Meg's shoulder.

It was an instrument, a metal pole with a circular wand at one end with a square display box below the handle. Meg peered down at it. "A metal detector?" she asked. "That's what you're searching for?"

Adam swung back around to James. "I thought you were looking for Kieran."

"I'm just as surprised as you are—but that explains why Kieran is out here." James turned and swept the flashlight around the field, starting from where the metal detector had been. "Come out, Kieran," he shouted. "No more games. You might as well show yourself."

Adam's eyes narrowed. "Why would he be using the metal detector in this storm?"

"Because he knows I found a potential site yesterday." James turned slowly back around, rain glittering in the flashlight's glow. "There, I've admitted it. I found a site, but it has nothing to do with Kieran or his ideas. Only Kieran—I don't know. Maybe he figured out he's getting fired, and he's desperate. Or maybe he wants the credit. Maybe he just wants to make trouble—it's what he's good at doing."

There was fury in James' voice but also a hard edge of panic that made Meg shift in front of Adam and put herself between them. The nape of her neck prickled at the idea of

Kieran hiding among the grass and furze and rocks behind her, volatile and unseen, but every nerve screamed a protest at the thought of turning her back on James.

"When?" Adam didn't take his eyes from James. "If you're saying he came out here, tell me when he took the metal detector. You're the one who checked the lab in the village, and you said there was nothing missing. And where has he been all day? Why didn't anyone else see him?"

"What?" James shook his head. "Why does it matter when he took it? This afternoon—or this morning. Gemma was working on sheep bones at the dig site most of the day, so I couldn't leave the volunteers to go do site surveys. The equipment was locked in the village, but Kieran has a key. He could have taken it anytime. I didn't check every item in there—the place was dark and the shovels and GPR and the tablets were in their usual places. It looked all right, but you're right. I should have checked more carefully."

His words, his actions, everything was possible, plausible. Meg had seen him herself at the dig off and on all day, working with the volunteers, checking any little thing that anyone found, inspecting what remained in the sifting screens, slicing fresh sod away from the soil to expand the excavation grid. And Kieran was the one who was volatile and dangerous—she had seen that, too.

She wanted to believe James, she did, but still there was that prickle on the back of her neck that she'd learned long since was usually her subconscious mind noticing details or anomalies that her conscious self couldn't process quick enough.

And it was James who Adam disliked, not Kieran, and Adam had watched them both for weeks.

She pulled out an old reporter's trick. "Well, we're not going to figure this out here. We should head back. We're getting cold and wet, and it's a waste of time standing in the field when Kieran isn't here. I'm sure we could all use something warm to drink."

"Exactly," James said, nodding with evident relief.

Meg took two steps back toward the village, then she paused. "Out of curiosity, though, James—and I'm sorry, it's just that I don't understand archaeology very well. Wouldn't it have been easier to give Kieran what he wanted all this time and get him to stop pestering you? Why didn't you want to survey out here?"

"This again?" The beam of the flashlight blinded her as James moved his hand impatiently. "It's not that I didn't want to—look, there's a reason metal detectors are illegal in Ireland. We have to be licensed to use them even for an archaeological site because it's the only way we ensure a methodological framework. Documentation. Context. All that takes time and patience. Somewhere like Dursey, that's even harder, right? There could be important sites across most of the island. St. Michael's was thirteenth or fourteenth century and built over a much older church. There's the ruined monastery by Oileán Beag and a place name in the middle of the island suggests a possible third church site. Then there are holy wells, Neolithic standing stones and artwork, probable Bronze Age burials, a hill fort with a series of tunnels. Another separate tunnel may have been part of the Corr Áit complex where Morty Óg O'Sullivan kept the men he was taking over for the Irish Brigades. That same site was likely also used by the Viking slavers, but its origin is prehistoric. There could be finds anywhere—not rich, glamorous ones probably, but that doesn't mean they don't deserve attention."

"And that's not what Kieran wanted?" Meg asked.

"He wanted to prove his theory. That's not what we're supposed to do." The wind stripped the emotion from James' voice, making it even harder to read, and with the beam of the flashlight in front of him, Meg still couldn't see his expression. Rain dripped from her hood, running in cold streams down her face. Mingling with the salted wind, it stung her eyes and the raw skin beneath her stitches.

She switched on the portable lantern Adam had given her and pivoted to scan the soggy field where the brush rustled and swayed and the grass was being pummeled by the downpour. There was no sign of Kieran, no movement, no luminous figure that might have been anything at all— Kieran with a flashlight or a *bean sidhe* or a figment of Meg's imagination. In the pressing darkness she sensed only wind and rain and the distant sheep and a story she would have bet her soul was there, somewhere, lurking in the shadows. The kind of story that made her heart quicken, but it was also more than a story: it was real, with real people, real problems, and fear of what it all meant was already beginning to make her stomach roil.

"Okay, we really should get back," she said, meaning it this time. "I'm sorry, Adam, but even if Kieran is out here, we're not going to find him. Not like this, and for all we know, he might be at the house by now. We can all check the village together on the way, make sure he isn't there, and then let's go get ourselves dried off and sit down and figure out what to do next."

James shone the flashlight around the field one more time, then he lowered it. "We need to find him," he said in an odd, strained tone. "We have to find him."

It was the first thing that he had said that had the ring of absolute truth, and Meg found herself wanting to reassure him as much as she wanted to reassure Adam. "We will," she said. "We absolutely will."

DAMP SKIN

"We're each of us alone, to be sure.
What can you do but
hold your hand out in the dark?"

URSULA K. LE GUIN
THE WIND'S TWELVE QUARTERS

THERE WAS NO EVIDENCE OF Kieran in Kilmichael, so they continued on to Niall's cottage in Ballynacallagh. Adam said nothing to James—he didn't speak at all but followed with a jutting chin and wary eyes when James settled in the kitchen, dropping into the chair across the table from him. He then refused to budge when Meg asked him to come help her with something in the living room, which worried Meg all the more because she couldn't question Adam meaningfully in front of James. Fortunately, within fifteen minutes, Niall arrived.

He was preoccupied as he stepped inside the cottage, kicking off his boots in the entry before removing his dripping coat and not even noticing that the floor was already wet enough to soak his socks. He didn't notice that the kitchen door had opened, either, and Meg stood watching him, relieved and happy to see him, and nervous about that happiness.

But then he looked up and spotted her, and his tired preoccupation lifted, giving way to the smile that made her feel lighter, too. "Well, hullo," he said. "You're a welcome sight."

Her own smile grew wider without permission. Too wide, probably, and too foolish, so she went straight to business. "Did you find anything?"

"I take it that means you didn't?" He closed the distance between them until they were mere inches apart.

Still not sure what to say, she glanced back at the kitchen door. She had to tell him something, though, so she put her finger to her lips, then caught his hand and tugged him toward the stairs. Keeping her footsteps light, she led him up to the landing, then hesitated, standing there in the darkness with the sound of the rain on the roof and the smell of his damp skin and clothes making the air feel close.

"I'll be honest," he said, "this wasn't the way I imagined you coming upstairs."

There was a low note in his voice that made her aware of his fingers curled around hers, and she wondered if she had kept hold of his hand out of selfish weakness. Need. She let go but as she slid her fingers away, he caught them back and drew her into the bedroom out of sight from below. He picked up her other hand and held that, too.

How was it that such small gestures could be both hopeful and disconcerting?

With their fingers twined together, he made her aware of every inch of skin and of the miracle of sensation that was the human hand.

"What happened?" he asked.

She explained about finding James and the metal detector out in the Kilmichael field, leaving out her own odd impressions. Still, she had the feeling when she finished that he had heard her fears. For a long moment he was silent, and then he said, "You didn't believe him?"

"I don't know what I believe. It's clear that Adam is convinced he's lying—but I think Adam is hypersensitive to the idea of people not listening to each other right now. Everything James said was plausible."

"But it could have been he was searching for the metal detector and not for Kieran?" Niall asked, studying her.

"Why, though? And if he was, he didn't know where it had been left, so I don't think he was the one who put it there. The question is, what do we do now?"

"We talk to Adam. Or more importantly, listen to him—something I should have been doing better all along."

"And Kieran?"

Niall rocked back on his heels and released her hand. "If Gemma and Liam haven't found him by the time they come back, I'll go to Kilmichael and ring the police. Who knows if they can get a search team over here in this storm, but I think we need to try."

SWORDS

*"Scars have the strange power
to remind us that our past is real."*

CORMAC MCCARTHY
ALL THE PRETTY HORSES

ADAM TURNED TO JAMES AS soon as Meg had left the kitchen. "What did you do to Kieran? I know you did something. Where is he?"

James sat at the table, both hands curled around his glass. His eyes lifted to Adam's, then dropped again, and he raised the glass and swallowed the rest of the whiskey down. His voice was hoarse when he answered. "If he went out there somewhere with my equipment, it's not my fault. But that's why I went to look for him. I didn't want him caught in this storm."

Adam hated the make-believe sincerity, the bollocksness. James fooled everyone with that, the way he made himself a victim.

Without Meg the kitchen was heavy and cold, empty,

and Adam felt the weight of his own weakness in the silence. He should have made someone listen.

"Kieran told me you've been sneaking out at night," he said to James.

"Did he tell you he snores so loud it's impossible to sleep?" James retorted. "How about that he took the better bed and uses all the hot water in the shower and leaves his clothes around so it's like living in a pigsty? You can't sleep when your mind is cluttered."

Disgusted, Adam shook his head. "Why did you go back to Kilmichael? Why did you say the metal detector was in with the equipment when it wasn't?"

James' glass crashed into the table, liquid splashing out onto the wood. His face pinched into a snarl. "Niall needs to put a leash on you. Don't you think I get enough grief from Kieran? What do you want from me, Adam? Do you know what it's like having someone nagging at you all the time? Wearing away at you? You do know, don't you? You look the type to be picked on at school, so why can't you understand?" His eyes slid over Adam, and one side of his mouth lifted in a sneer. "Or are you one of the hangers-on? The ones so desperate to be accepted you're willing to make life hell for someone else."

Adam's gut twisted uncomfortably, but he looked away. "It was you who never gave Kieran a chance. You got everyone on your side."

"There shouldn't have been sides. This is my work, my career. And it's none of your business."

Adam stood up slowly. "Where is he? You know

something, I can tell."

"I don't—and anyway, I don't care! And that's it. I'm through answering questions. I've tried to make allowances because of your mother, but you're a bloody menace. You're meddling in things you can't begin to understand."

Adam wanted to pummel him—hit him and keep hitting him. He was sick to death of people treating him as if he didn't matter. As if his opinion didn't matter. "Kieran's my friend!"

"Don't be naïve. He isn't." James reached for the whiskey bottle again, and then he straightened and looked back at Adam with his expression gone blank and cold. "The Kierans of the world don't have friends. They have people who are useful to them and others they keep around to make them feel better about themselves. That's all you are to someone like him—an audience. You show him what he wants to see in himself so he doesn't have to face the mirror."

In his damp clothes with the rain bulleting against the wide-paned windows, Adam found that he was shivering. Tears that wouldn't reach his eyes burned in his throat and collected in a great pool deep inside his chest. He wanted to say James was wrong. And he was wrong. He was. Only what he'd said made Adam think of Declan and Rory at school, the way they'd hounded him until he'd started laughing with them so they'd leave him alone.

"You know what your real problem is?" James continued. "You're afraid you're more like me than you are like Kieran, that's your trouble. And you don't want to be.

You think siding with the Kierans makes you stronger. Makes you matter more. You think it's better to be stronger, that you'll save yourself that way. But you won't. That's why we're here now on this godforsaken island, why there was a massacre here. Because not enough people ever stand up to say something isn't right unless they get a return out of it, admiration or money or power. Meanwhile they go along, bend over backwards searching for the common ground with the people who are holding swords against their throats."

The empty glass glinted beneath the overhead light and the bottle of whiskey stood a few inches away on the table. The pressure of the tears Adam was holding back built up inside him until he thought his eyes would explode, everything that had happened in the last six weeks, his whole life, everyone telling him over and over how he didn't understand, how he was wrong.

James was twisting everything. Everything.

It hadn't been like that. It was Kieran who no one had listened to . . . wasn't it? And Adam had tried to stand up, that was exactly what he'd done. He'd tried, and everyone told him not to make trouble, to be good. They were always telling him to be good, and he'd done his best. He'd tried not to mind when things were crap and nothing ever got better, when it only got worse and worse and then Ma was gone and he did mind. He minded everything, and he hated James and all those people who'd lied to him and all the pressure building inside him, building and building and building, the pressure and the emptiness of knowing something was wrong and no one would listen to him because he was just a stupid kid. But they were adults and they couldn't see. They wouldn't see. And he'd tried to tell them. He had, and they hadn't listened.

Only maybe James wasn't wrong, either, not completely. Because after a while, he'd stopped hating Declan and Rory, hadn't he? He'd stopped hating that he had to laugh while they pantsed Aidan Wells or took photos up Kathleen Farrell's skirt or made Tariq Ahmed give them his new trainers. He'd stopped hating them and he'd started hating Aidan and Tariq and all the other stupid kids who didn't fight back.

Snatching the glass off the table, Adam threw it against the wall as hard as he could. He threw that, and he threw the half-empty bottle, and the explosions shattered the pressure inside him and left him breathing hard while the fragments rained down against the table and the chair and the floor and the honey, vanilla, and pencil eraser smell of the whiskey filled the air until he couldn't breathe.

IMAGINATION

"Many that live deserve death.
And some that die deserve life."

J.R.R. TOLKIEN
THE FELLOWSHIP OF THE RING

T HEY FOUND THE BODY IN the morning before the sun
had fully risen. Niall awoke on the sofa downstairs to
an unfamiliar weight pressing on his shoulder and the
sound of someone banging on the door. Blinking the sleep
out of his eyes, he realized the warm weight was Meg curled
against him, and for a moment he resented whatever had
woken him. But she raised her head and looked at him, then
brushed two fingertips along his cheek as if she was as
surprised and delighted as he was to find themselves waking
up together.

Then the banging came again, and reality crashed over
him like a wave. "Kieran," he said, jumping up and running
to the door. "That has to be him."

It wasn't Kieran, though; it was the police. A man and a

woman in fluorescent yellow garda coats, who must have come over in the boat once the storm had broken.

"Niall Sullivan?" the woman asked.

Niall nodded, feeling a queasy sense of déjà vu that left his heart pounding and his mouth dry with more than morning breath. He glanced up the stairs where Adam was—hopefully—finally asleep and pulled the door open wider. "Have they found him?" he asked. "Is he safe?"

"I'm Sergeant Harrington and this is Garda Foran," the woman said.

And Niall, recognizing the quiet tone of voice, gave a heavy nod. "You'd better come in, so."

They wiped their feet on the still sodden mat inside the door but made no move to remove their coats or shoes. Mindful of Adam, Niall led them toward the kitchen, past Meg standing beside the sofa, doing the best she could to smooth down her clothes and hair.

In the kitchen, Niall stopped awkwardly. "Can I get you some tea? Or coffee?"

The kitchen was colder than the sitting room, the glass of the windows still beaded with rain, but the sky was already lightening to lavender and the sea was stained red by the sun approaching the horizon. When the police had said they'd welcome tea, he gestured them toward the chairs at the table and went to the sink to fill the kettle.

Meg hovered by the door. "Are you just getting here?" she asked the guards. "Or have you found something already?"

The two gardai exchanged a look, and it was the sergeant

who answered. "They've had the helicopter out from Shannon," she said gently, "and I'm afraid they've spotted a body in the water. They haven't been able to reach it yet, but they've got boats coming. It shouldn't be much longer."

It. A body.

Niall took a deep breath, thinking of Kieran and what a sod he'd been, but no one deserved to die alone in a storm, at twenty-seven, with their whole lives stretched out in front of them. He imagined how cold and dark it must have been. How lonely.

He'd left his hand on the kettle too long with it on the burner, and the fact that it was hot finally penetrated his brain fog. Jerking back, he realized his palm was red and stinging, and he stared down at it with a strange sense of disconnection. "They're sure it's a body?" he asked. "There's no chance of a rescue?"

"I'm afraid not." Sergeant Harrington had removed her hat but not her coat, and her face reminded Niall of one of his teachers from secondary school, the lines around her mouth and eyes and between her brows a mixture of scowls and smiles, as if her nature couldn't decide whether to be prone to laughter or inclined to shout at people. Of course, that was half of Ireland for you. One or the other or both at once.

Sod Kieran for not living long enough to even find out which he was going to be.

"Is there anything we can do?" Meg asked, looking lost. "What should we do?"

Her face was pale, her gray eyes dark and enormous in

her face with faint bruises beneath them from the lack of sleep. The fact of death had settled over her features, too, crept into her voice with a wave of the deep compassion that had so surprised Niall as he'd grown to know her, compassion that was too well coupled with imagination to let her do anything but feel for Kieran, to picture Kieran's body floating, from that brief answer the garda had given.

The gardai turned to her, Garda Foran with a hint of an eyebrow lift while Sergeant Harrington hid whatever she was thinking behind a professional mask. Meg unfolded her arms as though she wasn't sure what to do with them. "I'm sorry," she said, visibly trying to compose herself. "I should have said—I'm Meg Cameron. One of the volunteers at the dig."

Sergeant Harrington nodded, and her glance took in both Meg and Niall together. "We'll need to get statements from everyone. But to start with, can you tell me when you last saw the deceased?"

"Personally saw him, or when he was last seen?" Niall asked, getting mugs down from the cupboard.

"Both, if it's not the same answer," Garda Foran said. He pulled a blue notebook and a biro from his pocket.

"James Donovan saw him yesterday morning at the house where they're all staying, and Liam Richards and Gemma Brown heard him in the shower as they were leaving. Apart from Kieran, they were the last out of the house. Speaking for myself, I haven't seen him since about ten o'clock in the morning on the day before." He glanced at Meg for confirmation of the time.

"Maybe a few minutes earlier, but not much," she

acknowledged.

"And was that unusual?" Sergeant Harrington asked. "To go so long without seeing him?"

Niall wasn't certain what to say, quite how much to tell her. His eyes met Meg's, and hers were clouded with sorrow and confusion. Well, it was all going to come out anyway, he told himself. There was no avoiding that since the volunteers had seen the incident and its aftermath, so he sighed and said, "Kieran had an argument with some of the staff at the dig site on Oileán Beag—that's the small island with the white tent that you would have passed on your way here from the boat harbor, if you came up that direction. Kieran went off in a huff afterward. I spent most of the day yesterday trying to reach him, and when I couldn't, I assumed he'd gone to the mainland for something at the university."

Sergeant Harrington tipped her head and studied him with the air of someone whose focus is sharpening. "Would he have done that without telling anyone?"

"I thought he might have been embarrassed for the volunteers to have seen what happened," Niall said heavily. "The truth is, I was trying to work out alternate employment for him."

"So you were going to fire him?" Sergeant Harrington asked.

"Not in those words exactly."

"But close enough to amount to the same thing?"

Niall rubbed the back of his neck, feeling tired. "More or less."

The sergeant waited for Garda Foran to finish writing,

then she asked, "And what was the argument about?"

Niall turned off the kettle as it whistled. Then he poured boiling water into the teapot and removed milk from the refrigerator which he set, along with the sugar bowl, on the table before retrieving the tea and mugs. The tea needed to steep longer, but so did his thoughts, and he was afraid . . . afraid of too many things, answers that he needed but might not want. Afraid of believing Adam and afraid of not believing in James. Afraid that he could have done something if only he'd been paying closer attention.

"We'd had a difference of opinion," he admitted, "about the work we are doing here. Part of our aim is to excavate the old fortress on Oileán Beag, but we're also trying to locate other potential areas for excavation on the island that might provide answers about the O'Sullivan massacre in 1602. Kieran strongly believed there could be a mass burial on land that had belonged to the St. Michael's church, and the rest of us prioritized other sites for investigation."

Sergeant Harrington leaned back against the edge of the table. "He 'strongly believed,'" she repeated. "Was that enough to fight over?"

"In my opinion? No," Niall said. "We would have gotten to all the sites sooner or later, but Kieran wouldn't let it go, and after that things got heated."

"How heated?" Garda Foran asked, looking up from the notebook.

Niall didn't want to hold anything back, but Kieran was dead. The cold fact of that word—its reality—caught Niall in the gut all over again, and he had to pause and draw breath deeply several times. It was instinctive to want to protect the dead, and these days you never knew what was going to be leaked to the press. He glanced at Meg on that thought, processing for the first time, really, that she was a reporter and this was a story—an enormous story. The thought should have filled him with fear, but it didn't. He trusted Meg to be fair, he realized. And while, growing up as he had, his own feelings about the gardai were mixed, Malcolm O'Rourke had taught him that the police were like anyone else—some were mostly good, and some were mostly bad, and all of them were as prone to be fallible as any other member of the human race.

"Kieran left in a huff, as I've already told you," he said, "and in the process, he physically pushed the staff out of the way."

"Which staff?" Sergeant Harrington asked, her attention sharpening again.

"All three of them at one point or another—but it wasn't serious, and no one was hurt. Again, it was really more about Kieran being embarrassed than anything else, but it's a bit of a sensitive issue. You already know who he is, don't you?"

Sergeant Harrington tipped her head up to meet his eyes, and beneath the light the gray strands in the dark hair she had pulled into a bun at the nape of her neck stood out. "That his father is Callum Stafford, who's about to take office as the next prime minister of Ireland? Yes, my chief superintendent did mention that," she said in a dry tone. "Now, is Kieran the sort who'd consider taking his own life?

ABSOLUTION

*"... you have to study and learn so that you can
make up your own mind about history and everything else
but you can't make up an empty mind."*

FRANK MCCOURT
ANGELA'S ASHES

MEG FOUND IT UNCOMFORTABLE BEING inside an unfolding story instead of helping it unfold. Standing in the kitchen watching Niall, she could imagine the guilt and the responsibility he felt, and she couldn't help wondering if Kieran's body had already been over the cliff and in the ocean while she and Adam had been talking to James in the field. And how? Why? Had he jumped? Fallen in the darkness? Run over it by mistake, trying to get away? Or had it been something more sinister?

She had a hard time picturing James as a murderer, so surely it had to have been something else? On the other hand, she'd interviewed two murderers in the course of her career, and both times she had been struck by how human and ordinary they had seemed. One had been a twenty-five-year-old mother about to lose custody of her young boys who had killed them so that her husband wouldn't win. The other had been a dentist who'd murdered his mistress because he was afraid his wife would cost him too much in alimony when she found out he'd been unfaithful. Sane, ordinary people who had killed for reasons that didn't seem remotely sane. Maybe anyone could be pushed into killing.

"What do you really think?" she asked Niall quietly as he and the police were preparing to go back out to speak with Liam, Gemma, and James. "Could James have had something to do with Kieran's death?"

"I just don't see it from a physical standpoint if nothing else. But I suppose anything is possible." He glanced at the officers then bent his head swiftly and kissed her. "I'm sorry about all this. With any luck, I'll be back before Adam wakes up. If I'm not . . ."

"I'll play it by ear. Do you mind if I tell him about Kieran if he asks, or should I wait for you to do it? He'll suspect with the police all over the place, and I don't want to lie to him."

"No, don't lie. That's the last thing he needs. He shouldn't have to face any of this. But thank you for being here for him."

He tugged his jacket back on and followed the policemen out to lead them to the other rental cottage, and Meg stood in the doorway with her arms wrapped around herself for warmth and her hair billowing in the wind. Yellow-coated police in blue hats were searching the road to Kilmichael, and she imagined there were more along the cliffs and in the nearby fields. How would they hope to find anything after the rain, as heavy as it had been?

She took the time while Adam slept to do her best with a washcloth and soap in the bathroom, to brush her teeth and put on clean clothes. Tea didn't begin to fulfill the caffeine requirement, so she found coffee and a French press in the cupboard and forgave herself for exceeding her one-cup quota. What she actually craved, though she'd never been a smoker in her life, was one of Adam's cigarettes. She couldn't fathom why.

At seven o'clock, she tried to phone her mother to explain, and ended up having to go out on the patio and stand on top of the drystone wall between the house and the adjacent field before she got a signal. Even then it fluctuated from one bar to two and the call dropped three times. Her mother's voice went from just-out-of-a-deep-sleep to full-throttle irritation during the explanation.

When Meg had finished, Ailsa was silent a long, uncomfortable moment. "It was the boy, wasn't it?" she asked. "I told you he was dangerous."

"Don't be ridiculous. I was with him the whole time," Meg said.

"How do you know when it happened?" Ailsa sniffed. "You don't have any idea."

"Exactly. The rescue crew hadn't even taken the body out of the water yet when the police were here, so we have no information. What's the point of making accusations?"

"Well, he didn't end up dead in the water by himself, did he—" A muffled rumble in the background made Ailsa break off the conversation and shush someone, at least, that was how it sounded.

Since her mother had grumbled at her for waking her up, it didn't take much of a leap to figure out the situation. "There's a man there with you?" she couldn't help asking. "Someone spent the night?"

"None of your business," Ailsa said, and the line dropped again, leaving Meg standing on the wall with the brilliant Irish light spilling over silver-blue water and the green, green quilt of stone-stitched patchwork fields patterned by yellow furze and purple heather. A gray-winged herring gull had landed on the edge of the picnic table and hunkered down, watching her with its head dropped low and its eyes curious, as though she might at any minute pull a fish out of her pocket. It was an intent stare, an insistent one, and Meg turned her back on the bird when the phone rang, bracing herself as she answered.

"When are you coming over here?" her mother demanded without preamble. "There are boats and police everywhere—both on Dursey and down at the parking lot by the cable car station. I can see them from the window."

"I don't know when they'll be done with us."

Her mother paused. "You don't mean to tell me you want to stay there?"

Meg turned in the direction of the mainland, but a low hill blocked her view and she could see only the yellow and blue dots of police moving against the white backdrop of the laboratory tent at the excavation site. "I think I need to stay. I want to find out what happened, and Niall—"

"If you're going to say Niall needs you, don't. I need you."

"You'll be fine—take some time to relax," Meg said, wishing that every conversation with her mother didn't feel like she was trying to walk a tightrope. "Or take the car and go into Allihies village. It's supposed to be charming. They won't be allowing anyone to come over here the rest of the day, so there's no point hanging around. I know it doesn't make sense to you that I want to help Niall and Adam, but I do. And then, too, it's a story, isn't it? Stories are what I do."

"Not in Ireland."

"But I'm here, so I can't ignore the fact that something's happened—and clearly you have a friend to keep you company."

Ailsa gave an irritated chuff of breath. "That was a mistake. You upset me dredging up the past the way you did, making all those accusations when all this time I was only trying to do the best for you and your sisters and your father. That's all I've ever done."

Whether it was the clear quality of the Irish light or the reminder in the night that life was just too damn short to waste, Meg had suddenly had enough. She let out a deep slow breath. "Mom, I love you," she said. "I will always, always love you, but I will not accept responsibility for your mistakes. Anna and Katharine and I never asked for you to make yourself miserable. We didn't need you to spend all your time taking us around to pageants and lessons. Anna and I didn't, anyway; we would have been fine. All we wanted was for you and Daddy to stop arguing, for you to be happy, for us to be a family. That's all any child ever wants. But you did do all those things, and you gave us good foundations and independence, and I'm going to use that to make my own choices. I can't ignore the fact that Niall and Adam need some help right now—that's not the kind of person I want to be. They need me more than you do, and I'll come back over and see you when I can."

It was the hardest thing she'd ever said to her mother, to anyone really, and when she finished, there was silence on the line. Silence and no explosion. "I may not be here when you show up," her mother said a few beats later. "I think I'm tired of Ireland anyway. I'll find a cab that can take me to Cork and go home to Cincinnati."

Meg's heart twisted in her chest. "Don't do that, Mom. Please, don't."

But the line had dropped again, or maybe her mother had hung up. Meg checked the bars on the phone and there weren't any, and by the time the planets or gods of the cellular towers had shifted themselves back into alignment, Ailsa's phone went straight to voicemail. Meg left a message asking her not to leave, but she didn't expect that to make much difference. Her mother would do just as she liked. She always had. And apparently she'd spent a lifetime running from her problems instead of facing them.

Meg turned to jump down off the wall, and she found Adam in the open kitchen door. A half laugh at the way he'd startled her vanished beneath the reminder of everything that had happened.

"Where's Uncle Niall?" he asked.

"He's gone with the police," Meg said. "Up to the house to talk to the others, I think."

Adam studied her, his head tilted and his eyes as insistent as the herring gull who was still roosting on the picnic table watching her, too. "They found Kieran," he said bleakly. "Didn't they?"

Meg swallowed a lump in her throat and nodded. "Yes, I'm sorry. I know he was important to you."

"When did he die? Was it while we were in that field? Did James do it? He did, didn't he?" Adam's voice rose with every question, both in volume and in pitch.

Meg jumped off the wall and hurried toward him and folded him into her arms, cautiously in case he wanted to pull away. But he didn't. He went stiff and then his narrow shoulders began to shudder, and in that moment he was only a child caught in bottomless grief. She could feel every bone and every fear and every scrap of vulnerable longing in him, and then he drew back, and he was a teenager again, aloof and alone and angry.

"Tell me what happened," he said. "Tell me the truth."

Meg wished she knew how to help him, wished there was a pill or a potion that would take away adolescence—or just pain. So much pain. "We don't know anything yet. Except that there is nothing you could have done. It wasn't your responsibility to fix things or prevent what happened. That's both the hard part and the advantage of being fourteen. It's frustrating to feel like you don't always have a seat at the grown-up table, as if people don't see you or hear you. But you're not responsible for the mistakes the adults in your life are making, Adam. You couldn't have known what was really going on in Kieran's head, or James', much less what was happening between the two of them. It was a horrible night last night, and if Kieran was out poking around in that storm, he wanted whatever he was looking for so badly that he wasn't being rational—or safe. That was his responsibility, not yours. And if James was involved, again, that wasn't something you could have foreseen. No one else expected it, either."

BURIAL

*"It was the first time that I came
face to face with madness
and feared it and was fascinated by it."*

EDNA O'BRIEN
COUNTRY GIRL

T HE POLICE COMBED THE FIELDS and cliffs behind Kilmichael, marching across in a double row, searching for any hint of what had happened. They found only a scrap of wool caught on the stone wall, but it matched the sweater in which Kieran's body had been discovered. There was nothing else, not there and not anywhere along the cliffs from the cable car to the ruined beacon on the western tip of Dursey. Not in the rental cottage that they'd sealed up with crime scene tape, not in the other house that they'd allowed Niall and the others to clear so that Gemma and James and Liam would have a place to sleep. The detectives who'd arrived a short time after the rest of the police—Detective Inspector Miller and Sergeant Singh—kept them all answering questions or out of the way indoors until mid-afternoon, so Niall had missed seeing the recovery of Kieran's body. The start of Kieran's journey home. It seemed to Niall as though he should have stood witness to that. Said goodbye.

Someone should have.

It was mid-afternoon with the sun flying at kite level above the horizon before they were allowed back out in the field. Not the field where Meg and Adam had found James the night before, but the next one over, closer to the cliffs.

James had only gotten cagier and more . . . Niall shook his head, finding it impossible to define James' mood as he watched him lead the sergeant through the grass, Adam, Meg, Liam, Gemma, and Sergeant Singh following in his footsteps single file. Even James' movements were sharp and unnatural, tight with tension, his eyes fever bright and his right hand rubbing the knuckle of this left thumb like a worry bead while he walked.

The gardai, Niall suspected, missed none of that. Especially DI Miller, who had the air of missing nothing at all. Niall hadn't liked the man from the moment he'd ducked his head to walk into the cottage, his dark gray suit rumpled and his tie crooked. He tried too hard to be good-natured and regular-blokeish, in contrast to Sergeant Singh, who was buttoned up and by the book. But there was a still and watchful quality about Miller that reminded Niall of a chameleon whose protective cover lured in its unsuspecting prey only to dart out its long tongue and swallow it whole. A gray-suited chameleon in a black overcoat and muddy Wellington boots, and where Meg observed people, it was with that bottomless compassion and desire to understand—with humanity. Miller's approach made Niall wonder if letting them come out to see whatever it was that James had found wasn't an elaborate trap designed to get a speedy result, their reactions on display to be dissected and assessed and reassembled after the fact like pieces in a puzzle.

James stopped at the head of a pile of rocks and vegetation off to the side of the field, not far from the wall that bordered it on the right, and he turned to Niall. In the sunlight, his face looked nearly as young as Adam's, eager and vulnerable with blond stubble sparse along his jaw and upper lip and the lack of sleep painted in a wash of blue beneath fever-bright, reddened eyes. "Do you see it?"

His wave included the mound of rubble in front of them and similar piles that stretched down the field toward the road for fifty odd feet or so.

The mounds didn't look like much that would have drawn attention—remnants of a hill fort or barrows or burials or even sections of a wall. Beneath the grass and clumps of prickly dwarf furze, they were almost invisible, and Niall was reminded of the old stories in which furze with its fierce thorns was said to protect the mounds and dwellings of the *sidhe*.

Maybe it had protected these—because James was right. Taken individually, each mound might have been nothing more than a pile of rocks generations of farmers had cleared out of the field through the centuries. But taken together, the mounds added up to a shape that narrowed to about two feet where Niall stood, then widened until the span in the middle was seven or eight feet across, then narrowed again until it reached the opposite end some fifty feet away in the direction of the road. Even with gaps in between where stones had probably been removed to be reused elsewhere, the symmetry was clear and too deliberate to be insignificant.

The shape itself niggled at the back corner of Niall's mind, familiar, but at the same time like nothing he had ever seen. Then his hands tingled as an idea clicked, and a flood of adrenaline shot through him, followed instantly by guilt. It seemed so wrong to be excited about archaeology when Kieran was dead. But Kieran had possibly—inconceivably—died for this.

"A Viking longship? Is that what you're thinking?" He glanced up at James, then crouched down to look over the mounds from a lower eye level.

Behind him, Gemma and Liam huddled closer, and he glanced over his shoulder at them to see his own shock reflected on their faces. Even Adam had stopped slouching, and Meg . . . Meg had her eyes locked on James.

"It could be, couldn't it?" James was breathless, and he crouched down beside Niall, absently plucking a blade of grass and running it between trembling fingers. "There's ash mixed in with the soil underneath—I took a sample. The metal detector found a cluster of objects at one end, so if they burnt the body and then added offerings, it would have been a very elaborate burial."

DI Miller's tread was heavy but quiet as he stepped closer. "What do you mean 'the body'?"

He'd hung back, so still that Niall had almost forgotten

he was there, and Niall suspected that quietness was deliberate. Again, he had the sense of being toyed with.

He straightened to his feet and pushed his hands into his pockets, not sure how to protect James—or even whether James needed or deserved protection. He was upset by the news of Kieran's death, clearly—he'd run to the bathroom and thrown up when Niall had first arrived with the police to tell the staff, and he'd stood over the bowl and heaved for a good five minutes. But afterward, it was as though that purge had given way to relief and he'd become almost manic, insisting he had to show them the site he'd found, that he couldn't just describe it.

"There were Vikings here—we know that. They used an enclosure a few fields over from here to hold Irish captives before taking them away to sell in the Middle East, and there were large Viking settlements in Cork, Waterford, and Dublin. But we haven't found a ship burial—not like this— in Ireland yet. There's only one in the UK at all, so if that's what this is, it would have been someone very important."

"The find would be significant then," DI Miller prompted. "With treasure?"

Niall transferred his attention back to James, still crouching beside the mound. "Not necessarily in gold or valuables. But it could still be one of the most significant finds of the century, depending on circumstances."

Gemma cleared her throat and moved up to stand at Niall's elbow. "What we know about Viking ship burials was just turned on its head last year. DNA evidence proved that what's been considered the 'ideal' example of a Viking warrior's burial since the 1880s wasn't a man at all but a woman. A female warrior. Every archaeologist who examined the site assumed the bones were male, despite the telltale markers in the pelvis and other indicators, because it never occurred to them it could be anything else. They ignored all the evidence about the existence of female warriors, including a tenth-century chronicle that records *Inghen Ruaidh*—Red Girl—leading a fleet to Ireland."

"That's why this could be doubly important," Niall added. "Not because—if it proves to be a burial at all—it would necessarily be the grave of a warrior 'princess,' but because we would have the opportunity to look at it with entirely objective eyes, making no assumptions."

"You do see." James was smiling, but instead of becoming more excited by the recognition of what the find could mean, he seemed to Niall to be deflating, as if just getting to this field and showing them had taken every last bit of strength he had.

Niall nodded at him. "Of course."

James tipped his face up toward the sun hanging in the west. Even the inevitable wind had died, dwindled to a breeze after having scoured the sky free of clouds. The air smelled of wet earth and salt and the coconut scent of furze, and behind them gulls and gannets and storm petrels called out as they soared above the cliffs.

"Everyone missed it," Liam said, shaking his head slowly, and looking down the length of the mounds. "We all walked past it, and so did the previous archaeological surveys on the island. Anywhere else, the stones might have all been moved or reused, but this was one of the old church fields."

Niall didn't take his eyes from James. "Whatever it turns out to be, fair play to you, James. It's a grand catch."

He felt itchy beneath his skin watching James, though he couldn't have said why. Something about the way James had grown detached and oddly deflated . . . Niall glanced at Meg and saw that she had come alert, too. And Adam—

Adam's eyes were narrowed to slits and wary.

He flushed as he caught Niall looking at him. His brows snapped together, and his hands balled into fists. "How do you know it was James? Because he says so? It could have been Kieran."

"It wasn't bloody Kieran!" James swung to his feet and spun around. "I'm the one who found it, and he would have . . ."

"Would have what?" DI Miller prompted him to finish. "Tried to take the credit for your discovery?"

James rubbed his temple. "That's not what I said."

"But he did, didn't he?" DI Miller insisted. "So you had to stop him? You didn't have a choice."

"No." James shook his head and backed a step.

"How did Kieran end up in the field? It wasn't last night, was it? It was the night before, and you ran the shower to make Liam and Gemma think he was still alive."

James whipped back toward him, his eyes wide and his breath coming hard and fast. "What? N-no."

"But Kieran knew you'd found something?" Sergeant Singh asked, peeling away from the rest of the group behind James and moving closer.

James backed another step toward the wall. "I didn't tell him."

"He thought it was the burial he'd been searching for, didn't he?" DI Miller insisted, moving forward a step himself. "Is that what happened, James? He saw you were excited after Niall sent you down here to check the cemetery. Anyone would have been, but he came down here with the metal detector himself and tried to cut you out of the discovery. Only he didn't know where to look, so what did you do? Follow him? Find him in the other field, getting closer?"

James shook his head and continued shaking it as if he couldn't stop, and Sergeant Singh moved up another step. Caught between him and DI Miller, James looked panicked and defeated and empty, and Niall was trying to decide whether he owed it to James to intervene or to Kieran to let the police do their work when Sergeant Singh took another step.

James bolted into the crowd behind him, heading for the narrow opening between Meg and Adam. DI Miller caught at the back of his shirt, and Sergeant Singh was closing the distance from the side.

James wrenched free of Miller's grasp. His hand flashed into his pocket and emerged holding the knife he used for cutting sod. Niall ran toward him, but James grabbed Adam and spun him around, the sun flashing on the six-inch blade as he held the knife to Adam's throat.

"Stop," he said, and everybody froze.

Niall's heart froze mid-beat. His muscles felt like they

weren't his own, but his brain made the automatic calculation of distance and speed that equaled recklessness and impossibility, and he stayed where he was, changing gears from action to trying to decide what he could say.

Beside Niall, DI Miller was already talking, his hands held up in front of him in a gesture of surrender, his face a smooth, sallow mask. "All right, look here, lad. There's no reason for anyone to get hurt here, so why don't we all calm down? You tell us your side of the story. That's all you need to do. Tell us what you want."

James' eyes shifted back and forth from DI Miller to Sergeant Singh, who gestured for Liam and Gemma and Meg to move away. Niall felt as though he was staring through the wrong side of a picture and the image was fractured and out of focus. As if he was missing the key that would put it all back together. This wasn't James, his brain tried to tell him, but it was James, and it was Adam, and he couldn't let Adam get hurt. He'd already let Adam down enough. Why hadn't he found a way to listen better? To make Adam see that he could listen?

How did this end in anything but disaster?

"James," he said. "DI Miller's going to step away, and it'll be just us, right? You and me."

DI Miller grunted an objection but Niall threw him a quick, silent plea and stepped forward.

"You tell me what you need, James," Niall continued. "I can imagine you're feeling pressured and pushed into saying things that aren't true. We can stop talking altogether and get you a solicitor, if you like. If you think that would help you.

Only you need to let Adam go. Now. He's a kid, James. Adam—this is Adam. You know what he's been through."

"I'm not going to hurt him," James said, glancing at the knife that had already nicked Adam's skin and left a trickle of blood snaking along his neck.

Niall's stomach gave a painful squeeze, not at the blood but at the light in James' eyes, the rapid breathing, and the way his thin chest heaved, rustling the fabric of his shirt. His glasses had slipped down his nose again, but he didn't try to push them back. Instead he tightened his grip around Adam's chest, and Adam's entire body became a wordless scream of shock and fear and anger, his nostrils flaring as he fought for breath. The sight of him like that had Niall's own breath rasping through a throat that had gone too tight.

It was Meg who spoke up from where Sergeant Singh had moved her. "But James, you are hurting him, don't you realize that? You're making him feel just like Kieran made you feel, and that isn't what you want to do, is it?"

"I never meant any of this to happen," James said, his voice cracking.

Meg nodded as if she understood. "I know. Kieran made you angry, didn't he?"

"He picked away at everything like a buzzard. Knew exactly what to say to . . . ."

"To what, James?" Meg asked.

James blinked, as though he didn't understand the question. "Just leave me alone!" he cried. "Why can't you leave me alone? Don't you understand? I can't go to prison. I won't."

Niall felt even colder hearing the words, and he glanced at DI Miller, but the detective was watching Meg with narrowed eyes, assessing what she was doing, watching James react to her. Biding his time.

Meg held her hands up, away from her body. "I understand. No one said anything about prison. The police haven't arrested you. We just need to do what Niall said and get you a lawyer."

James backed Adam farther down the field, the trickle of blood at Adam's throat running faster, pooling in the hollow beneath his collarbone. Niall felt helpless, and standing there, doing nothing when he wanted to do something, anything, was one of the hardest things he'd ever had to do.

James had moved past the sergeant, past everyone, with only the one stone wall between him and a clear stretch to the cliff's edge, and Niall put his own hands up and walked forward, brushing aside DI Miller's restraining hand as the detective reached out to stop him.

"We've lost one life already, James," he said. "Nothing we do is going to bring Kieran back, but we don't have to lose anyone else. Think, mate. As long as there's life, there's always a solution somewhere. There's possibility. Whatever's happened, you can be forgiven for it."

James shook his head. "What if I can't?"

That was the problem with despair, Niall thought, it was a tunnel so deep and long and cold that once inside it, there didn't seem to be any way through to the other side. But there was always light. Somewhere, James needed to find a glimmer of light to cling to.

Meg moved forward. "Tell me what you felt when you first found the ship, James. That moment when you realized what the mounds might be. What did you think?"

He had reached the wall, and Niall saw the instant when James discovered he didn't know how to get to the other side without letting Adam go. James' white-rimmed stare moved from DI Miller to Sergeant Singh and then to Niall, calculating—clearly—how fast he could climb over, how far he might get if he ran.

"Release Adam," Niall said, his throat strangling the words, his mind refusing to think beyond just having Adam safe. "Please, James. He's just a kid."

Meg nodded. "Put the knife down, James. You don't need Adam. But if you're considering making a run for that cliff, I think that would be a tragedy. A mistake."

"I can't go to jail."

"Then at least tell us what you want us to say to your family. The world. What do you want everyone to remember?"

From the corner of his eye, Niall saw DI Miller move his hand, brush his coat aside. He reached for the gun holstered at his waist, and Niall didn't think, just stepped in front of him. Blocked him.

"Let Meg talk," he snapped. "Trust her."

Unable to see Miller, or the gun, he didn't know what the detective was doing behind him, but Meg kept talking.

"Come on, James. Aren't you curious about what you found? About what's underneath those rocks?" She gestured to the mounds behind her. "I heard the way you talked last night, and I can't imagine you making a discovery like this and not being around to find out how much it changes what people know about the past. Never finding out. You probably think you're not strong enough to go to jail and face whatever mistake you made, but you are. Your curiosity is stronger than your fear. We're all afraid. If we're human, we all are—of the future, the things we've done, what we should have done but didn't. But too few people are genuinely curious the way you are. We see only what affects our own small corners of the world, and when we're looking that narrowly, the bigger picture loses focus. Human beings may be smart, but we're not that smart. For most of us, however hard we try, anything we accomplish is at best a ripple in the strands of the universe. You're different. You want to do more. To unveil the truth. It's what you've dedicated your whole life to doing. Isn't it?"

James had turned to look at her, his eyes still fevered but quieter, more like himself and less like a cornered creature. Silently, he nodded.

Meg smiled at him, that wide, bright smile. "Then you know the value of truth. Not just long-buried truth, but the truth about what happened yesterday. You can imagine what it would be like for Kieran's father never to know what happened, and for your own parents, for Niall, your friends, not to get the chance to understand. And I know—I know—you don't want to hurt Adam for your own mistakes. You don't, do you?"

James shook his head, so faintly that the movement was

barely visible, but Niall felt for the first time in minutes as if he could fully fill his lungs with air.

Meg took a step forward. "I'm going to come to you, James. You see? Just me. I'm walking over, and you and I are going to put that knife away together, because it's what you want to do. It is, isn't it? You don't want to hurt Adam or yourself, and you want people to know the truth. You want to have the chance to be around to find out whether you were right, which means you have to be strong enough to face what's happened. And you are. You can be."

She'd continued moving forward, a step at a time, her hands held up and visible, her smile warm, and Niall's heart thundered as James watched her coming. Niall didn't know what to do, go forward and stop her or let her go because it seemed to be working. But James didn't know, either, and then Meg was standing there beside him, with her hand on James' hand, and they were both gripping the knife, together. The knife came away from Adam's skin and James' other arm came down.

Adam, released, bolted toward Niall, who grabbed him and held him while he trembled, and Meg put her arms around James and held him. James and Adam both stood stiff in their arms as if neither of them knew what to do with the human contact. People could so easily be broken.

"You're all right, now," Meg said quietly. "You're all right."

Niall took a shaking breath.

James' eyes filled with tears that brimmed over and slipped down his cheeks. "I didn't mean to k-kill him," he said. "I didn't. I saw him out here with the metal detector and I knew he would spoil everything. Take it away from me. It's what he did—how he was. I came back to the house, and he asked where I'd been. Gemma and Liam told him I'd been out here, thinking it would make him stop nagging if he knew you'd sent me. I hadn't told them I'd found anything yet, because I wasn't sure and I wanted to have a look with the GPR before I said anything. But he knew somehow, he could see how I felt, and I woke in the night and the room was too quiet. He wasn't snoring, and I turned on the light and he was gone. Someone was moving down the road with a flashlight, so I followed him and he was in the field by the time I got there. He laughed and said everyone thought I was the smart one, but he'd been the one to figure it out. Only he hadn't. He was in the wrong bloody field—but it wouldn't have mattered in the end. He would still have made it all about him. You do see that?"

"Of course I do. And it must have been hard to hear that, to think of that coming true and not feeling like you could do anything about it."

Niall couldn't see Meg's expression, but over her shoulder, James' eyes were so bleak that Niall wanted to cry himself. He told himself that Adam was all right, though. Adam was all right, and that was enough. In a lot of ways, it was a miracle.

"I only pushed him—that's all I did," James said. "I r-ran at him to shut him up, and he tripped and fell backward, and he didn't get up. I tried to think what to do, and I couldn't think. He was dead, and I knew no one would listen if I explained. His father wouldn't let them listen, so I carried him to the cliff on my back and dropped him over. It took me ages, and I had to run to get back before Gem and Liam woke up, and I made coffee and changed my clothes and turned the shower on and left. Only I forgot about the metal detector, and Gem was busy with the bloody sheep all day and I barely had time to leg it to the house to turn the shower off. I couldn't get away to search the field."

Niall pressed Adam's head into his chest and kissed the top of it, and he thought about stupid choices and senseless mistakes. He thought about what Meg had said to James, and what she'd done for all of them, and when Sergeant Singh had gently taken James from her, Niall left one arm around Adam and went and put the other around her.

"Thank you," he mouthed. "Are you good?"

"Not remotely," she said, and Niall realized two things at once—first, that neither Meg nor Adam had moved away, and second, that he had no intention of letting them go, either one of them.

WISDOM

*"People do not change,
they are merely revealed."*

ANNE ENRIGHT
THE GATHERING

I T WAS EVENING AT THE Bay Point, and Meg's mother
insisted she was making good on her threat to leave first
thing in the morning. Lying on the wooden lounge chair
at the edge of the cliff, a blanket across her knees and a glass
of cabernet in her hand, she turned to Meg and said, "Come
with me."

In the lounge chair beside her, Meg took a sip of her
own wine and drank in the endless view of the green island
and the sky and sea, breathing in peace after the triple horror
of Kieran's death and Adam's ordeal and James' confession.
She had never been impulsive. She'd planned everything—
the one-year plan, the two-year plan, the five-year plan,
writing the story of her own life as carefully as she wrote
anything else. But there was something about Ireland that

had shifted her thinking, made her feel as though she had been only half-alive with all that planning and living in the moment when there was so much mental landscape to be had in the past and in the future. Days seemed like a lifetime here, and four hundred years passed in the blink of an eye, not one instant of it, not one horror or resentment or moment of joy forgotten. That Irish circular concept of time was seductive, the slow pace of making a doughnut or getting together to sing. Even the police, efficient as they were still crawling over Dursey Island, seemed to move more politely and unhurriedly through their duties, happy to drink a cup of tea while they took down answers to their questions.

Not that there were answers yet.

Meg couldn't leave without them. James' story was still unfinished, his fate yet to be decided, and there was the Viking burial and whatever lay beneath the earth. But she knew also that she and Niall had a story. Their own story. She was certain of that, though she couldn't guess what kind of story it would turn out to be or how long it would run. For once, she was in no hurry to find out. It could play out as slowly as it needed.

At home, there was only her apartment to take care of— and Ruben. What to do about him remained another question mark, but in some measure the situation between Kieran and James had decided that for her, too. Some stories were black and white, but most were painted in shades of gray, in questions answered and questions left unasked, in questions phrased to elicit the answers that you wanted. All Meg wanted was the truth. She needed to find out the kind of man Ruben was, and whether what he had done with her was a one-off, or whether he'd had work relationships with other women in the past and bullied them into staying quiet—or pushed them out of their jobs when they wouldn't. She'd spent weeks questioning how much of what had happened between them had been her fault, how much she had contributed to the problem. Probably every woman questioned that.

However much she had made mistakes and willing choices, though, Ruben was the one who had cheated, lied, and been willing to destroy her career. If she was the only one to whom he'd done that, she could take responsibility for herself. Save her own dignity. But her mother had been right. Men who hit women didn't stop at hitting once. And men who cheated and lied and used their power over others didn't do that in isolation. If there were other women, Meg needed to know that. If there were others, she needed to speak up and stop Ruben before he did it to anyone else.

She didn't need to be in New York full-time to get that investigation started, though.

"Meg?" Ailsa rolled to her hip in the lounge chair. "Did you hear me? Are you listening?"

"Hmm? Sorry. I was thinking."

"I said I refuse to sit here and wait for God knows how long until the police finish. Why don't you come back to Cincinnati with me until your vacation is over? I've been considering buying a different house. Or a condo. Making a complete change. Maybe I'll get a horse."

"You can't buy yourself a different life," Meg said.

Ailsa's lips went hard. "There you go again. Ireland's made you mean."

Meg laughed at that, a warm bubble of laughter that felt utterly alien on a day that had been filled with so much grief. "Ireland's made me consider what's important. Things I knew all along but had let myself forget. And what about Brian Sheehan?" she asked more seriously. "I assume that's who was in your bed this morning. He seems very nice. Why don't you stay and get to know him better?"

She had the pleasure of watching her mother blush at that, and for a brief moment, she wondered if Ailsa wasn't simply looking for encouragement—a chance to talk— someone to tell her it was all right to let herself open up for once. That she deserved to have a little fun.

"Stay, Mom," she said. "Stay here. Have a real adventure."

"You don't know what you're talking about," Ailsa said.

Meg raised an eyebrow. "Are you saying it wasn't Brian in your bed this morning?"

"We have nothing in common. He's a farmer."

"You seemed to have plenty to talk about the other night."

"That's what you don't understand. You can talk to anyone for a few minutes when you're physically attracted to them. The very fact that they're nothing like you only adds an element of intrigue, keeps you from seeing deeper. But eventually, it's like riding two elevator cars side by side. Imagine riding beside someone who has to stop when you want to continue climbing. You're stuck there between floors, looking up at where you could be, but you can't pull that other car with you. It's too heavy."

Meg's heart cracked with a pain that felt almost like another death. She couldn't look at her mother. "That's where we're different, I guess. In your version of life, there's an elevator car climbing up by itself with only one person inside, and I think that's the saddest story I've ever heard. Wherever I'm going, I don't want to be alone in my elevator. I want to fill it with people, and we'll lift each other, because that's what people do. Because no one should be alone. You shouldn't be alone."

"Come home with me, then. That's what I'm asking you."

Even then, Meg was torn. She'd been angry at her mother for so long without even knowing it that she'd almost forgotten how much she loved her. But just because you loved someone didn't mean that you could change them. People couldn't be fixed; they needed to repair themselves.

She turned back to the view of the ocean that sprawled out in front of her, the ever-changing water and Dursey Island with Oileán Beag swimming along like a whale calf beside it. In Irish, Dursey was called Oileán Baoi after the goddess Baoi, an incarnation of the hag aspect of the triple goddess who lived in the water and the rocks and the animals. The *Cailleach Bhéarra*, the Hag of Beara, was sovereignty and fate and the phases of life, meant to be venerated equally when she was young and beautiful and when she was wise and old, for she held the promise of all of those things within her at once.

The mind needed to be open, though, to allow itself to be filled with wisdom.

"No," Meg said. "I'm not coming back. I need to stay here in Ireland. For a while anyway. Maybe a long while."

Her mother's glass clinked against the metal table between the two lounge chairs as she set it down unsteadily. "Don't be stupid. What about your job? You can't be irresponsible now. You've worked your whole life to get to where you are."

"Exactly." Meg didn't turn her head. "And for once, I know I'm where I'm supposed to be. I have a few stories I want to write here, some things I want to explore. After that, I'm not sure. I suppose time will tell."

ELECTRICITY

"Love looks not with the eyes,
but with the mind,
And therefore is
winged Cupid painted blind."

WILLIAM SHAKESPEARE
A MIDSUMMER NIGHT'S DREAM

T HEY WALKED THE CIRCUMFERENCE OF Dursey the
second week in August, just Meg and Niall and Adam,
with a basket lunch for three. The ruined signal tower
at the top of the island was Napoleonic, square and roofless
with staring windows that stood sentinel over the miles and
miles and miles of ocean broken only by an occasional ship
scooting in or out of Bantry Bay. Below the ruin, the markers
that had spelled out EIRE in World War II to deter bomber
pilots from hitting neutral Ireland looked like little more than
the foundations of broken buildings.

"So many different people fighting over such a small
spot of ground," Meg said, standing with her hand in Niall's.

"True, but it's a grand spot of ground, don't you think?"

He smiled down at her, and sometimes the sight of that smile that shone from the depths of his soul made her heart expand all over again.

Meg was certain it had expanded over the months, stretched to make room for Niall and Adam and all of Ireland. An enormous amount of room, and maybe the heart's capacity to stretch was limitless.

A gull screeched overhead and Adam came back around the corner of the tower and stopped beside them. "Did you ask her yet?" he said to Niall. "What did she say?"

"Go away, eejit," Niall said.

Adam grinned. "That's not what she said."

"It's what I said. Now leg it, mate."

Adam's grin widened even more, and he ambled off slowly, very slowly, back toward the tower.

Meg studied Niall's face, the now familiar planes and shadows, the white lines of smiles and sunlight etched around the corners of his eyes. "What was it that you were supposed to ask me?"

"Will you come with us?" He ran the back of his thumb across the blade of her cheekbone and made her shiver.

Her laugh was nervous and hopeful, and she took in a deeper breath. "I *am* with you."

"I mean to Dublin when this last session ends. We've been ignoring the subject all these weeks, and if you go to New York for good, I'll visit you—Adam and I will visit you—but will you consider staying here? Stay and take a chance."

Meg hadn't believed in fairy tales before coming to

Ireland, but she had come to believe in the *sidhe*. She'd come to love the lichen-flecked standing stones that had stood in the same place for some five to six thousand years and sometimes felt, in moonlight, as though they could pick themselves up and move. She'd discovered the magic of holy wells with Bronze Age cup marks, of ancient ruins, and Viking warrior ship burials complete with swords and cauldrons and intricate game pieces that museums were already fighting over, and of a history so brutal that it had left its marks of faith and fury on every inch of embattled ground. More than anything, she had fallen in love with the man who stood beside her. He wasn't perfect, but he worked harder to be good than anyone she had ever met, and that alone was worth a gamble.

She'd been thinking a lot about the nature of love—which was such a nebulous word with so many various meanings. But she had decided that the definition was much less complicated than people made it out to be. Love wasn't about any particular kind of electricity, any specific feeling. It was, quite simply, what happened when you opened the inner vault of your heart and threw it wide to let another person enter, when you laid bare every dark and cobwebbed corner of your soul. When you wanted to be a better person for someone, even when they didn't ask you to change—when they didn't ask you for anything except a little faith.

She'd had electricity with men before. Her brief marriage had started with a firestorm of that, which had quickly burned out. She'd met men who could make her ache with need, men who could make her smile, men who made her think and made her laugh. But all that rarely came wrapped up in a single package, and wasn't that what love really meant? The package deal.

Turning back to Niall, Meg looked up into eyes that shimmered as blue and deep as the wild Atlantic, and she asked him, "Why do you want me to stay?"

"Because I can't imagine a time when you weren't with me, and I can't bear to think of a future without you in it," he said, without hesitation, and he brought her hand up against his chest and pressed her palm against the thin fabric of his T-shirt. "Because wherever you decide to live, wherever you go, you will always be alive right here."

Beneath her fingers, his heartbeat was strong and steady, and she fisted her free hand in his shirt and pulled him down to her, felt his pulse quicken even before their lips met. Kissing Niall was like scraping all the light from the sky and the ocean and the brightness of the yellow furze bushes and cramming it inside her until it made her feel like a beacon, so filled with light that it threatened to burst out through her skin.

"Yes," she said. "I'll come to Dublin with you. Dublin and anywhere else you want to go."

THANK YOU FOR READING

I hope you enjoyed *Echo of Glory*, and if you did, I hope you will take the time to write a brief review wherever you normally buy books online or on Goodreads. Even a single sentence shared with other readers can make an enormous difference in the success of a book and in my ability to keep writing new books.

For additional reading, *Lake of Destiny*, *Bell of Eternity*, and *Magic of Winter* are all stand-alone novels in the Celtic Legends Collection based on similar blends of romance, history, family, mystery, suspense, and food as *Echo of Glory*. *Heart of Legend*, coming later in 2018, will be set in Wales. And if you're interested in more of the history and legends behind these novels, or in the recipes or music mentioned, please sign up for my newsletter to get a free limited-time copy of *Welcome Home*.

http://martinaboone.com/index.php/free/

Author's Note

The Beara Peninsula in County Cork, along the shores of Bantry Bay and out to the Atlantic, is one of the most beautiful places in Ireland, which is one of the most beautiful of all places in the world. This was once the seat of the O'Sullivan Beare clan, of whom two of the most famous chiefs were Donal Cam O'Sullivan, Prince of Beare, and Morty Óg O'Sullivan Beare, known as the Captain of the Wild Geese.

Dursey Island with its ruined O'Sullivan fortress lies at the very tip of the Beara Peninsula. I usually change the names of the settings I include in my fiction to give myself a little more freedom to fictionalize the landscape, but in this instance, I decided that the history of Beara and Dursey Island was such a big part of the story that I left as much of the location intact as I could. I've changed little, except that there are rather more visitors crossing to the island over the cable car than I've described. Once the cable car stops running, there really are only a handful of year-round residents in the three abandoned villages on the island, though. The Dursey Sound and the Atlantic that beats along the island's cliffs can be as treacherous as they are in *Echo of Glory*, and there are no trees on the island, either, only windswept tufted grass and gorse and heather, along with the sheep, cows, and a variety of seabirds that soar above the steep-sided, ruffled cliffs.

The cable car ride takes about fifteen minutes round-trip, and there is only one box. If you cross over and there are a lot of people on the island, you need to be ready to leave in plenty of time to wait through the queue to get off again, because there are no shops, hotels, or restaurants.

Inside the car, there really is a bottle of holy water and a copy of Psalm 91. This doesn't encourage confidence as you swing over the wild water, but the trip is—in spite of all of this—relatively easy. The car, however, smells vaguely of sheep and cow. This is because livestock has the right of way. One doesn't usually have to share with them, but you may have to wait until they've been transported back or forth.

Off the coast of Dursey, slotted alongside the main island like a piece of a puzzle, lies the smaller island of Oileán Beag. And on this small island is the scene of an unspeakable tragedy in the long series of tragedies that is the history of Ireland at the hands of English monarchs.

From the Norman conquest until the time of Henry VIII, the English Crown had made few inroads into subduing the rebellious Irish clans. By Henry's time, English influence had mostly drawn down to an area around what is now Dublin and a bit south along the coast. This section of Ireland came to be called the "Pale," after the custom in Europe of staking off areas that one could control and leaving all the uncontrollable, undesirable people on the other side of the pickets.

The "Old English" settlers, as the incomers (foreigners to the Gaelic Irish) had come to be called, had grown comfortable after a few centuries. They managed a tense relationship with the Gaelic chiefs, and the chiefs and clans warred among themselves and, when they could, hit back at the Old English. Every now and then, the Old English would take more land, demand even more in taxes, impose some even more oppressive rule, rub someone the wrong way, cheat someone, or abuse someone—or vice versa—and there would be a fresh cycle of rebellion and retaliation. From an English perspective, the Irish weren't "civilized," which is to say that they weren't behaving as if they were English, and from an Irish perspective, the English were stealing their land and taking away their rights and means of keeping their families fed.

Into this environment stepped the Protestant Reformation. In some ways, the reform was less about religion—in terms of faith—than it was an outbreak of populism, a bit like we are experiencing now in many places in America and Europe. The institution of the Catholic Church, headed by the pope, had for centuries been getting more and more corrupt, failing its mission to serve the faith and help the poor and ordinary people, and leaving its clerics and officials to enrich themselves instead. Henry VIII took advantage of the resentment being stirred up by people like Martin Luther and John Calvin to settle a disagreement with the pope over his need to annul his own marriage to Catherine of Aragon, and he set up his own religion with himself as the head of the "Protestant" (Protesting against the abuses of Catholicism) Church of England. For Catholic Ireland, this was to have serious consequences in the coming centuries, and it allowed religion to become a rallying point and an excuse for many other disagreements.

By the time Queen Elizabeth I, Henry's second (Protestant) daughter, ascended to the throne of England and Ireland, a policy of increasingly brutal crackdowns under Henry and his children had pushed the Gaelic Irish and many of the Old English Irish too far. Elizabeth decided she had better send more troops over to Ireland to help get those feisty Irish under control, and the Irish Parliament simultaneously enacted even stricter laws, based on which Elizabeth's soldiers were legally allowed to treat the Gaelic Irish in seriously terrible ways.

The Gaelic Irish had never been thrilled with English rule, but now they decided just about anything would be an improvement. The king of Spain was all too happy to help weaken England's position around the world. The pope, too, would have been delighted to have Ireland remain safely Catholic. Even a few of the Old English Irish within the Pale—many of whom were Catholic—were sympathetic.

Led by the "Great O'Neill," the Earl of Tyrone, along with the "Red" O'Donnell, and the Maguire, the Irish chiefs launched a revolt that came to be called the Nine Years' War, or Tyrone's Rebellion. Due in part to material support from the king of Spain, who saw the Irish conflict as an opportunity to strengthen his campaign against English colonial supremacy, interrupt English shipping, and further his fight against Protestant encroachment in Europe, it was a far harder war to win than Queen Elizabeth envisioned. By the time it was said and done, this "rebellion" cost England 30,000 men and much of the treasury.

Because there were global implications, as well as her Irish interests at stake, though, Elizabeth couldn't afford to give up. She was spending three-quarters of England's annual budget to maintain and supply a standing army of 20,000—over a third more than through most of England's history to that point—with the majority engaged in fighting across the sea in Ireland.

Increasingly desperate as the war dragged on, she ordered her commanders to use any means necessary to get the rebels to lay down their arms. Mainly, this involved killing anyone who resisted, making examples of entire families, butchering livestock, and burning homes and crops as a warning and an incentive for the Irish to finally fall in line.

While this campaign of terrorism and—basically—genocide had some effect, it also made the Irish even more determined.

The pope had been supposed to send some actual troops for a while by that point, though that hadn't gotten very far. The king of Spain had sent two separate armadas to provide fighting men, but the weather hadn't cooperated and they'd turned back. Now, in 1601, he finally managed to land 4,000 men over under Don Juan del Águila at Kinsale south of Cork in the realm of the O'Sullivan Prince of Beare. Águila massed his troops at Kinsale and also garrisoned the O'Sullivan and O'Driscoll castles of Dunboy, Baltimore, and Castlehaven.

Now things grew more tense. The Irish, facing greater numbers of trained soldiers under Elizabeth's commanders, had avoided large, pitched battles, opting for more creative hit-and-run tactics instead. At Kinsale, though, Elizabeth's commanders sent in a force roughly double the size of the combined Spanish and Irish forces, forcing a traditional "battlefield" fight while the English ringed the Spanish position at Kinsale and laid it under siege.

The Irish fought ferociously to get through the English lines, but ultimately they were overcome by the English cavalry. The Spanish, after having held Kinsale for three months with the help of the Irish, surrendered. And unlike the Irish, to whom the English gave no quarter, the Spanish retired with their own flag flying and peacefully left under terms of truce, having also agreed to turn over the additional Irish garrisons once English troops under Sir George Carew arrived to hold them.

Most of the surviving Irish fled north to Ulster with O'Neill and O'Donnell. But some remained in Cork to continue fighting alongside the O'Sullivan, the O'Driscoll, and the McCarthy.

Donal Cam O'Sullivan Beare did two things. He wrote to the king of Spain, complaining about General del Águila's behavior and asking for new reinforcements, and he swept down to Dunboy to take his castle back before the English could get their hands on it.

With a handful of men, he snuck into Dunboy and kicked most of the Spaniards out, though—tellingly—quite a number decided to stay and fight for him instead. They all dug in and prepared for the English to arrive in force. Knowing the ensuing battle would be ugly, Donal sent his family and the families of his men to his cousin Diarmuid's fortress on Oileán Beag, the small island alongside Dursey, with a force of forty soldiers to protect them.

These days, there's nothing left of that fortress. The placement of the drawbridge that used to span the narrow channel between the islands is still visible, and here and there, differences in the color and elevation of the grass reveal where foundations used to be. All else is gone.

At the time, though, in 1602, the fortress was thought to be virtually impregnable, protected by high cliffs and challenging seas.

And it might not have fallen, had not the English had some help.

It came down to tanistry and the interference of the English. Instead of the purely hereditary form of succession that created so many problems with regencies in England and Scotland, for example, under the tanist system, a chief was elected from among the eligible males in the line of succession. Some years earlier, when his father had died while Donal Cam O'Sullivan was still an infant, under the tanist system, Donal's brother Owen had been elected and he'd sought confirmation from English forces in Dublin. On reaching adulthood, though, Donal Cam challenged this and, again with confirmation from the English in Dublin, became the chief in his place.

Owen, unbeknownst to most of his clan, had been fuming over this ever since, and he ended up fighting on the English side against Donal in the rebellion.

As the English took their time getting down to Dunboy, the king of Spain finally sent money and more supplies, which arrived at the O'Sullivan castle on the other side of the peninsula. Donal Cam O'Sullivan went to retrieve it, leaving 143 of his best men to hold Dunboy and thinking his own family, and those of his men, would all be safe on Dursey.

George Carew sent 5,000 men and the English navy to retake Dunboy Castle.

He also received help from Owen O'Sullivan Beare,

who made the mistake of thinking that if he helped the English defeat Donal Cam, they would afterwards pack up and sail off home to England, leaving him in charge and in possession of Donal's lands.

Having learned from Owen of a weak spot near the main stairwell at Dunboy, the English forces began to bombard that section of the wall. After ten days of artillery fire, the walls were reduced to rubble, and under a flag of truce, Donal Cam's captain sent out a messenger to the English requesting terms. In response, the English made a show of hanging the man where those alive in what remained of the castle could see.

The remaining defenders barricaded themselves inside the cellar, which, too, was eventually breached. In the midst of bloody hand-to-hand fighting, Donal's captain tried to ignite the powder stores and blow up the invaders, but he was killed in the act. The last few survivors from the original 143 men were hanged from a single tree in the market square.

For the English, that still was not enough. Among the women and children that Donal Cam had sent to Dursey Island was Owen O'Sullivan's wife, apparently as a hostage to ensure Owen's good behavior. But that didn't work out exactly as Donal Cam had planned. Even before the fall of Dunboy, Carew sent his forces off to Dursey Island with instructions to raze the fortress on Oileán Beag level with the ground, and Owen O'Sullivan told them how to access the island and conquer the fortress that was meant to be impregnable, removing the threat to English shipping and supremacy that it posed by virtue of its strategic position.

The resulting massacre was documented, but mostly by Phillip O'Sullivan, the son of Diarmuid O'Sullivan who had built the fortress, from stories he gathered from the handful of survivors. Sir George Carew's secretary, Thomas Stafford—believed to be Carew's illegitimate son—inherited Carew's papers and published what was, for many centuries, considered to the definitive account of the "Pacification of Ireland." Stafford's book, *The Pacata Hibernia: Ireland Appeased and Reduced,* offers a soldier's pragmatic account of Tyrone's Rebellion, describing the battles and decisions that left 100,000 Irish dead, including 60,000 who starved to death in Ulster as a result of the English scorched-earth policy. It describes the Siege of Dunboy in detail, but on the subject of the Dursey massacre, it is relatively silent.

Echo of Glory describes the questions surrounding when the massacre took place, so I won't get into that here. To my knowledge, there is no real question about the dead being buried anywhere on the island, but that doesn't mean some weren't. Sir George Wilmot swept through the Beara Peninsula in 1602, after the Dursey fortress had fallen, determined to kill or capture Donal Cam O'Sullivan Beare once and for all. And while it is generally believed that it was Carew's men—who were mostly English soldiers—who perpetrated the massacre after the fortress fell, it is possible it was Wilmot's forces, arriving a little later, who were responsible. These troops included many Irish, mostly conscripts.

In the end, it probably didn't matter to the women who died whether they and their children were thrown over the cliffs by Englishmen or Irish. But for the story that I wanted to tell in *Echo*, the story that was inspired by the conversations we are having today about sexual harassment

ACKNOWLEDGMENTS

Once again, an enormous and heartfelt debt of gratitude goes to Erin Cashman, Susan Sipal, and my editors, Jennifer Harris and Linda Au. I need to also thank my wonderful early reader team, who always manage to catch something that has fallen through the cracks. I want to mention a special thank-you to Lesley Walsh for being particularly attentive on the last book. I can't begin to express my gratitude to all of you.

As always, thank you to my patient family and to all of my readers, whose support and enthusiasm makes me want to keep telling stories.

About Martina Boone

MARTINA BOONE IS THE award-winning author of the romantic Southern Gothic Heirs of Watson Island series for young adults, including *Compulsion*, *Persuasion*, and *Illusion* from Simon & Schuster, Simon Pulse, and of heartwarming contemporary novels interwoven with romance, history, and legend beginning with *Lake of Destiny*. She's also the founder of AdventuresInYAPublishing.com, a Writer's Digest 101 Best Websites for Writers site, and she is on the board of the Literary Council of Northern Virginia.

She lives with her husband, children, a too-smart-for-his-own-good Sheltie, and a lopsided cat, and she enjoys writing books set in the sorts of magical places she loves to visit. When she isn't writing, she's addicted to travel, horses, skiing, chocolate-flavored tea, and anything with Nutella on it.

More Information:

http://www.martinaboone.com/
Twitter: @MartinaABoone
Facebook: https://www.facebook.com/martina.boone/

Made in the USA
Monee, IL
03 July 2022

98940062R00208